Winter Solstice

那一年的冬至

容　非■著

Z. Z. Lehmberg■译

SPM 南方出版传媒

全国优秀出版社　全国百佳图书出版单位　广东教育出版社

·广州·

图书在版编目（CIP）数据

那一年的冬至／汉英对照／容非著；庄重（Z. Z. Lehmberg）译. —广州：广东教育出版社，2017.3
ISBN 978-7-5548-1398-0

Ⅰ.①那… Ⅱ.①容… ②庄… Ⅲ.①回忆录—中国—当代—汉、英 Ⅳ.①I251

中国版本图书馆CIP数据核字（2016）第273203号

策　　划：梁耀凤
责任编辑：严洪超　李杰静　姜树彪　范洪波
整体设计：陈国梁
责任技编：佟长缨　刘莉敏

那一年的冬至
NAYINIAN DE DONGZHI
广东教育出版社出版发行
（广州市环市东路472号12-15楼）
邮政编码：510075
网址：http://www.gjs.cn
广东新华发行集团股份有限公司经销
广州市岭美彩印有限公司印刷
（广州市荔湾区花地大道南海南工商贸易区A幢）
787毫米×1092毫米　16开本　16.75印张　335 000字
2017年3月第1版　2017年3月第1次印刷
ISBN 978-7-5548-1398-0
定价：34.80元
质量监督电话：020-87613102　邮箱：gjs-quality@gdpg.com.cn
购书咨询电话：020-87615809

目　录

Contents

前　　言

1968年，毛泽东主席发出了“知识青年到农村去，接受贫下中农的再教育，很有必要”的号召，在全国范围内掀起了一个大规模的知识青年上山下乡高潮。在短短的几年里，大约1600万城镇学生青年下放到全国各地的国营农场、生产建设兵团和广大的农村劳动和生活。

1968年11月，17岁的我和比我大一岁的姐姐带着行李，在一片欢送的锣鼓声中融入了一支有1000多名知青的大队伍，乘船从我们原来居住的大城市来到了中国南方水乡的一个农村当知青，踏上了人生中一段艰辛的历程。

我们插队的这个农村地处广东珠江三角洲平原，土地肥沃，物产丰富，河涌纵横交错，是一个“出门见水”的鱼米之乡。全村总共有600多人，其中有400多个劳动力，上山下乡知识青年16人。总耕地面积有600多亩，主要的农作物是水稻和甘蔗。

这里民风淳朴，中国传统道德文化的影响在人们的思想意识中根深蒂固。由于远离喧嚣的都市，村民们对当时那些时髦的政治活动态度冷漠，毫无兴趣，依然过着祖祖辈辈习惯了的“日出而作，日落而息”的生活。与大城市相比，这里显得那么的平静、安逸。

从大城市来到农村，我们这些知青面临着三个巨大的挑战：第一是过生活关——农村日常生活的衣食住行等条件都比较简陋、落后，无法与城市相比，我们要生存下去，就必须尽快地适应生活环境上的巨大落差；第二是要过劳动关——我们要从一个城市学生变为一个天天在田间辛苦劳作、自食其力的农民，其蜕变过程是异常艰难和痛苦的；第三是要过“前途关”——根据当时的知青政策，我们必须当一辈子农民，上学无望，回城无望，一辈子扎根农村。

正当我们这些知青陷入困境的时候，憨厚纯朴的村民们向我们伸出了援助的双手。在生活上，他们妥善地安排好男女知青分住的房舍，派人带我们到镇上去选购基本的生活用品及干农活的工具等，使我们很快地安顿了下来；在劳动上，他们不厌其烦，手把手地教我们干各种农活，帮助我们逐步成长为一名能干的农民；在精神上，他们经常主动和我们聊家常，对我们无奈离开城市、远离父母和家人的遭遇深表同情，并开导我们要向前看，不要自暴自弃。逢年过节，村里各家各户都不约而同地邀请我们去他们家吃饭团聚，以缓解我们对家人的思念。

村民们无微不至的关心和帮助像春风一样温暖着我们，他们的纯朴、正义感、同情心和追求幸福的热情深深地感染了我们。

我在这个村庄当了4年知青，经历了很多事情，品尝了人生中的酸甜苦辣。在这本书里，我想透过亲身经历的几十个故事，从不同角度向读者讲述40多年前中国南方水乡农村的文化生活、人情风俗以及插队知青的喜怒哀乐。

我插队当知青的那个农村是当时中国千千万万个农村的一个缩影，那里发生的事情在一定程度上反映了当时中国广大农村的实际状况。

我虽然离开那个村庄已有40多年，但一直把她当作自己的第二故乡，思念着那里的一草一木，牵挂着那些曾经朝夕相处的乡亲们。我曾分别在2002年和2010年回到那个村庄与村民们重逢，“有朋自远方来，不亦乐乎”——我们一起畅谈往事，吃饭照相，相见甚欢。

我非常欣喜地看到：经过40多年的努力，村民们的生活水平发生了翻天覆地的变化。如今，村里崭新的小洋楼林立，家家都有自来水——过去靠河水生活的日子一去不复返了，村里创办了灯具厂等企业，大大增加了村民的收入。

最令我兴奋和不可思议的是：我回村时竟然能与本书故事里提到的一些人物在阔别了40多年后又相遇了，其中有“打鸟”里的枪手阿根和阿真；“姓名趣事”里的黄狗女、麻糖发和蔡狗；“打篮球”里的农民高中生蔡锦森；“老知青” 里那个嫁给当地农民青年的阿妹，以及“搭食”里的主人公锦胜等。

40多年过去，弹指一挥间。在回忆、讲述这些故事的同时，我深深地意识到：不管经历过多少艰难曲折，人类社会一定会不断进步，人们的生活也一定会变得更加美好。“青山遮不住，毕竟东流去”，历史的洪流滚滚向前，势不可挡。

容 非

2016年2月于美国西雅图

Introduction

In 1968, Mao Zedong issued his decree: "Educated Youth should go to the countryside to be re-educated by farmers. This is very necessary." Immediately, an Up-to-the-Mountains-and-Down-to-the-Countryside Movement swamped the country. The goal was to send, within a few short years, about 16 million urban youths to live and work in remote regions, such as state farms, sites of production-construction corps, and rural agricultural areas, throughout China.

In November of 1968, at the age of 17, together with my sister, who is one year older than me, we joined over 1000 young men and women in our region and became *zhiqing*—Educated Youth. We boarded a boat that would take us to our new home, a coastal water village far away from our family and the city in which we grew up. Amongst a cacophony of celebratory drum beats and gong strikes, we began a challenging life-journey.

The water village to which my sister and I were assigned was located in the Pearl River Delta, an area of bounty, where rivers and streams crisscrossed land masses. It is known as the Land of Fish and Rice, where one saw water everywhere one looked. There were about 600 residents in the village at the time, about 400 of whom were farmhands. Sixteen zhiqing were assigned there. Together, we farmed the 600 *mu* (about 40 hectares) of farmland and grew rice and sugarcane.

The farmers' way of life was down-to-earth and they held tight to the traditional Chinese cultural and moral standards. Because the village was far away from the noisy and disorderly metropolises, most of the farmers were not interested in any of the popular political activities at the time. They followed their routine of working when the sun rose and quitting when the sun set. Compared to the cities, life in the village was quiet and peaceful.

However, we zhiqing faced three major challenges in the countryside. The first was the challenge of everyday life: Compared to what we were used to in the city, life in the countryside was backward and primitive. The second was the challenge of physical labor: As students from the city, we were not used to physical hardship. To survive, we had to learn to do farm work and become self-reliant. The process of changing our lifestyle was unexpectedly difficult and traumatic. The third was the challenge of the unknown: According to the policies of the time, we were supposed to be farmers for the rest of our lives, with no hope for ever going back to school or returning to the city. We were supposed to take root in the countryside, to which we had been banished.

Thankfully, while we were desperate and hopeless, the farmers extended their helpful hands. To help us with our daily living, they arranged male and female dormitory-like living quarters for us, and they helped us choose and purchase the necessary farm equipment and pots and pans. To help us with farm work, they taught us patiently and they became overjoyed when our farming skills improved. And to help us with our spirits, they often talked to us about our families back in the city, and they empathized with our situation, encouraging us to hope for a better future and not to give up on life. Whenever there was a holiday, they invited us to celebrate with their families so that we would not be too lonely or homesick.

Our hearts were warmed by the farmers. Their straightforwardness, honest sense of right and wrong, empathy and desire for basic human happiness affected us.

I was a zhiqing in my village for four years, where I experienced a spectrum of human misery and happiness. In this book, through lived accounts and from different perspectives, I hope to present to readers the culture, customs, and zhiqing life in a coastal water village in southern China over 40 years ago.

The village I was assigned to as a zhiqing was representative of the innumerable villages throughout China. What happened in my village was illustrative of what was happening everywhere else in China at the time.

Even though it has been over 40 years since I lived and toiled in the village to which I was banished, I have always thought of the village as my second hometown aside from the city where I was born and raised. I think of the farmers I befriended and I am even nostalgic for the grass and trees of the area. In both 2002 and 2010, I visited the village and got together with some of the farmers. As Confucius said, "How happy to have friends come from afar." My village friends and I reminisced about the past, had meals together, and took pictures. We were happy to see each other.

I was pleased to see that the living conditions in the village have improved drastically since I was there 40 years ago, as if heaven and earth had changed places. Today, family dwellings of two or more stories are everywhere in the village. Running water is in every household—the days of having to fetch water from the rivers are gone. The village is now operating various small enterprises, such as a factory that produces lamps and lighting fixtures. These enterprises help increase everyone's income.

However, what was most inconceivable and what made me the happiest was that I actually met up with some of the people I mention in this book. I had a reunion with Ah Gen and Ah Zhen from "Bird Hunting"; Dog Girl Huang, Thriving Sesame Chew, and Dog Cai from "Names"; the senior-high student Cai Jinshen from "Basketball Games"; Ah Mei, the girl who got married to a young farmer, in "Old Zhiqing"; and Jinsheng, my host in "Meals with Host Family."

Looking back, over 40 years went by just like that, in a snap of the fingers. I have learned, while writing this book, that no matter how difficult life is, the human world moves forward and we strive to better humanity. As this line from a Song Dynasty poem says, "Mountains cannot stop the eastward water." We move forward and our life will become better.

Rong Fei

Seattle, U. S. A.
February, 2016

译者自序

本书的作者和我都希望这本双语读物能够达到两个目的：一是把作者在中国南方农村插队当知青亲身经历的故事告诉读者；二是向读者提供一个挑战他们的中文或是英文语言能力的机会。我们相信，了解历史能帮助我们理解今天的世界，而学习语言最好能与应用语言结合起来。作为一个对各种语言感兴趣的人，我常常发现，对学习语言来说，各种双语读物能提高读者对语言学习的兴趣，也有助于读者的语言学习。我希望我的读者与我有同感。

因为作者和我的目的是要让中文和英文的读者都可以读这本书，特别是那些正在学习中文或英文的读者，当我翻译《那一年的冬至》一书时，我敏锐地意识到两种语言给予翻译者的挑战：我既想忠实于作者的故事和意图，又想要流畅地译成我们想要的那种语言——英文。可是，因为我们想把这本书作为学习语言的工具，我必须坦白地说，为了忠实于原文——中文，有些时候我不得不牺牲英文的流畅性，希望借此会对那些以通过读本书来比较和对照两种语言的不同为目的的读者更容易一些。我鼓励读者们尝试自己动手来翻译这本书——中译英或英译中，并对照我的译文和作者的原文。我相信，这样的语言翻译练习将会是一次有效的，也是有趣的语言学习经历。

我要感谢本书的作者容非给予我的机会以及信任我翻译他的作品。他不厌其烦地回答了我的很多问题。通过翻译《那一年的冬至》一书，我不但学到了中文和英文之间一些微妙的不同之处，还知道了本书故事中所提到的那些男女青年们的那段不平凡的经历。

我还要感谢我的大女儿Freya Lehmberg，因为她对中文和英文都有兴趣，她成了我的试验读者。我很感谢她十分仔细地阅读了所有的细节以及对我的要求的迅速反馈。每当我为要把一种语言转换为另一种语言而感到责任重大的时候，是她的鼓励支持着我。

翻译永无止境。我现在把对《那一年的冬至》一书的翻译暂时告一段落，是为了让大家可以阅读和体验这本书。

Z. Z. Lehmberg

2016年2月于美国马凯特市

Translator's Note

Both the author and I hope that this dual-language book will serve two purposes: one is to inform its readers of the story that the author experienced in a village in southern China as a zhiqing; and two is to provide its readers an opportunity to challenge their language skills, be it Chinese or English. We believe that history contributes to our understanding of the present world, and language study is best coupled with language use. As someone who is interested in languages, I often find bilingual books interesting and motivating for language learning. I hope my readers will, too.

As it is the author's and my intention for this book to be accessible to both Chinese and English readers, especially to those readers who are learning either Chinese or English, I was keenly mindful of two language issues when I was translating *Winter Solstice*: I wanted to be faithful to the author's stories and intentions, and I wanted to achieve fluency in the target language—English. However, because we want this book to be a language learning tool as well, I must confess that I have sometimes had to sacrifice English fluency in order to be faithful to the source text—Chinese, hoping to make it easier for those readers who are reading the book for the purpose of comparing and contrasting the two languages. I encourage readers to try their hand at translating this book—from Chinese to English or from English to Chinese—against the backdrop of my translation and the author's words. I guarantee that the translation exercise will be a stimulating language learning experience.

I want to thank the author, Rong Fei, for giving me the opportunity and trusting me to translate his work. He was never tired of my many questions. Through translating *Winter Solstice*, I learned not only the nuances of Chinese and English, but also the extraordinary experiences of the young men and women whose stories constitute this book.

I also want to thank my first daughter, Freya Lehmberg, who served as my test-reader because of her interest in both English and Chinese. I am grateful for her careful eye for detail and her quick responses to my inquiries. Her encouragement supported me whenever I felt the heavy responsibility of carrying one language across to the other.

A translation is never finished. I now pause my translation of *Winter Solstice* so that others may read and experience this book.

Z. Z. Lehmberg

Marquette, U. S. A.
February, 2016

作者简介
Author Bio

容 非

本书著者容非出生在中国广东省广州市。

1968年至1972年，容非到广东南方某农村插队当知青。在此期间，他除了和农民、知青同吃、同住、同劳动外，还被他所在的公社借调到公社报道组全脱产工作了半年，并参加了公社和县上山下乡知识青年先进代表大会的筹备工作，撰写了很多知青先进个人和先进集体代表的材料等。借工作机会，容非穿村过户，探访了很多知青，深入了解他们的思想，搜集了生活中的很多人和事，为本书的写作打下了坚实的基础。

1972年，容非被招工回城当了一名码

头工人；1978年，他参加了全国大学统考，并考入了一所全国重点大学，读工程力学专业；1982年，他大学毕业获得了工学学士学位并留校任教。

1985年，容非到美国留学，获得了工程力学硕士和博士学位，并在国际学术刊物及会议上发表过数篇文章。他先后在其工作的两家世界著名跨国公司有两项发明，其中一项已获得美国专利，另一项正在美国国家专利局审批。容博士现任职于美国波音公司，是该公司的科学家和高级工程师。

容博士虽然是搞科技工程的专业人士，但他在海外30多年来一直致力于弘扬中国文化。他曾应邀到美国和中国的大学演讲，与听众分享他的生活和工作经验；他曾担任过美国纽约州罗彻斯特市中文学校校长，出席了1995年在美国俄亥俄州哥伦布市举行的第一届全美中文学校校长大会，并做了演讲。

容非博士的著作《我愿你起舞》一书，2015年8月由广东教育出版社出版。在这本书里，作者讲述了教育培养女儿的心路历程以及他年轻的女儿在美国读书、创业的成功经历。该书获得了2015年冰心儿童图书奖。

Rong Fei

Rong Fei, the author of this book, was born in Guangzhou, Guangdong Province, China.

From 1968 to 1972, Rong Fei was a zhiqing in a coastal water village in southern China. In addition to working with the farmers and other zhiqing in the fields, Rong Fei spent half a year as a member of the news bureau of his production commune. One of his assignments at the news bureau was to help organize the annual Meetings of the Outstanding Representatives of Zhiqing at the commune and county levels. Because he was responsible for writing a lot of the publicity materials for the noteworthy individuals and groups chosen for these meetings, Rong Fei got to visit and interview hundreds of zhiqing in different areas. The stories and information he collected at the time provided a solid foundation for this book.

In 1972, Rong Fei was hired as a porter by a company from his home city. The hire effectively ended his life as a farmer. Then in 1978, Rong Fei took and passed the newly revived national college entrance exam in China. His high scores guaranteed him a spot in a top notch university in China. He became a college student, majoring in engineering mechanics. Rong Fei graduated in 1982 with a B.S. degree, and he taught as a college instructor at his alma mater.

In 1985, Rong Fei went to the U.S. for further studies, eventually earning an M.S. and a Ph.D. in engineering mechanics. In addition to holding two U.S. patents, Rong Fei has also had papers published in international journals and presented at international conferences in his discipline. Dr. Rong is currently working as a scientist/senior engineer with the Boeing Company in the U.S.

For the 30 years that he has been in the U.S., besides being a successful engineer in his field, Dr. Rong has always engaged himself in promoting the Chinese culture. He has been a guest speaker at different universities in China and the U.S., sharing his life and work experiences. In 1995, as the president of the Rochester Chinese Language School in Rochester, New York, U.S.A., he attended and presented at The First U.S. National Chinese School Presidents Conference held in Columbus, Ohio, U.S.

Dr. Rong Fei is also the author of *I Hope You Dance,* published by Guangdong Education Publishing House in August of

2015. A memoir, the book is about raising his daughter. It includes stories of his daughter's schooling in the U.S. and her successful entrepreneurial experience in Silicon Valley. The book won the Binxin Children's Literature Award in 2015.

Z. Z. Lehmberg

本书译者Z. Z. Lehmberg是位于美国密歇根州马凯特市的北密歇根州立大学英文系教授。她在中国出生和成长。赴美留学前，她在中国从事了两年英文教学工作。Lehmberg博士先后在北密歇根州立大学获得了工商管理学士学位和英文创作写作硕士学位，在韦恩州立大学获得了英语作文应用语言学博士学位。

作为一名教授和学者，Lehmberg博士曾多次在美国和中国召开的专业年会上做了关于英文作文、写作教学和对外英语等方面的演讲。Lehmberg博士一直对英文写作和中译英有着极大的热忱和浓厚的兴趣。她曾经发表过英文散文以及中国诗词的英文翻译。在美国北密歇根州立大学英文系，Lehmberg博士主要教授英文作文、文学、中文和中文翻译等课程。Lehmberg博士还是马凯特市儿童中国语言和文化学校的创始人和校长。她在美国教美国学生学中文和在中国教中国学生学英文的经历，以及她对语言和作文教学的兴趣，促使她和容博士合作完成了这本中英双语读物。

Z. Z. Lehmberg

Z. Z. Lehmberg, the translator of this book, is currently a professor of English at Northern Michigan University in Marquette, Michigan, U.S.A. She was born and raised in China, and taught English in China for two years before going to the U.S. to further her education. Dr. Lehmberg earned her B.A. in business administration and M.A. in creative writing from Northern Michigan University, and a Ph.D. in composition and applied linguistics from Wayne State University.

As a professor and scholar, Dr. Lehmberg has given numerous presentations (at professional conferences in both the U.S. and China) on writing, teaching writing, and teaching English to speakers of other languages. She has always been interested in writing in English and translating from Chinese to English. She has had creative nonfiction essays and English translations of Chinese poetry published. She currently teaches English composition and literature courses as well as Chinese language and literature in translation courses at Northern Michigan University. Dr. Lehmberg was also the founding teacher and president of the Marquette Children's Academy of Chinese Language and Culture. Her experience teaching American students Chinese in the U.S. and Chinese students English in China motivated her to work with Dr. Rong on this bilingual book.

一

进村第一课

1968年下乡插队，进村后的第一件事就是由生产队长领着我们全体知青逐家逐户认“阶级”——悠悠万事，唯此为大，千万不要认错了门牌号码。一听介绍，我们大吃一惊：我们插队落户的这个村子共有600多人，居然有30%的人家庭成分是地主、富农。后来听了村民们的解释，才明白了其中的原因。

旧社会时，这个乡有一个恶霸，他原来只是一个上无片瓦、下无插锥之地的雇农。一天，他借了地主的一条船给田里施肥。中午时分，他用锄头在田埂上挖了个炉灶做饭，结果一不小心，煮饭的瓦锅穿了底，米和水全都掉进了炉灶里，与草木灰混在一起。午饭吃不成了，一气之下，他卖了地主的船，得钱后买了一杆枪，做起了剪径的行当。此人从此一发不可收拾，最后成了远近闻名的土匪恶霸，有大片的田地和1000多人的私人武装，常与邻县的另一个恶霸大打出手，争夺地盘。“一人得道，鸡犬升天。”该恶霸有一个外甥是我村人氏，原来家徒四壁，此时摇身一变也成了地主恶霸，他的族人也跟着沾光，所以村里的富人就多起来了。土地改革时，尽管村里评成分的条件放得很松，还是评出了30%的地主、富农。

我所在的生产队副队长是下中农成分，与我关系很好。我问他旧社会过得如何，他说农忙时比较辛苦，忙不过来就请短工帮忙。有空会到茶楼去饮饮茶、抽抽鸦片。我听了不禁愕然，这怎么与我们从书上了解到的相去甚远?

离我村大约5公里，有一个200多人的村子，全村人都特别穷。土地改革评成分时，该村硬是按指标在“矮子中间挑高佬”——评了一户地主，其余的全是贫下中农，没有中农和富农。我村的农民不无遗憾地说，那户地主其实也很穷，若在我们村就肯定被评为至少是下中农成分。

在那个年代，下中农成分与地主成分有着天壤之别!

我所在的村子规定：地主、富农每年要给村子义务劳动三天，而且时间往往安排在春节期间。

春节期间，春寒料峭，村里灯火通明，炊烟缭绕，家家户户都在暖烘烘的屋里准备美味的食物，大人、小孩的欢笑声此起彼落。此时，人们会听见村治保主任敲着铜锣沿街吆喝，要所有的地主、富农自带工具到村里的大礼堂正门口集中，准备参加义务劳动。

有一天，我冒着寒风细雨穿过村里的街道时，十分惊讶地看见在地主、富农义务劳动的人群中，所有地主、富农的子女都有说有笑地干着活，丝毫不知按照政策，他们不是地主、富农，而是属于“可以教育好的子女”，是不用参加地主、富农的义务劳动的。可当地土政策把地主、富农的儿女与地主、富农等同起来，如俗话所说的：“龙生龙，凤生凤，老鼠生儿打地洞。”

那时，我们村地主、富农的儿子多为光棍，因为贫下中农的女儿是不会嫁给地主、富农的儿子的。地主、富农的女儿则会嫁给贫下中农，因为这样可以永远甩掉地主、富农的“帽子”—— 有谁会愿意让子孙后代永远戴着地主、富农这顶“帽子”呢？！

相比之下，我很庆幸自己生长在城市里，我人生道路上的许多坎坷也显得那样的微不足道，我再也没有任何理由去怨天尤人了。

Chapter 1

First Lesson in the Village

The first thing we did after arriving in the village where we were sent in 1968—and it was the most important thing above all else—was to go around making "class identifications" with our production team captain. Don't make a mistake, we were warned. Astonished, we found out that out of the six hundred or so residents of the village, thirty percent of the families belonged to the class categories of landlords and wealthy farmers. We found out later that there was a reason for this high percentage of wealth in my village.

In the area before 1949, there was a tyrant who used to be a poor farmhand. He was so poor that he was said not to have a pot to piss in. One day, he borrowed a boat from a landlord to bring fertilizer to the fields. Around noon, he dug a hole in the ground so that he could cook his rice, but unfortunately, his ceramic pot leaked and all of the water and rice seeped out into the hole that was used as a stove. The mixture of water, uncooked rice, and ashes was no lunch. The farmhand was so mad that he sold the landlord's boat for a gun. He started to rob. Unstoppable, he eventually became a well-known tyrant far and near, owning a vast amount of farmland and a private militia of 1000 men, who often fought with neighboring tyrants for land control. The saying "When a person gets his way, even the status of his chickens and dogs gets raised" fits this farmhand perfectly. The farm-hand-turned-tyrant had a nephew from my village. This dirt-poor man also became a tyrant after his uncle. Anyone who was related to this nephew in my village got rich as well, which was why during the Land Reform, when class categories were determined according to wealth, thirty percent of the families in my village got the classification of landlords and wealthy farmers even though the selection criteria were not followed closely.

I was good friends with the assistant production team captain who was identified as a lower-middle peasant. When we talked about life before 1949, he told me that he was busiest during planting and harvesting seasons. He would hire other farmhands to help when he could not do everything himself so that he would still have time to enjoy dim-sum in a restaurant or smoke an opium pipe now and then. I was shocked by the stories of his life before 1949 as they were so different from what I had learned from my textbooks at school.

There was a 200-resident village about five kilometers from my village. Everyone there was very poor before 1949. During the Land Reform when class categories were created, their village managed to assign one family as the landlord family and all the others as poor and lower-middle peasants. They did not have anybody in the middle nor any wealthy farmer classes. People in my village could not help telling me that the landlord in that village was actually quite poor. If he were in our village, he would have gotten the classification of a lower-middle peasant only.

During the Cultural Revolution, there was a difference of day and night between the classes of a lower-middle peasant and a landlord. In my village, landlords and wealthy farmers were assigned three days of voluntary labor each year and the time for such a punishment was usually around the Chinese New Year.

Each year at Chinese New Year, when the village was lit up and everyone stayed indoors from the spring chills outside, enjoying good food and family bliss, we could hear the shouting and gong beating of the village security director. He would be calling all the land owners and wealthy farmers to bring their own tools to report to the village meeting hall. It was time for their "voluntary service."

One day, I walked through the village in chilly rain and gusty wind. I was

surprised to see that, among all those working, there were also the children of land owners and wealthy farmers. They were working cheerfully, oblivious of the government policy that actually classified them differently from their parents: They belonged to the class of those "who can be re-educated" and they did not have to join their parents to do voluntary service. But unfortunately, the local policy told them something different: Children of

land owners and wealthy farmers are the same as their parents. Local policies at the time followed this saying: Dragons are born dragons, phoenixes are born phoenixes, and baby mice know how to dig holes. In other words, an acorn does not fall far from the tree.

At that time, most of the sons of the village's landlords and wealthy farmers were single because the daughters of the poor farmers did not want to be married to them. The daughters of the landlords and wealthy farmers, however, could get married to the sons of poor farmers and change their social and political status forever. No one would want their dependents to be labeled landlord or wealthy farmer for the rest of their lives!

Compared to them, I felt fortunate that I was born and raised in the city. No matter how difficult my life's path ahead of me would be, compared to the sons of the landlords and wealthy farmers, I had nothing to complain about.

二

打　鸟

南国水乡的深秋，依然骄阳似火，万里无云。秋收已近尾声，湛蓝湛蓝的天空下，那片曾令知青们心惊胆战、无边无际的金色稻浪早已荡然无存。在灿烂的阳光下，灰蒙蒙的田野一望无际，空空如也，宛如一块巨大无比的灰色地毯，一直延伸到天边，唯有那几片零星散布在河涌附近的甘蔗林仍然郁郁葱葱，犹如镶嵌在一块灰色地毯上的几颗小巧玲珑的绿宝石，格外引人注目。

傍晚时分，火红火红的太阳落到了远处巍峨的山头上，夜幕渐渐降临了。村里的小伙子阿根和阿真邀我晚上一起去打鸟。他们对我说，吃饱了秋天稻谷的鸟儿现在都长得肥肥的，特别好吃，被当地人称为“禾花雀”。一到傍晚，白天吃饱喝足了的禾花雀要找个安全的地方睡觉，可田野里到处都是光秃秃的，无奈的鸟群只好投宿在那几片残存的甘蔗林里——这是打鸟的最好时机。太阳落山之前，阿根和阿真就分头到村外去侦察，远远地用目光跟踪着那几群频繁飞来落去的禾花雀，看准了它们最后落脚的那几片甘蔗林，就马上回村互通情报。经过讨论，阿根和阿真决定晚上到河中心一个小岛的甘蔗林里打禾花雀。

晚饭后，村里华灯初上，村外一片漆黑。阿根和阿真带上了打鸟的气枪、子弹、装鸟的布袋，还有装着三节电池的强光手电筒就来找我。我当时是个一穷二白的知青，无枪无弹，只拿了一个两节电池的手电筒跟着他们两个。

在村的小河岸边，我们登上了生产队的一艘小艇。阿根在船头划桨，我在船中央划桨，阿真则在船尾掌舵，大家齐心协力地向河中心的小岛划去。水乡的秋夜，皎洁的月光静静地洒在柔和的河面上，远处的渔火时暗时明，四周万籁俱寂，只听见船桨轻轻的划水声。我们默默地划着，谁也不愿意惊扰这秋夜的宁静。小艇在水面上像箭一样滑行，在船尾留下了一串串迅速远离而去的旋涡。

到了小岛，我们把小艇拴在岸上，就静悄悄地钻进了那片甘蔗林。阿根和阿真兵分两路，各选了一个方向前进。因为我没有枪，阿根让我跟在他的后面拾“战利品”。

甘蔗林里密不透风，甘蔗长得比胳膊还粗，约有两米多高，宽大的甘蔗叶横七竖八，叶子的边缘长满了锯齿般的刺，我们稍不小心，就会被锋利的叶子拉一道口子。借着天上的月光，我猫着腰从下往上看，每隔三四步，就有一只或两只禾花雀站在甘蔗的叶子上睡觉。阿根不愧是打禾花雀的高手，他用右肩紧紧地顶着枪托，右手握着枪把并按着扳机，左手拿着手电筒并托着枪的前半部，把枪管伸到离禾花雀的脑袋只有几厘米的距离才开火。当然是一枪一只，百发百中啦。据说，在强光的照射下，禾花雀会感到四处都是一片漆黑而无法辨别逃跑的方向，只好站着不动，任人宰割了。

霎时间，甘蔗林里手电筒的光柱四处摇曳，枪声此起彼落，打破了秋夜的宁静。我跟在阿根后面三米左右，借着手电筒微弱发黄的光柱，把一只只落在地上的禾花雀捡起来，放在阿根给我的布袋里。不一会儿，装禾花雀的布袋就显得有些沉了。

在银色的月光下，甘蔗叶上的禾花雀就像一尊尊银白色的泥塑小鸟，纹丝不动。看着这些伸手可得的禾花雀，打鸟哪还要用枪啊——我决定“徒手捕雀”。很快，我的手电筒照到了一只肥肥的禾花雀，站在与我齐眉高的一片叶子上酣睡。我看准目标，屏住呼吸，迅速地伸手往上一抓就逮住了它。徒手捕雀的成功让我兴奋不已，我如法炮制又抓了几只。突然间，我发现了一对禾花雀肩并肩地站在一片叶子上睡觉。虽然无从知道它们到底是一对夫妻，一对情侣，或是一对母子，但它们睡得是那样的深沉甜蜜，对即将降临的灭顶之灾还一无所知。罪孽深重的我轻轻地往上一跃，就把那对禾花雀捞在了手里。

我插队前住在大城市郊区，也曾用过弹弓、手电筒和气枪打鸟，但常常是空手而回，毫无斩获。相比之下，在这里打禾花雀实在是太容易了。我和阿根边打边走，最后与阿真在甘蔗林的另一头胜利会师。阿真把他打的禾花雀全部倒进我的布袋里，也不征求阿根的意见就爽快地对我说：“你们知青没什么肉吃，你把这些禾花雀都拿走吧。”我原来只是想跟着他们玩儿的，根本没想过要瓜分他们的战利品。于是，我连忙说了几个“不”，可阿真坚持要我拿走所有的禾花雀，阿根也叫我不要推让。“恭敬不如从命”，我只好把他们的好意收下了。

回到村里，我们在河边拴好了生产队的小艇就分头回家了。阿根与我同路，我们俩边走边聊。快到我的住处时，阿根很不好意思地结结巴巴地对我说：“我想要几只禾花雀哄哄我哥那5岁的女儿，可以吗？”我马上说可以，并让他多拿。但他只拿了几只，还告诉我说：“你要马上把禾花雀连夜弄熟，否则变坏就不能吃了。”40多只肥肥的禾花雀，让我们姐弟俩美美地享受了好几周“食有肉”的幸福生活。

农村这个广阔天地的生活虽然艰苦，但农民兄弟对知青的深情厚谊却让我终生难忘。

Chapter 2

Bird Hunting

In southern China, even in late fall, the sun does not cease to burn from the cloudless blue sky. I remember how it was that year, when we were almost finished with our first ever fall harvest. The once challenging and to us zhiqing—terrifying—golden rice plants had been harvested and removed, exposing the rich soil underneath. The bare rice paddies now looked like a massive dark rug, extending to the horizons. The most eye-catching sights in this open field were the alluring green sugarcane patches dotting the river banks, resembling precious emerald stones scattered on grey flooring.

One day in the evening, as the bright red sun disappeared behind the mountains in the distance, darkness hugged my village. Two young men from the village, Ah Gen and Ah Zhen, invited me to go bird hunting with them. They told me that the birds had been feasting on the ripened grain throughout fall, making themselves most plump at this time of year. The locals called the birds Rice Blossom Sparrows. Ah Gen and Ah Zhen told me that the best bird hunting time was evening because after gorging themselves all day, the Rice Blossom Sparrows would want to find a comfortable and safe place to sleep. Since the rice plants had been cut and the rice paddies were now bare, the sparrows could only rest themselves on the sugarcane stalks. Earlier that day, Ah Gen and Ah Zhen had gone separately to the outskirts of the village to scout the

Rice Blossom Sparrows. They observed several flocks of Rice Blossom Sparrows coming and going and finally disappearing in the sugarcane fields. After a quick discussion, Ah Gen and Ah Zhen decided on a patch of sugarcane on a small river island—we would do our bird hunting there.

After supper, as the lights went on in the village and darkness cloaked the outskirts of the village, Ah Gen and Ah Zhen knocked on my door, each bearing an air rifle, pellets, a cloth sack for storing the kill, and a mega flashlight with three D-cell batteries. I was a destitute zhiqing, who had neither a gun nor pellets. I could only grab my flashlight (with only two D-cell batteries) and follow them.

By the river adjoining our village, we boarded a small row boat belonging to our production team. Ah Gen positioned himself at the bow while Ah Zhen took up the stern, leaving the middle for me. In the moon light, we rowed toward the island where our targets were resting. Other than the blinking lights on fishing boats in the distance, all was quiet and still. The only sound we could hear came from our paddles stroking water. We paddled without speaking; no one wanted to break the peacefulness of the night. Our boat broke water like an arrow, leaving only ripples fast disappearing behind.

When we reached the island and after we had secured the boat, we made our way into the thicket of the sugarcane forest. Ah Gen and Ah Zhen chose to go toward different directions, but since I did not have a gun, Ah Gen asked me to follow him so that I could pick up his "war booties."

It was a dense sugarcane forest, impenetrable even by wind. Each sugarcane stalk was about two meters tall, a little bigger than my arm, and the huge leaves jutted out from the stalks in disarray. If we were not careful, the sharp saw-like teeth on the edges of the leaves would slash us, leaving painful and bloody gashes. Hunching my back and taking advantage of the moon light, I looked up to see that, every two or three steps, there was actually one or two Rice Blossom Sparrows sleeping standing on a sugarcane leaf. No wonder An Gen was thought of as a superb Rice Blossom Sparrow hunter. With his right hand, Ah Gen propped his air rifle on his right shoulder, his index finger at the ready on the trigger; and with his left hand, he held his flashlight while supporting the front of the gun. He did not pull the trigger until the gun barrel was only several centimeters away from each sparrow's head. Of course it was one shot one sparrow. He had one hundred percent accuracy. I had heard that bright lights would blind the sparrows so that they would be stunned to stand still, not knowing which direction they could take flight. They could only wait to meet their fate.

Upon our arrival on the river island, the quiet and still fall night broke into chaos, lights flashing everywhere and gun shots firing continuously. I stayed about three meters behind Ah Gen, picking up the sparrows that had been shot. My flash light provided only a weak yellow light beam, but it was enough to help me put the dead sparrows into the cloth sack Ah Gen had given me. The sack became heavy in no time.

Under the silver moon light, the Rice Blossom Sparrows on sugarcane stalks looked like silver bird sculptures on display—not moving at all. No guns are needed, I thought, looking at the birds within my reach. I decided to try my luck with my hands. Quickly, my yellow light beam found a fat Rice Blossom Sparrow sleeping on a sugarcane leaf right at my eye brow level. I held my breath, aimed, and snatched the bird. I was so excited by my victory that I captured several more in quick succession. Suddenly, I found a pair of sparrows sleeping shoulder to shoulder on a leaf. I could not tell whether they were husband and wife, lovers, or mother and child. They were sound asleep, not knowing death was looming. What sin!—I extended my arm and jumped up lightly. The pair ended up in my sack.

I used to live in the suburb of a big city before coming to the village, and I had bird hunted with slings or flashlights and air rifles, but I often went home empty-handed. Compared to those prior bird hunting experiences, this Rice Blossom Sparrow hunt was just too easy. Ah Gen and I made our kills as we walked across the sugarcane patch. Soon we met up with Ah Zhen on the other side, gloating. Ah Zhen filled my sack with all of his Rice Blossom Sparrows, and without discussing it first with Ah Gen, he said to me, "You zhiqing don't have enough meat to eat. Take all of the Rice Blossom Sparrows." I never thought I would end up with any of the birds when I decided to go hunting with them—I only went because I thought it would be fun.

"No, no, no," I stammered. But Ah Zhen insisted that I take all the Rice Blossom Sparrows we killed that night. Ah Gen also agreed. I remembered a saying: obedience is better than politeness.

I received their kindness without protesting further.

After we rowed our boat back to the village and secured it in its original place, we went our separate ways home. Ah Gen and I went the same way so we chatted while we walked. When we were almost at my place, Ah Gen said to me sheepishly, stuttering a bit, "Would it be all right with you if I took a few of the Rice Blossom Sparrows home to treat my older brother's five-year-old daughter?" I asked Ah Gen to take as many as he would like, but he only took a few. He also told me that I should clean and cook the sparrows right away. "Otherwise," he said, "they will spoil and you can't eat them anymore." Later, my sister and I feasted on the 40 Rice Blossom Sparrows for several weeks and we had a good taste of what life would have been like for us if we had meat in our diet.

Even though life was hopeless, desperate, and difficult in the village, my farmer brothers were always kind and generous toward me. I will never forget the friendship they showed me and the other zhiqing in the village.

三

自　留　地

在“农业学大寨”“割资本主义尾巴”的火红年代，农村实行的是严格的计划经济。全村600多亩地，种多少亩水稻、多少亩甘蔗、多少亩黄麻等经济作物，上面都有严格的规定。为了解决农民吃蔬菜的需要，按政策农民每人分得两厘（约13平方米）自留地。自留地，顾名思义即是可以“自由支配的保留地”，这是村民们赖以维持生计的宝地。

我村与一个大镇子只有一河之隔，镇上居民的日常蔬菜基本要依赖镇子周围的几个村子供应。我村自留地种的蔬菜除了村民自用外，全部都由各家各户拿到镇上的自由市场卖。卖菜是村民经济收入的一个重要来源，日常的油盐酱醋等支出都得靠卖菜所得。每天清晨，村民们就到自留地里收菜，并在穿村而过的小河里把菜洗得干干净净，然后挑着一担担翠绿鲜亮的蔬菜往镇子里赶。

与村民们一样，知青不种自留地也就没有蔬菜吃。有的村民知道知青们一不会种菜，二没有搞自留地的工具，三吃不了种自留地的苦，就与知青们做交易：让知青把自留地给他们经营，他们则让知青每天到他们的自留地选蔬菜食用。对我们知青来说，要应付生产队日常的劳作已经苦不堪言了，收工后哪还有心思和能量搞自留地啊？与其让自留地荒废，还不如拿自留地与村民们换蔬菜。这样，很多知青，特别是劳力较弱的女知青，都愿意用自留地换蔬菜。

我那时血气方刚，也想尝尝搞自留地的滋味儿。各村一般都把紧靠村边，且比较肥沃的地划为自留地，以便于村民们收工后去打理。我用锄头把自留地黝黑的土翻了翻，分成两垄，但不知道种什么菜比较好，几个青年农民朋友就为我出谋划策，告诉我先种哪些菜，后种哪些菜，以保证自己长年有菜吃。他们还拿来了自家的蔬菜种子供我选择。在他们热情的帮助下，我在一垄地种上了一棵冬瓜，一些长豆角、丝瓜、生菜等；在另一垄地则全种上了比较省事儿的甘蔗。为了让我省钱，这几个农民朋友还给我拿来了生产队里剩余的甘蔗苗。这样，种自留地的战斗就打响了。

每天干完生产队的活，我就拖着疲惫不堪的身子来到自留地里干活。除了下雨外，浇水是每天最基本的活儿了。因为没有工具，我得等到别人都浇完水才能借用他们的浇水工具。浇水工具是用一根扁担挑着一对木水桶，水桶壁上斜插了一根打通了的竹管，就像一个茶壶一样。我照本宣科地学着农民浇水的架势，挑起一担借来的木水桶走到小河没膝深的地方，弯腰把两个水桶往水里一按，待水桶装满了水，就直起腰来，憋着一股劲儿，挑着满满的担子踉踉跄跄地向自留地走去。幸好自留地离小河不远，到了我的地盘，我挑着水担子走在两垄地的中间，两个壶嘴分别对着两垄地，双手左右开弓地把两个水桶往下一摁，只见两股清水射向菜地。我尽可能保持匀速直线运动，让水均匀地洒在菜地上。很快，菜叶上挂满了晶莹的水珠，在夕阳的照射下五彩缤纷，分外夺目。望着那片日新月异、绿油油的自留地，我心花怒放，充满了成就感，一天劳作的艰辛也不翼而飞了。

村民种自留地有一套理论。各家各户都把自留地的蔬菜分成两种：一种是留给自己吃的；另一种是拿到自由市场卖的。对自留的蔬菜，只施人粪、尿等有机肥，不施化肥，不打农药；对拿到自由市场卖的蔬菜，则是化肥、农药双管齐下。所以，自留的蔬菜长得比较丑陋，且叶子上满是虫眼；而拿到自由市场卖的蔬菜则长得绿油油的，光彩照人。由于知道内情，我们到镇上的自由市场买菜时，都挑选叶子上有虫眼的菜买——虫子吃了没事儿的菜，我们会比较放心。

为了解决自留地有机肥的问题，家家户户都八仙过海，各显神通地收集人粪、尿。村民阿胜买了两个米缸放在男知青住的楼里收集小便，定期上门把缸里的尿收走。我们男知青也图个方便，不用出楼就能解决问题。但有了自留地后，“肥水不流外人田”——知青们也开始收集自家的尿了。我们男知青楼一夜之间就新添了好几口知青尿缸。

一天，村民阿胜来到知青楼对我说："我挑着尿桶来收集你们知青楼尿缸里尿的时候，看到知青河民在他的尿缸旁的墙上贴了一首打油诗，我识字儿不多，不懂诗的意思。我估计是河民不满意我收集了他尿缸里的尿。要是这样，跟我说一句话就行了，何必写打油诗呢？你去看看那首打油诗是不是这个意思。"

我随着阿胜来到河民的尿缸旁，果然看见一张巴掌大的纸贴在墙上，纸上有三行秀丽工整的钢笔字儿：

自家肥田肥又肥，

管人薄地草不生，

尿缸一倾去若空！

为何只有三句？我笑得差点晕倒，只好对阿胜说他的猜测没错。自从这场尿缸风波之后，就再也没有村民敢来知青楼收集尿了。

俗话说，"种瓜得瓜，种豆得豆"——我从自留地收获的豆角、丝瓜和青菜吃也吃不完。那株冬瓜藤也顺利地开花，结了一个有4公斤多重的大冬瓜。根据农民朋友的建议，我把那个大冬瓜去皮后，再刨成一片片晒干，制成冬瓜干，以备在蔬菜青黄不接时用来煮冬瓜汤。村民们还建议我把多余的蔬菜拿到镇上的自由市场卖，挣几个零花钱。我们那时哪拉得下面子抓杆秤到自由市场去卖菜呀！阿胜的母亲松姨知道我爱面子，就主动提出替我到自由市场卖菜。

天刚蒙蒙亮，我就到自留地里收菜，在河里把菜洗干净后整齐地放在两个平底的竹筐里，然后用扁担挑起满满的两筐蔬菜，踏着晨曦，摇摇晃晃地沿着田埂向渡口走去。这时，年近60的松姨已在渡口等着我了。她抽着卷烟，背上背着还在熟睡的孙子，二话不说就接过我的担子上了渡船。那条河约有100米宽，过河后还得走大约半里路才到镇上的自由市场。每次卖菜回来，松姨都交给我几块钱，并告诉我，她来回过河的四分钱渡船费已从卖菜所得的钱中扣除了。

我种的一垄甘蔗，由于施肥少，虽然长得比较“苗条”，可也有两米多高。甘蔗浑身都是宝啊——甘蔗叶子可以做柴火；甘蔗秆可以榨糖；榨糖后的甘蔗渣子还可以用来做猪饲料。

秋后，我把甘蔗砍下来，用甘蔗叶子把甘蔗捆成一把一把的，每把大约有25公斤重。晚饭后，我借了生产队的一条小木船，把船系在靠近自留地的河边，到自留地把捆好的甘蔗扛在肩上，走大约几百米后，再把甘蔗卸在船上。

硬硬的甘蔗秆儿压得我的肩膀疼痛难忍，但丰收的喜悦却让我感到欢欣鼓舞——这毕竟是我有生以来第一次自食其力的劳动成果啊。在明亮的月光下，我一边摇着橹，一边哼着小调，驾着沉甸甸的小船缓缓地驶向镇上的榨糖厂。到了榨糖厂，我把甘蔗一把一把地卸下来，摆在榨糖厂的大秤上一称，出乎意料地居然有500多公斤。按榨糖厂的规定，每10公斤新鲜甘蔗可换1公斤糖。遵循村民的教导，我在船上早就准备好了一口新缸用来装糖。榨糖厂的人把50多公斤糖装进我的糖缸后，我就吱丫吱丫地摇着橹胜利返航了。

那个榨糖厂给我的既不是白砂糖，也不是红砂糖，而是很稠很稠的黄褐色的糖浆，看起来像一团黄褐色的泥巴，表面还有一层黄色的泡沫，散发出浓浓的甜味儿，还略带点儿发酵的酸味儿，当地人食用的基本都是这种糖。

不知是特别珍惜还是吃腻了，那缸自留糖我和姐姐吃了很久很久也没吃完。

Chapter 3

Private Plots

Painstaking planning was practiced during the years of "Learn from *Dazhai* in Agriculture" and "Sever Capitalist Tails." Self-sacrifice was practiced and glorified. Of the 600 *mu* of arable land in the village, how much of it should be used for growing rice, sugarcane, or jute was carefully planned and followed. As for vegetables for human consumption, the policy was to give each resident about two *li* (about 13 square meters) of farmland so that farmers could do what they wanted with their private plots, which became each family's livelihood.

My village was separated from a big town by only a river. The town's people depended on the bordering villages for their supply of daily vegetables. Farmers from my village grew vegetables for their families in their private plots but more importantly, they sold the vegetables at the free-market in town. The money from the vegetable sales was an important income for the farmers, who could use the money to buy cooking oil, salt, soy sauce, and vinegar—daily essentials. Early each morning, the farmers would harvest vegetables from their private plots, wash the vegetables in the river that meandered through the village, and then carry the fresh vegetables on shoulder poles to board a ferry to the market in town.

Like the farmers, we zhiqing would not have vegetables to eat if we did not grow them in our private plots. Aware of our difficulties, such as not knowing how to grow vegetables, not having the right equipment, and not knowing how to deal with the demand of managing a private plot, some of the farmers made an exchange with us. They asked us to let them cultivate our private parcels of land in exchange for supplying us with our daily vegetables. To us, especially to the female zhiqing who were not too robust, this was a good exchange. We were not prepared to work in our private plots physically or mentally. It was hard enough for us to handle the required daily work assignments from the production team.

However, I was a hot blooded young man eager to know what it was like to work in my own parcel of land. Most of the private plots occupied some of the most convenient and best soil in the village. Farmers usually worked in their private plots right after working in the fields belonging to the production team.

Imitating the farmers, with a hoe, I dug up the soil in my plot and divided it into two rows, but I did not know what to plant. Several young farmers helped me by suggesting which vegetables to grow first and which to grow later so that I would have vegetables to eat year round. They also brought me seeds from home. With their enthusiastic help, I planted winter melon, long beans, luffa, and lettuce in one row; and in the other, for the sake of convenience, I planted sugarcane with the starter plants my friends brought me from what was left over from the production team's fields. Thus I began a battle with my land.

Every day I dragged my body to my parcel after finishing my work for the production team. Watering the plants was a daily must-do unless it rained. Because I did not have any tools, I had to wait for everyone else to finish before borrowing their equipment. What we used for watering was a shoulder pole and two wooden buckets that looked like two huge teapots because a section of hollowed bamboo had been inserted into each bucket to make a spout. Like the farmers, I carried my borrowed wooden "teapots" to the river where the water came to my knees. I bent forward while pressing the "teapots" into the water to fill. Then holding my breath, I would straighten my back and carry the two buckets of water to my land. Fortunately the river was not too far from my parcel. Walking between the two rows of plants, each hand grabbing onto one of the two "teapots," I would aim the bamboo spouts at my plants. I tried to walk steadily and at an even pace so that I could water my plants evenly. This way, water pearls would collect on the leaves, reflecting the sun light and exhibiting a colorful display. I always felt a great sense of accomplishment when I saw how healthy my plants were and how they grew each day. I would forget my weariness.

The farmers had a way of managing their private plots. Each family divided their vegetables into two kinds: one was for self-consumption and the other was for sale at the free-market in town. To grow the vegetables for self-consumption, the farmers used only human waste or other organic compost. They would not use any chemical fertilizers or pesticides. But to grow the vegetables for sale, the farmers used both chemical fertilizers and pesticides. As such, the vegetables for self-consumption would usually be smaller and full of bug bites while the vegetables for sale would be healthy looking and attractive. Because we knew the secret, when we went to buy vegetables from the free-market in town, we would always choose those vegetables that had a few bug bites. We figured that it would be safe to eat the vegetables that bugs liked.

To ensure that they had enough organic fertilizers for their private plots, each family came up with its own ingenious ideas to collect human waste. Farmer Ah Sheng installed two earthen jugs in the male zhiqing's dormitory to collect urine. He came collecting the urine on a regular schedule. We liked it that way since we would not have to leave our dorms to relieve ourselves. But since some of us had our own private plots as well, we did not want our "treasured liquid" to go into other people's fields—we started collecting our own urine. As a result, almost overnight, several earthen jugs appeared in our dorms.

One day, Farmer Ah Sheng came to me and said, “I noticed a poem on Hemin’s urine jug when I was collecting the urine from your dorms. I don’t know how to read but I guessed maybe he wasn’t happy with me collecting the urine from his jug. Why didn’t he just tell me? There is no need to write a poem about it. Could you go read the poem to see what it says?”

I followed Ah Sheng to Hemin’s urine container. There I found a piece of paper as big as my palm pasted to the jug. Three lines of beautiful calligraphy were written on the paper:

Happiness is having a fertile plot,
I do not care if other’s soil is too lean for weeds.
Desolation follows the tipping over of my urine pot!

Why weren’t there more lines? I almost passed out from laughing. I could only tell Ah Sheng that his guess was right. Ever since, no farmer came to our dorms to collect urine again.

The saying about how “One gets what one sows” is definitely true. I had more than enough long beans, luffa, and other leafy vegetables that year. The winter melon seed I planted gave me a big melon weighing about four kilograms. Following the suggestion of a farmer friend, I peeled and sliced the melon so that I could make dried melon for when I did not have fresh vegetables. It was also suggested to us that we should sell our surplus vegetables at the free-market in town so that we would have some spending money, but we found it too embarrassing to do that. Ah Sheng’s mother Aunt Song recognized my predicament so she volunteered to sell my vegetables for me at the free-market.

I would go to my private plot to harvest my vegetables when it was still dark in the morning. I would then wash the vegetables in the river and fill two flat bottomed bamboo baskets with the vegetables. With my two baskets of vegetables on a shoulder pole, I would go to the ferry crossing at dawn. There, with a hand-rolled cigarette in her mouth, Aunt Song, who was almost 60 years old, would be waiting for me with her sleeping grandson in a sack on her back. Without saying anything, she would take over my shoulder pole and baskets of vegetables and walk onto the ferry. The river was about 100 meters wide and one had to walk for about half a *huali* (250 meters) to get to the market after crossing the river. Every time after she came back, Aunt Song would give me a few *yuan* as earnings from the vegetable sale and tell me that she had deducted four *fen* for the ferry ticket.

My row of sugarcane grew well even though I did not fertilize the soil enough. The stalks grew to about two meters tall. Every part of the sugarcane could be used so sugarcane was considered a treasured crop. The leaf could be used as firewood, the juice from the cane could be extracted to make sugar, and the pulp could be fed to pigs.

In late fall that year, I cut down my sugarcane stalks and divided them into bundles weighing about 25 kilograms each. I tied each bundle with sugarcane leaves. One day after supper, I borrowed a wooden boat from our production team and rowed it to my private plot. I carried my sugarcane bundles on my shoulders to the boat. Even though my shoulders hurt from the heavy weight of the sugarcane—there were several hundred meters between my private plot and the boat—I was happy and encouraged by my harvest. It was the first time I produced something from my labor. Under the bright moon, humming a song, I rowed the boat to the town's sugar mill. When I got to the mill, I unloaded the sugarcane bundles one at a time onto the mill's scale. To my surprise, my sugarcane weighed over 500 kilograms. According to the purchasing policy at the mill, ten kilograms of sugarcane could be exchanged for one kilogram of sugar. As suggested by the farmers, I had already prepared a big container for the sugar I would get for my sugarcane. After collecting over 50 kilograms of sugar from my harvest, I rowed the boat back victoriously.

However, the sugar I collected from the primitive sugar mill was neither granulated sugar nor brown sugar. It was some heavy yellowish, brownish syrup, resembling runny mud with yellow bubbles on the top. It gave off the fragrance of fermentation. The locals called this syrupy substance sugar.

I don’t know if we were sick of the sugar or if we found the syrupy substance precious, but my container of sugar lasted a long time. I do not think my sister and I ever finished it.

四

夏　收

南方水乡，每年种两季水稻。夏收、夏种是最繁忙最辛苦的农时季节。为了不误农时，以便收割后马上犁地、抢时间插秧夏种，夏收时稻田里的水还是满满的。

我村大部分的田地在远离村庄的大围地区，走陆路或摇船走水路都得花一个多小时才能到达。大围，顾名思义就是四面环水，被堤坝围起来的田地。当河水涨潮时，围外的水位比围内的地面还要高。

为出征大围，我们每天早上4时左右就得起床洗洗刷刷，匆匆忙忙地做饭、吃饭，然后带上镰刀、草帽、禾撬和煮饭锅，在6时前赶到停泊在生产队大晒场旁的几艘木船上。每条木船上都黑压压地坐满了村民，人声鼎沸，好不热闹。很快，满载着人和工具的几艘木船就沿着弯弯曲曲的小河前行，穿过村里的水闸，驶进了水面宽阔的大河。

到了大围，太阳才刚刚升起。站在堤坝上极目远眺，大围内那一望无垠的稻田，除了金黄色，还是金黄色！稻田里的水刚好漫过了脚踝，我们卷起裤腿跳进稻田里排成一行，每人负责收割6行稻子，从田头往田尾横扫过去。

我是左撇子，平时习惯用左手，但由于没有为左撇子专门设计的镰刀，且用左手挥镰会很容易与在我左侧用右手挥镰的人相碰而造成危险，所以我只得改用右手握镰了。当地镰刀的形状像一个问号一样，月牙般弯曲的部分是用铁制的刀，刀刃上有一排锋利的锯齿；问号的笔直部分则是手握的木把。割稻子时，右手用镰刀钩住前后排两棵稻子靠近根部之处，左手马上抓住那两棵稻子的中上部，右手再用力往斜上方一拉把稻子割断。不断地重复着这一动作，直到左手抓满了稻子为止，才抽空把手里的稻子放在人的左侧。我们周而复始，一遍又一遍地重复同样的动作，缓缓地向田尾推进。为了割得快些，我们的左手都尽量地抓更多的稻子。我的手掌较小，则先用大拇指和食指抓，再用食指和中指，而后用中指和无名指，最后用无名指和小拇指。

有时割稻子时不小心，手脚就会被锋利的镰刀划伤。一次，由于割稻时用力过猛，我的镰刀在左手的小拇指尖儿上拉了一道深深的口子，指甲也被削掉了一片，鲜血直流。村民锦胜看见后，马上从自己的烟盒里拿出烟丝敷在我小拇指的伤口上，并从自己的衣服上撕下布条为我包扎伤口。据村民们说，烟丝有消毒、止疼和止血的作用。俗话说“十指连心”，再加上烟丝的刺激，小拇指伤口的疼痛犹如雪上加霜，我的前额冒出了豆大的汗珠。锦胜帮我包扎好伤口后让我歇着。但我谢绝了他的好意，又继续干了起来。因为这件事情，锦胜在生产队年终评工分的大会上力排众议，使我评上了知青中最高的工分。

南方水乡的五六月，暑气袭人，没有一丝风，狠毒的太阳像要把一切都烤干似的。我们人人头戴草帽，身穿长衣长裤，汗流浃背地劳作在那金黄色的田野里。农民们穿的是清一色的黑衣、黑裤，妇女们则在草帽里加放一条毛巾，用毛巾下垂的两端来遮挡照射在脸颊两面的阳光，以保护脸上白嫩的皮肤。按理说，黑衣黑裤会吸收更多的热量，不利于消暑散热。可在那买布凭票定量的年代，用更耐脏、更不易褪色的布来做衣裤则更实用。

我们割完了一块又一块地，浑身上下都湿透了，腰酸背痛，骨头架子都像散了一样。可望望四周，那些被我们消灭掉的几片稻田就像沧海一粟，不见踪影，周围还是那片一望无际的金色海洋——真是“苦海无边”啊！

中午，我们从船上拿来随身携带的煮饭锅，在河水里淘淘米，用锄头在堤坝上挖一个炉灶，架上饭锅用干稻草烧火做饭。我的午饭很简单——一个咸鸭蛋，几根咸菜和米饭。饭后虽有半小时休息，可在这赤日炎炎的大围，堤坝上连一棵小树也没有，堤坝下除了稻田还是稻田，哪有地方遮阴啊！幸好附近有个牛棚，虽然地上到处是臭烘烘的黑牛粪，我们也顾不了那么多了，抱来一大把稻草铺在牛粪上，倒头就打个盹儿，伸伸快要断了的腰，可真是天大的享受啊！

短暂的午休后，我们又回到田里，用两把稻草打个“禾抱结”作为绳

子来捆稻子。我们把上午割下来，还躺在水里的水稻捆绑成大约有25公斤重的一捆，再用两头尖的禾撬挑起两捆稻子扛在肩上，东倒西歪地蹚着田里的泥水走上田埂，又摇摇晃晃地挑着沉重的担子踏上那只有一尺来宽的跳板，把稻子撂在停靠在河边的船上。水稻还未全部弄到船上，我的肩膀已被担子压得又红又肿，火辣辣的生疼。我那补丁打补丁的衣裤都被汗水湿透了，整个人就像被从水里捞出来的一样。为了消暑解渴，我只好拼命喝水，因为体力消耗很大。

下午4时多，装满了一捆捆稻子的几条船显得沉甸甸的，船沿离水面只有三寸高了。每条船上只留两个男劳动力摇橹撑船，从水路把稻子运回村，其余的人则肩扛禾撬，禾撬上挑着中午煮饭的锅，从陆路步行一个多小时回家。

自从学会撑船、摇橹后，我都主动要求承担运稻子的任务。我们运稻子的几个小伙子让船在小河里拐几个弯后，就停在一片茂密的甘蔗林旁边。大围前不着村后不着店，只有蓝天、大田和小河。我们把湿淋淋、浸透了汗水、散发着氨味儿的衣裤脱下来扔在船上，就赤条条地跃入清清的

河水里，深深地扎几个猛子。那种透心凉的舒服让我暂时忘却了疲劳，忘却了所有的痛苦，此时此刻简直就是“河阔凭鱼跃，天高任鸟飞”啊！

当我们从河里爬上来时，原来被汗水湿透了的衣裤也被太阳晒干了。我们钻进甘蔗林里穿好衣裤，顺手掰一根胳膊般粗的甘蔗就大嚼了起来。我们一边聊着天，一边把甘蔗渣吐到河里。突然，几个农村小伙用手指着漂浮在河里的甘蔗渣大笑起来，说我吐出来的甘蔗渣下沉得特别快，而他们的甘蔗渣则久久地浮在水面上。他们笑我太浪费了， 要我用牙齿把甘蔗里的汁榨得更干。听了他们的话，我也不禁开怀大笑了起来。

把稻子运回村里已是下午5时多了，我们赶紧回家做饭、吃饭。晚上7时又得用禾撬把船上的一捆捆稻子卸到村里的大晒谷场上。卸船完毕，男劳动力把一把把的稻子放进电动脱粒机里，女劳动力则站在电动脱粒机出口处的两边，用禾叉把脱粒后的稻草叉到草堆上。在电动脱粒机的出口处，经常会有一些谷子随着稻草喷射出来，打得人的皮肤很痛。尽管天气又闷又热，叉草的妇女们还是穿着长衣长裤，头戴草帽，并在草帽里放一条毛巾来保护脸部。通常要到晚上10时多才把打谷的工作干完。我们洗好澡睡觉时，已是11时了。第二天清晨四五时，我们又得爬起来上工。这样的作息循环要持续一个月左右。

这是一年中最艰苦的30天，也是最令知青们心惊胆战的30天，简直就是在地狱的炉火里熬炼人的意志。有的知青吃不了这种苦，夏收前就回城，等夏收结束后才回村，因而引起了农民的公愤，有的生产队就不给这些知青分口粮。不给分口粮，这些知青就破罐子破摔——干脆回城再呆久一些，如此恶性循环，与农民的关系越来越紧张。

Chapter 4

Summer Harvest

Two crops of rice can be planted in southern China's coastal water villages each year, so the summer harvest-planting time is the busiest and most labor intensive season each year. To ensure optimum planting conditions for plowing and the transplanting of rice seedlings, water is not drained from the rice fields at the summer harvest.

Most of the rice paddies that belonged to our village were far away from the village. It usually took over an hour to walk or row a boat there. The area was called *dawei*, which meant that the rice paddies were in the middle of embankments that were surrounded by water. When it was high tide, the water level beyond the embankments would be higher than the water level in the rice fields.

To get to the dawei for summer harvest and planting, we had to get up around 4 a.m. to wash and eat breakfast. Then each of us would bring a sickle, a straw hat, a *heqiao* (a shoulder pole with tapered ends), and a cooking pot to board, by 6 a.m., one of a few wooden boats waiting by the production team's grain sunning ground. Filled with chattering male and female farmers, the boats would be like "boiling cauldrons with voices" moving on the village's winding river, passing the village's floodgates, and entering the big river leading to the dawei.

The sun would be just rising when we arrived at the dawei. Standing on an embankment, I could see that the rice paddies within the embankments reached beyond the horizon. All I saw was the color golden brown. Water in the rice fields came up to our ankles. We rolled up our pant legs and lined up horizontally along one end of a rice field, each person being responsible for harvesting six rows of rice plants. We moved forward side by side toward the other end of the field.

I am left-handed, so normally, I would hold a sickle with my left hand, but because there were no sickles made for left-handed people and I might clash with the right-handed person to my left if I held the sickle with my left hand—we could hurt each other, I had to hold my sickle with my right hand. Our sickles were shaped like question marks. The quarter-moon shaped blade was made of steel and had saw-like teeth. The wooden handle was the straight part of the sickle. To cut the rice plants in the fields, one would hook a few stems with the sickle in the right hand, grab the hooked stems with the left hand, and slash upward with the sickle. One would keep on hooking, grabbing, and slashing until the left hand could not grab anymore. Then one would lay the handful of cut rice plants on the ground to one's left. We repeated these motions as we advanced to the other end of the rice field. To speed up the process, we always tried grabbing as many rice stems as we could in our left hand. My hands are small comparatively speaking so I devised a method that enabled me to grab the rice plants between my thumb and index finger, then my index finger and my middle finger, and last my ring finger and little finger.

If not careful, the sharp sickle could cut our hands and legs easily. Once because I was slashing too hard, my sickle sliced the tip of my left little finger and cut through its fingernail. Blood gushed. When farmer Jingsheng saw me, he took some tobacco from his pocket and put it on my wound. He then tore off a strip of fabric from his shirt and wrapped it around my tobacco-covered wound. According to the villagers, tobacco could be used as a disinfectant, painkiller, and blood congealing agent. That day, I understood why people say that "Fingers are connected to the heart." The pain from the cut and the irritation from the tobacco on the wound were like adding frost to snow—adding insult to injury. Pea sized sweat beads formed on my forehead in no time. Jingsheng told me to rest after he dressed my wound, but I thanked him and continued to work. Because of my bravery, at the year-end income allocation meeting, Jingsheng convinced the others that I should be given the highest income among all the zhiqing that year.

It is usually quite hot in May and June in southern China's coastal water villages. There is usually no wind and the savage sun scorches everything. We worked in the golden yellow fields sweating profusely, each wearing a straw hat, long pants and long shirts. The farmers all wore black, and the females usually put a hand towel on their heads inside their straw hats. The two sides of the towel would drape on their cheeks protecting their faces. Technically, black clothes absorb more heat from the sun and are, therefore, not good for keeping one cool, but at the time, because fabric was rationed, it was more economical to make clothes with dark colored fabric—stains would not show easily and dark color would not fade quickly.

After working for the whole morning, we would be tired and sore. I often felt as if my bones were going to detach themselves from my body. But to our disappointment, the rice plants we cut down simply disappeared among the standing rice plants in the fields. What surrounded us would still be a sea of golden yellow, which reminded me of the phrase, "The sea of bitterness has no bounds."

At noon, we would fetch our cooking pots from the boat so that we could make our lunch. We went to the river to rinse our rice, dug a hole in the ground to function as a stove, and put some dry straw in the hole to serve as a heat source. My lunch was simple—a salty egg, pickled vegetables, and rice. We usually got half an hour to rest after lunch, but there was never a tree around to provide shade under the scorching sun—there were just rice paddies after rice paddies! Fortunately, there was a cow shed nearby. Even though there was cow manure everywhere in it, we would simply put an armful of straw on the darkened cow manure and take a nap. Nothing could bring us more comfort than to be able to stretch our sore—and almost broken—backs on the straw!

After a short rest, we would go back to work again. We would first tie two handfuls of straw together using a *hebaojie* (straw knot). The straw would then become twine that could be used to tie up the rice plants we cut down but left in the water in the morning. Each of the gathered bundles would weigh about 25 kilograms. We would then stab our heqiao into two of these bundles, one on each end of the heqiao, and we would put the heqiao on our shoulders. We would then carry the bundles from the muddy rice paddies to the boats. We had to be careful when we walked on the one-foot wide springboards that connected the shore to the boats. My shoulders would become red and swollen long before the boats were filled. My clothes, which had been mended many times with patch over patch, would be soaked in sweat, as if someone had just lifted me out of a river. To ward off thirst and dehydration, we had to drink water constantly.

Around 4 p.m. in the afternoon each day, our boats would finally be full of bundles of rice plants, which would weigh the boats down to about three inches above water. Two males would be assigned to each boat to row them back to the village. The rest of us would have to walk for about an hour back, carrying our heqiao and cooking pots on our shoulders.

Ever since I learned how to row and pole a boat, I always volunteered to transport rice plants at the end of the day. My fellow boatmen and I would row the boats to a lush sugarcane field where no one could see us. There was only the blue sky, the fields, and the river. We would strip ourselves and dive into the river. The cool, soothing water would make me forget my exhaustion and all suffering. Momentarily, I would feel as if I were a bird or fish—so free!

Our sweat-soaked clothes would be dry by the time we got out of the river. We would usually collect some sugarcane to chew while putting on our clothes. We laughed and talked while chewing our sugarcane and spitting out the fiber. I remember some of my fellow farmers once laughed at me as they noticed that the fiber I spat out was sinking while theirs was floating. They said that I was being wasteful since I did not give my sugarcane a good chew. We enjoyed teasing each other.

By the time we got back to the village, it would usually be after 5 p.m. We had to hurry home to make supper, eat it, and then at 7 p.m., we would have to go back to work to carry the bundles of rice plants from the boats to the village's grain sunning ground, where males would put the bundles into the electric threshers while the females would stand on either side of the machines to remove the rice straw. They used pitchforks. Very often, rice grains would shoot out with the rice straw at the exit point, hitting and hurting those who stood nearby. Even though it was often hot and humid, to protect themselves from the bullet-like rice grains, the females had to wear long sleeved tops, long pants, and a straw hat. To protect their faces, they put hand towels inside their hats so that the towels could drape down their cheeks. We usually did not finish working until about 10 p.m. By the time we finished washing and went to bed, it would usually be past 11 p.m. We had to get up around 4 a.m. or 5 a.m. the next morning to go back to work. This work routine would last for about a month during the summer harvest period.

The summer harvest period—the 30 days or so out of each year—was the most harsh and most frightful time for us zhiqing. We felt as if we were being tested in hell. Some zhiqing could not take the unforgiving condition so they would go back to the city before the harvest time and return when everything was over. Their escape would anger the farmers, who would then refuse to give these zhiqing their food rations. Such conflicts often resulted in a vicious cycle, making the zhiqing-farmer relationship quite tense.

五

夏　种

夏收结束了，紧接着是夏种。刚收割完的稻田马上灌水、犁好、耙平，原来金黄色的田野摇身一变又成了白茫茫的一片——插秧开始了。

按分工习惯，已婚且家有小孩的妇女负责打秧——即从秧田里把稻秧拔下来，用水草捆成一把把垒在秧担子上，由男劳动力挑到田里散发给负责插秧的人。插秧由青年妇女和男劳动力承担。与收割相似，插秧时每人负责插横向6株秧一排，从田头一直插到田尾。

我们左手拿着一捆稻秧，右手飞快地从稻秧中抽出几根秧苗，用食指和中指把秧苗插进泥里。我们头戴草帽背朝天，腰像一根弹簧似的，不知疲倦地上下左右摆动着，一簇簇稻秧从指间飞进泥土里，缓缓地染绿了一块又一块水田。我最希望插秧的那块水田短一些，插完后可以伸伸腰，并借着转移阵地时，可以让疼痛难忍的腰得到喘息的机会。大囤有一块很大、呈狭长矩形的稻田，即使是插秧高手也得插一上午，才能从田头到田尾走一趟。我们知青都把那块地看作是“滑铁卢”，若摊上了插那块地的

秧，就只好自认倒霉了。

我第一次到“滑铁卢”插秧，干了数小时，腰酸背疼，可田尾还是那样的遥远，真不知何年何月才能插到田尾啊！正在暗自悲伤时，生产队的副队长大牛好像看出了我的心思，招呼我跟他一起走到田埂上坐下来。正当我疑惑之际，大牛从衣服兜里掏出一包褐黄色的烟丝、一叠烟纸和一盒火柴，说：“来，抽口烟吧。”原来，按当地的规矩，烟民们干活时停下来抽烟是天经地义的、合理合法的。所以，为了延长抽烟的时间，用烟纸慢慢地卷烟丝是一个好办法，况且烟丝比包装的香烟更经济呢。

我学着大牛的样子，把一小撮烟丝放在烟纸上，把烟纸卷成圆锥形，然后用舌头舔舔烟纸的接口处，再用牙齿咬去纸烟的锥尖，最后把纸烟夹在嘴唇之间，点着了火就抽了起来。虽然那烟呛得我直咳嗽，但只要能救救我那累得快要断了的腰，再呛也值啊！

我由衷地感激大牛，心里也暗暗地为那些不抽烟的女同胞们抱不平。

有的农民还把用竹筒做成的水烟带到田里，我也跟着抽了几回竹筒水烟。抽烟时听着竹筒里咕咚咕咚的水声还蛮有情趣的呢！

插秧没有收割辛苦，白天收工回家后就能歇着，晚上不用再干活了。

Chapter 5

Summer Planting

Immediately after summer harvest, summer planting would begin. We would flood the rice fields and plow and till the soil to prepare it for planting. The landscape of golden grey would turn whitish grey as if in an instant. Summer planting would thus begin.

Following tradition, the job of rice planting was divided into three categories: seedling preparation, transportation, and planting. Married women with children were responsible for seedling preparation, which required them to pull the rice seedlings from the nursery, tie the seedlings into bundles, and arrange the bundles on shoulder poles. Then male farmers would carry the shoulder poles with seedlings to the rice paddies to distribute the seedlings to the people in the fields. Younger women and other males would then plant the seedlings, the same way they harvested the rice plants, standing side by side, each planting six seedlings in a row, moving from one end of a field to the other in unison.

Our left hands would hold handfuls of rice seedlings, our right index and middle fingers would do the planting—choosing rice seedlings from the left hand and sticking them into the soil. Looking at us from afar, one would only see our straw hats bobbing up and down, left and right; our backs springing rhythmically;

and rice seedlings descending from our hands to the soil steadily. This way, we "painted" the rice paddies green one paddy at a time. I often hoped for small paddies for planting so that I could straighten my back in between paddies and give my sore back a rest while walking from paddy to paddy. There was a huge rice paddy that was longer but narrower than the others in the dawei. It would take an expert planter an entire morning to plant six columns of seedlings from one end of the paddy field to the other. We zhiqing likened planting in that paddy field to fighting in the Battle of Waterloo. We could only blame our bad luck if we were assigned to plant in that field.

The first time I was assigned to plant there, I could not believe my eyes: Even after I had worked there for several hours, the other end of the field was still out of sight! Just as I was sinking into a self-pitying depression hole, as if he knew how I was feeling, one of the vice-captains of our production team asked me to take a break with him. While I was puzzling over his kind gesture, Big Ox (as he was called) rolled a cigarette for me and said, "Come. Have a smoke." I found out that according to the local customs, it was perfectly all right for farmers to take a cigarette break every now and then. Rolling one's own cigarettes not only lengthened the break time but also made smoking more economical as it was cheaper to buy tobacco than cigarettes.

Imitating Big Ox, I took a pinch of his tobacco, put it on a piece of tobacco paper, and rolled the cigarette into a cone shape. I licked the end of the paper so that it would stick to the cigarette. Then I bit off the pointy end of the cigarette before putting the cigarette between my lips. I inhaled a mouthful of air as soon as the cigarette was lit. The smoke choked me to a coughing fit but I thought it was worth it since smoking gave my half-broken back a necessary break.

I was grateful to Big Ox from the bottom of my heart but at the same time I was most incensed thinking how the females could not smoke. Some of the farmers brought their water pipes to the fields so I learned to smoke a water pipe, too. I enjoyed listening to the rumbling sound the water pipe made when I smoked.

Summer planting was not as hard as summer harvesting as we did not have to work in the evening. We could rest at home after a full day's work.

六

姐姐的眼睛

夏收的一天晚上，我和姐姐吃过饭就到村里大晒谷场的河边卸船。晒谷场上灯火通明，村民们正在有条不紊地用禾撬把几条船上一捆捆的稻子挑到村里的大晒场上。不一会儿，卸下来的稻子就堆成了一座小山。

像往常一样，我们男劳动力每人手里拿着一把稻子，排着队轮流把稻子放进电动脱粒机里；女劳动力则站在电动脱粒机出口处，用禾叉把脱粒后的稻草叉到草堆上。姐姐头戴草帽和保护脸部的毛巾，穿着她那洗得发白、略带花点的长上衣和蓝长裤，站在最靠近电动脱粒机出口处叉草。她们干活时都低着头，尽量侧着脸，借着草帽和垂在脸部两边的毛巾来遮挡从电动脱粒机里喷射出来的谷子。新鲜的稻谷不但两头尖，壳上还布满了芒刺，打在手上都直生疼。突然，姐姐“啊”的一声，就停止了干活，我赶忙走过去看她。只见她闭着左眼，脸上满是汗水，说是有粒稻谷射进了她的左眼。我从未遇到过这种事儿，正在不知所措之时，生产队的副队长温竟坤马上走过来，问周围的村民谁有指甲刀。有人马上递给他一把指甲刀，他就用指甲刀钳住那粒稻谷的一端，把稻谷的另一端从姐姐的左眼皮之间慢慢地拉了出来。村民们说，电动脱粒机喷射出来的谷子打到人眼睛

的事以前也发生过，所以他们使用脱粒机时都随身带指甲刀以防万一。姐姐用毛巾擦干了脸上的汗水和泪水， 继续干活。收工后，她回到宿舍，往左眼滴了点氯霉素眼药水就去睡觉了。

眼睛受伤后的两天，姐姐还照常早出晚归地参加农忙。第四天，她对我说她的左眼很疼，怕亮光，要我陪她去县城里的医院检查眼睛。我当时觉得姐姐娇气，连这点苦都吃不了，心里很不愿意陪她去县城。姐姐看出了我的心思，伤心地哭了，我就用不高兴的语气说明天跟她去县城。

村庄距离县城有十多公里，不通汽车只通船，步行则要一两个小时。次日清晨，我们坐上6时开往县城的机动客轮，一张全程的船票要花6角钱。我们有个表舅母在县城医院工作。她毕业于上海的一所医学院，其学历之高在县城医院的医生中当属凤毛麟角，而且她的医术在县城里也挺有名气的。

船到了县城的码头，已是上午7时多了。我们走了15分钟就来到了县城医院附近。这时，姐姐的眼睛可能痛得难受，她想先到县医院等我，让我自己到表舅家找表舅母。表舅母家离县医院大约有15分钟的路程。不知什么原因，我就是不同意，坚持要她跟我一起先到表舅母家再说。姐姐大概越来越觉得不舒服，再加上我又不体谅她，一边走一边就轻声地哭了起来。那时的我自诩为“理智型”青年，看透了世态炎凉，有意识地压抑内在的同情心，表情冷漠。姐姐的伤心和眼泪丝毫打动不了我的那颗冷酷的心， 我反而觉得她太娇气，吃不了苦。我于是加快了步伐，把她甩在身后十几米远……

我们好不容易走到了表舅母家，可表舅母已经上班去了。无奈之中，我们只得由原路返回县医院。在医院里， 我们找到表舅母，她帮姐姐挂好五官科的号，姐姐就去看眼科医生了。经医生诊断，姐姐左眼瞳孔的外缘被稻谷打伤处已经感染化脓，临床观察可以看到一个半粒米大的白点。医生马上给姐姐打抗生素加外滴眼药水控制感染，并说若脓点继续增大，最后撑破瞳孔外缘的表面，眼睛就会变瞎。医生建议姐姐马上转到省城的眼科医院进行治疗。听了医生的话后，我马上把姐姐送到县城的长途汽车站，买好车票，让她回家后尽快到眼科医院看医生，我则赶乘下午的客轮回村参加夏收夏种。

回省城后，姐姐的眼伤很幸运地得到了时任眼科医院副院长、一级教授毛医生的及时诊治，感染得到了控制，脓点逐渐缩小直到最后消失，左眼瞳孔的外缘只留下了一个小小的瘢痕。谢天谢地，姐姐的左眼终于保住了，但是视力从1.5降到了1.0。

以后每每回想起这件事，我都深感内疚，总觉得欠了姐姐很多很多。每当姐姐因为我帮过她而感谢我时，我总是说：“不用谢，我们在一起患过难啊！”

Chapter 6

Sister's Eye

One evening after supper during a summer harvest, my sister and I went to our village's grain sunning ground to unload boats. The sunning ground was lit up as if it were day time. Farmers were unloading bundles of rice plants from the boats in an orderly manner. Soon the unloaded rice plants formed a small mountain on the sunning ground.

As usual, the males lined up to feed the electric threshers with handfuls of rice plants while the females stood on either side of the threshers with their pitchforks to collect the exiting rice straw. My sister had on her straw hat and protective towel. She was wearing a long sleeved top with small flower patterns on a whitish background—the top seemed white due to the wear-and-tear and repeated laundering. She had on a pair of blue pants. She worked closest to one thresher. The females all worked with their heads bowed and their faces turned away from the threshers, hoping their straw hats and the towels draped along their cheeks would protect their faces from the assault of the rice grains. Fresh rice grains are pointy on both ends and the rice hull is prickly. It hurts when the rice grains hit even just one's hand. "Ah!" my sister shrieked all of a sudden and stopped working. I hurried over to see that her eyes were closed and her face was covered with sweat. She told me that a rice grain had gotten into her left eye. I had never encountered a situation like that before. I was at a loss. One of the vice-captains of our production team, Wen Jingkun, rushed over right away. He asked if anyone had nail clippers. Someone handed him a pair. Carefully with the nail clippers, he snatched the rice grain from between my sister's left eyelids. The farmers told me later that they knew rice grains would sometimes get into their eyes so they always brought along nail clippers when working next to an electric thresher. Wiping her sweat and tears dry, my sister continued to work. She put a few drops of antibiotic eye drops in her left eye before she went to bed that night.

My sister continued to participate in the busy summer harvest but on the fourth day after her injury, she told me that her left eye hurt and it was sensitive to light. She asked me to accompany her to the county hospital to see a doctor. Annoyed, I thought my sister was a crybaby who was not tough, but when she started to cry knowing that I did not want to go with her, I told her agitatedly that I would go to town with her the following day.

Our village was over ten kilometers from town. One could only go to town by boat. No bus route existed. It usually took one or two hours if one walked the distance. Early the next morning, we boarded the 6 a.m. motorized passenger boat to town. The round trip ticket was six *jiao* each. One of our aunts worked in the county hospital. She graduated from a medical school in Shanghai, which made her one of the better trained doctors in the hospital. She was somewhat well known in the county.

It was past 7 a.m. by the time we docked. It then took us 15 minutes to walk to the neighborhood of the hospital. Maybe her eye was hurting her badly. My sister asked me to get our aunt from home while she went directly to the hospital. I do not know what possessed me, but I insisted that my sister walk the fifteen minutes to go to our aunt's house with me. Due to the pain and discomfort in her eye and my lack of compassion, my sister sobbed while she walked behind me. At the time, I thought of myself as a rational being, who had known all the suffering in the world. I often purposefully suppressed my true feelings to present a detached and cold front to others. My sister's pain and tears could not move me. I thought of her as weak and insufferable. I walked fast and left her far behind.

By the time we got to our aunt's house, she had already left for work. Grudgingly, we walked back the same way we had come. At the hospital, we found our aunt, who then helped my sister see an eye doctor. The doctor told us that my sister's left eye was infected because of the rice grain injury. The doctor said that she could see a white dot off to one side of my sister's pupil—the dot was about the size of half a grain of rice. The doctor gave my sister a shot of antibiotics and some eye drops. She said that if the infection got worse—if the dot expanded to break onto the pupil—my sister's eye could become blind. The doctor suggested that my sister go to the provincial hospital for treatment. Without hesitation, I brought my sister to the bus station, bought her a ticket, and put her on a bus to go home to my parents. I told her to go to see an eye doctor as soon as she got home. I returned to the village to continue participating in the summer harvest and planting.

Luckily, my sister got to see an eye specialist in the city in time. Dr. Mao was a first-rate eye doctor and he was able to control the infection in my sister's eye. Today, my sister's left eye has only a tiny scar from the injury. Thank heavens! The only consequence from the injury was that my sister's left eye vision went from 20/13 to 20/20.

I felt a twinge of guilt every time I thought of the incident as if I owed my sister. Ever since, whenever my sister thanked me for having done her a favor, I would say: Not at all. We had struggled and endured together.

七

肝 炎

夏收刚开始几天，姐姐因左眼被电动脱粒机喷射出来的谷子打伤后感染化脓，回城治病去了。我只身留到村里，起早摸黑地参加农忙。平时不管农忙农闲，姐姐总是把烧饭做菜的活揽起来，极少让我下厨。这下可好，我每天收工后累得半死还得自己做饭，真是“屋漏更遭连夜雨”了。

南方的盛夏，天气酷热，我们穿着长衣长裤干活，大汗淋漓，就像从水里捞出来的一样。为了抗暑，我们每天都喝大量的水，喝得嘴巴里只有一股苦涩的味道，舌头上长了一层白白的、厚厚的舌苔。当地农民说，这是体内“湿”气重的缘故。舌苔厚，胃口就不好。俗话说：“人是铁，饭是钢。”——吃不下饭就干不了活啊。 我们只好往饭里加白开水再吞进肚子里去。为了去“湿”，我们照村民们的办法，到镇里的中药铺买一种毛茸茸状的、名字为“绵茵陈”的中草药煮水喝。但喝了一段时间，舌苔还是很厚。

知青中的张球和张强是兄弟俩，弟弟张强在夏收开始后一周就因病回省城了。他走得很突然，我们都是几天后才知道他回城治病的消息。至于他得的是什么病，我们也无从知道。哥哥张球则留在村里干活。

有一天收工回来，我发现张球躺在床上，连忙上前问他是否不舒服。他说他在发烧，浑身难受。我用手摸摸他的前额，很烫，觉得他烧得很严重，就问他要不要我摇船送他到河对岸的镇医院去看病，他说不用了，最好能找到大队的赤脚医生给他打退烧针。可当时天色已晚，大队的赤脚医生所住的村子离我村有半小时的路程，况且也无法与他联系上。张球也意识到找大队的赤脚医生不是个办法，只好作罢。我见张球躺在床上啥也没吃，就对他说想吃什么就告诉我，我给他做。他说不想吃干的，只想喝点清淡的汤。我马上到厨房用新鲜蔬菜做了一锅汤，给他盛了一碗送到他床边，我自己也喝了一碗。那天晚上，我一直照顾着张球，用湿毛巾放在他的额头上降温，希望能尽量减少他的痛苦，等天亮再去医院看病。后来看到张球渐渐地睡着了，我也去睡了，明天还得起五更干活呢！

第二天一大早，张球啥也没说，就自己收拾好东西，到镇上的码头乘船回省城了。我看着他远去的身影，转过身来拿着镰刀禾槌赶上了夏收的人群。

连日的苦战令我疲惫不堪，张球走后的第七八天，我开始感到胃部很不舒服，经常觉得好像有什么东西塞在胃里一样，只想喝水，没有胃口吃饭。为了保持体力开工，我就吃点水泡饭应付。有一天收工后， 我扛着农具随着大家往村里走时觉得憋尿，就故意走得慢一些，等收工的队伍走远了，我就站在田埂上小解。突然之间，我发现流进稻田里的小便像浓茶的颜色一样呈深咖啡色，把稻田里的一沱清水都染成了浅褐色。我想，这也许是出汗多，喝水少的缘故，只要注意多补充水，再坚持几天，夏收就结束了，我们也可借夏收与夏种之间衔接的一两天时间喘口气儿。

果然，几天以后，几百亩的夏季稻已收割完毕。为了等夏种的秧苗就绪，生产队安排大家到花生地里拔草。相比之下，拔草这活儿轻松多了。我们每人带着一张小板凳，坐在花生地里，一边聊天儿，一边用丁字形的小铲子除草。忽然间，我觉得心跳加速，额上冒出了豆大的汗珠，眼前一黑，差点就晕倒在花生地里。我赶忙定了定神，才又在凳子上坐稳了。村民们说我的脸色苍白，劝我马上收工回家休息。我心里也有点慌了，觉得事情不太妙，在花生地里稍事休息后就回家躺着，决定次日清晨到镇上乘小客轮去县城医院看病。

我到达县城后就直接到县城医院找到我的表舅母，她马上建议我检验肝功能。因为抽血后的第二天化验结果才能出来，表舅母嘱咐我晚上到她家住。我还有另一个表舅也住在县城里，我们称呼他为熙表舅。他是妈妈的亲叔叔的儿子，在县城的卫生机关工作。当天正好是熙表舅装修旧祖屋的完工之日，熙表舅请我和表舅、表舅母一家到他家吃饭，有鱼有肉，让我这多日闻不到肉腥味儿的知青打了一次牙祭。

次日早上，我到县医院检验科取到肝功报告后，马上拿去给表舅母看。表舅母正在儿科上班，身上穿着医生的白大褂，头上戴着白帽子，嘴巴上围着个白口罩，只有前额和两只大眼睛露在外面。她看我的肝功报告时，我发现她的前额渗出了一滴滴的汗珠。她轻声地对我说，你得了急性黄疸肝炎，可能要住院治疗，你赶快回省城去医治吧。我再看看我的肝功能检验报告：转氨酶800；黄疸指数12；血红胆质指数1.5；还有草酚浊度++++。我虽然不太明白这些数据的意义，但从表舅母脸上的表情来猜测，我的肝病还挺严重的。表舅母还说急性黄疸肝炎有很强的传染性，回家后要注意与他人的隔离。我马上意识到表舅母的前额为何会冒出汗珠：我昨晚与两个表舅家的大人小孩共进晚餐，且没有用公筷，饭后还在表舅家住了一宿——可表舅家有两个不满7岁的小孩啊！这时我心乱如麻，担心自己把肝炎病传染给亲戚们。我让表舅母要好好地消毒我在她家用过的东西，以免得肝炎病。我还考虑到表舅母已在上班，表舅和孩子们在家里并不知道我得了传染性肝炎的事，我得马上去通知他。离开医院后，我就直奔表舅家。到了表舅家，我只站在大门外告诉表舅我得了急性黄疸肝炎，要他们注意消毒我在他家用过的被褥和用具。表舅是医生，他笑着让我进屋说话，但我怕把病传染给他们，就借口要赶班船回村，屋也没进就离开了。

我坐了下午的客轮回村，收拾了一些衣物，第二天就乘船回省城了。回到省城的家，妈妈正好从五七干校回来探亲，知道我得了肝炎，马上带我去医院看病。医生给我开了中药，我每天都要用瓦锅熬中药喝，里面有一味主药叫苦楝子，把药搞得很苦，难喝极了。回家的头两周，我还得每天到医务室打B12，复合维生素B等针。后来我干脆从医药用品商店买来注射器和消毒盒，每天把针筒、针头、镊子等放在消毒盒里，加点自来水，然后用煤油炉把消毒盒里的水煮沸约20分钟。我用砂轮把B12，复合维生素B的玻璃瓶压一圈儿，再用镊子一敲玻璃瓶，就可以把粉红色的B12或褐色的复合维生素B药水吸进注射器里，在臀部肉比较多的地方涂些酒精，飞针一扎，缓缓地把药水注入体内。久病成良医，为了让臀部左右两边的针眼数均等，我很快学会了分别用左、右手给自己打针，实行打针轮作制。数年后，父亲病重从干校回家治病，我从农村回家照顾他时，我每天都给他打针。

在家吃了三个月的中药，我的肝功能基本恢复正常，只是血液检验报告上还有两个显示肝功能不正常的“+”号。但据医生说，那两个“+”没有太大关系，会逐步消失的。听了医生的诊断，我又义无反顾地返回了久别的广阔天地继续劳动了。

回村后，见到了张球和张强兄弟俩，才知道原来他们得的也是肝炎，而且张强下乡前就得过一次肝炎。我想，也许是张强的肝炎传染了他的哥哥张球，而张球的肝炎又传染了我，唉，谁让我们知青是一根藤上的苦瓜呢？

Chapter 7

Hepatitis

At the beginning of one summer harvest, my sister had to return to the city because her left eye got infected after it was injured by a rice grain that shot into her eye from an electric thresher. I stayed in the village to participate in the harvest day and night. Normally, my sister would cook our meals no matter how busy or tired she was. She hardly ever allowed me in the kitchen. Now that she was not around, I had to make my own meals after having worked in the fields all day. My situation confirmed the validity of the saying that "When the roof leaks, several days of continuous rain is sure to come." In other words, misfortunes never come singly.

It is extremely hot in the summer in southern China. To protect ourselves from the hot sun, we had to wear long sleeved tops and long pants to work. Every day we would sweat profusely; we looked like we had been lifted out of a river. To prevent dehydration, we had to drink a lot of water, so much so that a bitter taste remained in our mouths and a thick, whitish coating grew on our tongues. The local farmers said the bitter taste and heavy tongue-coating were caused by the imbalance of *qi* in our bodies—we had too much internal "dampness." They explained that people usually did not have a good appetite when they had a heavy tongue-coating. It is said that we humans are steel (crucial) but food is iron (indispensable)—meaning that no one could work without food. We had to force ourselves to eat, usually by adding water to cooked rice to make swallowing easier. To get rid of the "dampness" in our bodies, we did what the farmers did by purchasing something called *Mianyinchen*, a Chinese herbal medicine, so that we could boil it in water and drink the brew, but unfortunately, the coating on our tongues was still thick after several treatments.

There were two brothers among us zhiqing, Zhang Qiu and Zhang Qiang. The younger brother went back to the city only a week after the summer harvest had begun because of illness. He left in a hurry—we did not know about his absence until several days after he had left. We did not know how sick he was or what he had. His older brother Zhang Qiu stayed in the village to work with us.

One day after work, I found Zhang Qiu lying in bed. I asked him what the problem was and he told me that he had a fever and was uncomfortable all over. I felt his forehead and found it burning hot. I suggested that I could row a boat to bring him to the town's hospital, but he said that it was not necessary. He only wanted the production brigade's *chijiao* (barefoot) doctor to give him a shot to reduce his fever. But it was night time and the doctor lived in a different village about half an hour of walking distance from ours. There was no way we could know whether the doctor was even at home. Zhang Qiu realized that it was not the best idea to try to see the chijiao doctor. We decided to wait till daybreak. I told Zhang Qiu that I could make him something to eat. He said that he wanted some soup so I went to the kitchen and made him some vegetable soup. I gave him a big bowl of it and I had one, too. That night, I helped Zhang Qiu whenever he needed me. I kept a wet towel on his forehead to keep the fever down and hoped that it would make him feel more comfortable while we waited for daybreak. When I saw him falling asleep, I went to sleep, too, thinking that I would have to get up early to go to work.

Early the next morning, without saying a word, Zhang Qiu packed up a few things and went to the dock to catch a boat to the city. I watched him disappear in the distance before I turned around to grab my sickle and heqiao to join the farmers on their way to the summer harvest site.

The nonstop hard work during the harvest period exhausted me. About the seventh or eighth day after Zhang Qiu's departure, my stomach started to bother me. I did not want to eat anything; I only wanted to drink water. I felt as if something was stuck in my stomach. To help keep my energy level up, I forced myself to eat some cooked rice mixed with water. One day after work, I had a sudden urge to urinate while I was carrying my tools and walking with the others. I fell behind so that I could be away from the others, but when I finally peed by the footpath, I noticed that my urine was a deep brown color similar to the color of strong tea that darkened the clear water in the rice paddy. I reasoned that the dark color of my urine was probably caused by my not drinking enough water after sweating so much. I'll drink more water, I thought to myself. The summer harvest would be over soon and I would be able to take a rest for a day or two before the summer planting began, I told myself.

As I had predicted, several days later, we finished harvesting the rice grain from the several hundred mu of rice fields. To wait for the preparation of the rice seedlings for planting, we were assigned to weed the peanut field for one day. Compared to harvesting or planting, weeding was a light job. Each of us brought a stool so that we could sit while weeding. We used a t-shaped tool to pull up the weeds while we bantered with each other. All of a sudden, I felt my heart racing and I noticed pea-sized sweat beads forming on my forehead. Everything went dark in front of me and I almost passed out in the peanut field. I steadied myself on my stool, but the others said that my face was ghost white. They asked me to go back to take a rest. I was scared, not knowing what was happening to me. After resting in the peanut field for a while, I went back to my dorm and crawled into bed. I decided to go to see a doctor at the county hospital early the next morning.

I went to my aunt directly after I got to the county hospital. She suggested that I should have my liver checked. Because the blood test results would not be ready until the following day, my aunt asked me to spend the night at her house. I also had an uncle in town. We called him Xi Uncle, who was the son of my mother's uncle. He worked for the Public Health Bureau in town. That day happened to be the day when he finished refurbishing his family home. He invited me and my aunt's family to have dinner at his place. The meal included fish and meat, the fragrance of which was something I had not experienced in a long time.

I got my test results back from the county hospital lab the next morning. I showed my aunt the report right away. My aunt was seeing patients in the pediatric unit at the time. She wore her doctor's white coat, a white cap, and a white face mask. I could only see her forehead and two eyes. As she read my test report, I noticed tiny sweat beads forming on her forehead. With a muted voice, she told me that I had developed acute icteric hepatitis and I might need to be hospitalized. She told me to go back to the city to see a specialist there. I took another look at my blood test report: alanine aminotransferase 800, icteric index 12, total bilirubin 1.5, and thymol turbidity ++++. Even though I did not know exactly what those numbers meant, I had a feeling that my liver was in trouble. My aunt also told me that acute icteric hepatitis was contagious and that I should be careful to quarantine myself from others when I got home. At that moment, I realized why my aunt was perspiring. The night before, I had dinner at my uncle's house with quite a few adults and children. We did not use any serving chopsticks as we were eating at home. I also spent last night at my uncle's—he had two children who were not even seven years old! I asked my aunt to sanitize everything I had used at her house. Realizing that my uncle did not know I had contracted such a contagious disease, I decided to go to tell him at his house. When I got to my uncle's house, I just yelled at the door to tell my uncle my condition and ask him to sanitize the bed covers and everything else that I had used. My uncle was also a doctor. He told me to go inside to talk but I was afraid of infecting them so I made an excuse that I had to catch a boat back to my village. I left without entering my uncle's house.

I took an afternoon passenger boat back to my village. Then I packed a few clothing items and boarded a boat to the city the next day. My mother happened to be home from *Wuqi Ganxiao* (cadre school) when I got home. Knowing that I had contracted hepatitis, she brought me to a hospital right away. A doctor there prescribed some Chinese herbal medicine. I had to boil it in water in a ceramic pot to make a broth. There was an herb in the concoction called bitter chinaberry that made the brew really bitter and impossible to drink. During the first two weeks of being home, I had to go to a clinic daily to get shots, such as a shot of B12 and B-complex. Soon I bought my own medical equipment from a medical supply store. Every day I disinfected my syringe, needles, and a pair of tweezers in a tin with some water. I would put the container on a kerosene stove and boil the water for 20 minutes. Then I would cut the glass bottle necks of the B12 and B-complex medicine with a small grinding wheel. A light tap on the bottle necks with my tweezers would then break off the tops of the medicine bottles. After drawing the pink B12 and brown B-complex liquid into the syringe, I would cleanse an area of my bottom and give myself a quick stab, slowly injecting the medicine into my body. Long illness makes one a doctor—I definitely could prove the validity of this saying. To give myself equal treatment on both sides of my bottom, I worked out a routine and quickly learned to give myself shots with both hands. Many years later, when my father got sick and had to go home from his cadre school, I went home to take care of him and I was able to give him shots every day.

After drinking the herbal brew for three months at home, I was basically cured except for the two "+" signs still showing up on my blood test reports; however, doctors said that I was healthy and the "+" signs would eventually disappear from my blood test reports. I immediately returned to my village, feeling that it was my duty to work in the fields. I was convinced that the vast farmland was giving me the re-education I needed.

When I saw the brothers Zhang Qiu and Zhang Qiang later, I found out that they, too, had hepatitis. I also found out that Zhang Qiang had an episode of hepatitis even before he first went to the village. He probably gave the virus to his brother Zhang Qiu and then Zhang Qiu gave it to me. Well, who said that we zhiqing were not bitter melons on the same vine? We definitely suffered and endured together.

八

“赛狗”

夏收夏种的农忙过后，农活就没那么忙了。日常的劳作以在稻田中耕除草、下河捞河泥给甘蔗地上肥、撒农药杀虫、积肥以及管理花生和黄麻等经济作物为主。据农民说，稻田中耕除草，当地传统的做法是人站在稻田里，手拿一根木棍插在泥里作拐棍，用一只脚在稻子的根部附近搅来搅去，把杂草除掉，把泥土弄松，累了就用另一只脚接着干。这活儿应该比较轻松，边干活还可以边聊天儿。

以前，我们地区的水稻亩产一般只有250多公斤。而在广东潮汕地区，水稻亩产却高达400多公斤。为了提高水稻亩产量，我们地区就从上到下全面地推广潮汕地区农民精耕细作的先进经验，其结果之一就是把中耕除草的站姿改为跪姿——即人的双膝跪在稻田的泥水里，用双手来除草和松土，一边干一边跪着爬行前进。殊不知潮汕地区是人多地少，人均只有不到一分地，平均每个劳力只负责几分地。要以这极为有限的土地来养活一大群人，只有在精耕细作上下功夫，拼命地设法提高水稻的单位面积产量。而我村虽说不属人少地多，但人均有一亩多地，是潮汕地区的十多倍，平均每个劳力要负责五亩多地，当然很难做到像潮汕地区那样的精耕细作了。我村有的农民说，如果我们只有像潮汕地区那么一丁点儿的地，要我们在田里绣花都没问题。

稻田里的水有3寸多深，又黑又臭，水里农药、化肥甚至人粪尿都有。稻田里的泥浆层约有4寸厚，也是黑乎乎的，散发出一股臭腥味儿。采用了潮汕地区中耕除草的先进方法之后，我们一连数周都是天天双膝跪在稻田的泥水里爬行，用双手在泥水里搅来搅去除草松土，膝盖、小腿和脚都被泥里的小瓦片或甘蔗头等划出一道道浅浅的伤痕，横的竖的，新旧交加，手指尖的皮肤上也布满了倒刺。皮肤上的小伤并不可怕，可怕的是这些伤口要天天泡在那“营养极为丰富”的黑水里，天知道会发生什么事啊。我当时也没想过伤口会感染等，只是有时会突然感到膝关节一阵钻心疼，担心膝盖一天到晚泡在水里会得关节炎。男知青尚且如此，女知青细皮嫩

肉，就更惨不忍睹了。

看着一群人在稻田里背向蓝天脸朝地排成一横排，双手双脚着地爬行，有的知青就联想到香港的赛狗场面，把这中耕除草的活儿叫作“赛狗”。从此以后，“赛狗”就成为知青词典中的一个专用词汇了。

Chapter 8

"Dog Racing"

We could slow down a bit after each busy summer harvest and planting season. We only had to till and weed around rice plants, collect river sludge to fertilize the sugarcane fields, spread pesticides to control pests, and gather manure. We also took care of our cash crops, including the peanut and jute plants. According to the farmers, the traditional way of weeding in the rice paddies was for each person to hold a wooden stick as a cane for support in the fields. The person would stand on one foot while using the other foot to stir the muddy soil and uproot any weed that was around each rice plant. The farmers said that the work was easy and one could alternate one's feet as weeding tools. People could also carry on a conversation with each other while weeding.

In our area in the past, the average rice grain yield per mu was a little over 250 kilograms, but in another area, Chaoshan, in Guangdong Province, their yield was as high as 400 kilograms per mu. To increase our production yield, we adopted the meticulous rice cultivation approach of Chaoshan. What happened was that instead of standing to weed in the rice paddies, we now had to kneel in the muddy paddies and use our hands to loosen the soil and pull up the weeds—instead of walking, we now crawled. We learned the Chaoshan method not knowing that each Chaoshan farmer was only responsible for a few fen of land because their population density was higher than that in our area—on average, each person there had only one fen of farmable land. To have enough food for themselves, they had to increase their per mu rice grain yield. In our area, even though we could not say that we had extra land, each person had at least one mu of farmable land. It was ten times more than what they had in Chaoshan per person. Each farmer in our area was responsible for over five mu. It was almost impossible for us to be as meticulous as the farmers in Chaoshan. Some of our farmers complained that if we only had that little bit of land to take care of as they did in Chaoshan, we would not mind even if we had to embroider our land as if it were a piece of silk.

The water in the rice paddies was usually about three inches deep. In addition to being dirty and smelly, the water was full of pesticides, farm chemicals, and even human feces. Beneath the water, there was mud, which was about four inches deep. The mud was dark and stinky. Ever since we adopted the Chaoshan approach to weeding, we had to crawl in the muddy rice fields for weeks, weeding and loosening the soil with our hands. Our knees, calves, and feet would be scratched constantly by broken roof tiles from who-knew-where or sugarcane roots appearing from nowhere. We would be covered by crisscrossing cuts and our finger tips would be full of slivers. What was worse than the cuts was how our wounds had to be immersed in the dirty water that was so full of "nutrients." Who knew what could have happened to us? I did not think about infections at the time. All I was worried about was getting arthritis in my knees as my knees sometimes gave me a shooting pain. The work was hard on the male zhiqing. As for the females, the damage to their delicate bodies was not a sight anyone would want to see.

The way we lined up in a row to crawl forward in the rice paddies, with our backs to the blue sky and our faces to the ground, reminded us of the dog races held in Hong Kong at the time. "Dog Racing" then became a phrase that we zhiqing used to describe the kind of work we had to do after summer planting, when we had to weed and loosen the soil around each rice plant, in the posture of dogs racing forward.

九

姓名趣事

我插队的那条村有陈、蔡两大姓，就人的名字而言，也没什么特别之处。男性的名字有：坤、森、文、锦明、灼才、金明等；女性的则是双名的多，例如：银好、银娇、金凤、银娣、凤娇、梅竹、梅桂等。但有几个人的名字却让我大开眼界，惊讶不已。

记得刚进村不久，有位村民向我介绍本村一个20岁左右的小伙子时说："他叫黄狗女。"我当时以为这位村民在开玩笑，就对他说："嘿，不要乱讲。"但那个小伙子却一本正经地对我说，他的大名就是黄狗女，小狗的"狗"，女人的"女"。我当时张大了嘴巴望着他，惊讶得说不出话来。但看到他那一脸认真诚恳的表情，我才信了。黄狗女在本村属外姓人家，很小时父亲就去世了，是守寡的母亲含辛茹苦地抚养他长大。我不知道他读过几年书，估计他也许就是小学水平吧。黄狗女人很憨厚，干活卖力，待人诚恳。村里的男男女女、大人小孩都亲切地叫他"狗女"，他也总是笑着答应，从未感到他的名字有什么不妥的地方。在我看来，"黄狗女"既不能用来做女孩子的名字，也不能用来做男孩子的名字。可令我

不解的是，村里所有的人，不论文化高低，都没有一个人觉得“黄狗女”这个名字难听。

有一位数年前从外村嫁到本村来的妇女，名叫“赖美女”。我到村里插队时，她已是几个孩子的妈妈了。我们在同一个生产小队里劳作。赖美女是一个很朴实的农村妇女，勤勤恳恳地干活、养儿育女。她长着一对小眼睛，单眼皮儿，塌鼻梁，大嘴，“哨牙”。平心而论，她的外貌实在无法与“美女”两字沾边。尽管村民们都“美女”长，“美女”短地称呼她，而我每次叫她“美女”时，心里就会觉得有点别扭。也许这就是受教育程度之间的区别吧。

在村民们看来，名字就是一个人区别于他人的符号，他们对其字面的意义并不像我们知青的感觉那么细腻、敏感。我想，一个人若生活在社会

的最底层，每天都要为柴米油盐去挣扎，哪还有心思去顾及名字的字面意义啊。“高贵者最愚蠢，卑贱者最聪明”——这也许就是我们知青小资要接受贫下中农再教育的原因吧。

村民们除了大名外，一般都有小名。女性的小名一般都是：阿娇、阿好、阿凤、小妹等。可相当多的男性小名就不堪入耳了，例如：大女、蔡狗、“咸湿狗”(当地土话是“肮脏狗”)、懵坤、麻糖发等。这其中的理由是：人们认为越低贱的动物就越容易饲养。用狗来作为男孩的小名，是希望借此能顺利地把男孩子养大来传宗接代。在男尊女卑的封建意识影响下，基于同样的逻辑，人们也认为女孩要比男孩更容易养，所以把男孩唤作“大女”。

Chapter 9

Names

The village to which I was assigned as a zhiqing had two large family clans, the Chen and the Cai. Most males in the families had names such as Kun, Sen, Wen, Jingming, Zhuocai, and Jinming, etc.; most females had these names: Yinhao, Yinjiao, Jinfeng, Yindi, Fengjiao, Meizhu, and Meigui, etc. There was nothing unusual about most of the names except for a few, which surprised me and broadened my understanding of rural cultures.

I remember when I first arrived in the village. A farmer introduced me to a young man about 20 years of age. "His name is Dog Girl Huang," the farmer said.

"Hey, don't be silly," I said, thinking that the farmer was joking with me. But the young man confirmed that his name was indeed what the farmer had said. His family name was Huang, and his given name had two characters, *gou* for dog and *nv* for girl, so his name was Dog Girl Huang. I looked at him with my mouth open, so shocked that I was speechless, but I had to believe him as he looked so earnest.

Dog Girl Huang's family came from another village. His father died when he was a child and he was raised by his widowed mother. I do not know how many years of schooling he had had but my guess is that he only had an elementary school education. Dog Girl Huang was a simple but honest man. He worked hard and was friendly to others. Everyone in the village, males and females, adults and children, all called him Dog Girl. He always responded with a smile, never appearing uncomfortable with his name. But for me, I did not think Dog Girl Huang should even be a name for a girl, let alone a name for a grown man. What puzzled me was that no one in the village, no matter how much education he or she had had, ever thought that Dog Girl Huang was an inappropriate and most offensive name.

There was a woman who came to our village through marriage. Her name was Beauty Lai. She was already the mother of several children by the time I arrived in the village. We worked in the same production team. Beauty Lai was a down-to-earth, hardworking woman who devoted herself to her children. She had a pair of incision-like small eyes, her nose bridge looked as if it had collapsed, and her mouth was big with buck teeth. Honestly, she was far from being good-looking. Although all the villagers called her *meinv*—beautiful girl, I often felt weird calling her Beauty. Maybe my discomfort was caused by the difference in cultural and educational experiences between me and the villagers.

To the villagers, names were used to distinguish one person from another. The farmers were not as sensitive to the meanings of the characters used in names as we zhiqing were. Perhaps when one had to live at the bottom of a society's social hierarchy, struggling everyday to make ends meet—stressing over firewood, rice, oil, and salt—one would not have any energy left to mind the meanings of names. The saying that "The sophisticated are foolish while the simple are wise" is perhaps true. Maybe there was a good reason for why we zhiqing were sent to the countryside to be re-educated by the farmers.

In the village, each person had a legal name and a nickname. Most females had nicknames such as Willow, Lovely, Phoenix, Little Sister, etc.; however, most nicknames for males were pretty nauseating, such as Big Girl, Dog Cai, Horny Dog, Ignorant One, or Thriving Sesame Chew, etc. One of the reasons for giving males such repulsive names was that the farmers believed that the lowly animals were easier to raise, so to give boys nicknames related to dogs would hopefully make it easier to raise the boys so that they could grow up to carry on family names. Following the logic of this feudal thought, females were considered inferior to males so farmers thought that it was easier to raise females than males; therefore, they often gave males nicknames that had something to do with females, such as calling a boy Big Girl.

十

施肥和撒农药

俗话说，“肥是农家宝”。农民种田没有肥料，犹如“巧妇难为无米之炊”。我村的肥料来源有三：一是买国家分配的化肥，例如尿素、硫酸铵、硝酸铵等；二是就地取材的有机肥，例如下河捞的河泥、生产队养猪场的猪粪、生产队鱼塘的塘泥等；三是到附近的城镇去买人粪尿。

一天，生产队派人到十几公里外的一个大镇买回来一船人粪尿，队长分配我和几个村民把这船人粪尿施到黄麻地里。装人粪尿的船停在河边，我们从岸上搭了一块跳板到船头，每人挑着两个木桶走到船舱里装人粪尿。我从来没干过这活儿，以为会有人在船上用带有长柄的木勺把船舱里的人粪尿舀到木桶里，我们再挑到黄麻地里。

谁知到了船上一看，我当场就傻了眼了。只见村民们个个光着脚丫，把裤腿卷到膝盖上面，挑着担子走进船舱，双腿泡在齐膝深的人粪尿里，弯着腰用双手把两个木桶按进粪水里，待木桶装满粪水后再把腰伸直，挑着担子走出船舱，向着黄麻地走去。

看到船舱里略带暗绿色的浑浊的粪水，上面漂着一团团咖啡色的大便，还有白色的草纸、小木棍之类的东西，我浑身的毛发都竖了起来，实

在无法把脚踏进那粪水里。那些粪水的臭味并不是太大，因为卖主为了多卖几个钱，早就在人粪尿里掺了大量的水——真是 “人心比夜黑”啊！我站在船头，把担子撂在一边，始终没有勇气走进船舱里。村民们看到我挺尴尬的，也没有责备我，就让我到岸上去帮忙把人粪尿浇到黄麻地里。从那以后，生产队再也没派我出工干这种施肥的活儿了。

因为村民们采用的这种施肥方式以及常年用人粪尿种自留地，钩虫病在当地十分流行。每次我们知青回城探亲，村民们都委托我们买一种叫“灭虫宁”的打虫药。村里的大人小孩从来不到医院去检查是否有钩虫病，每年都定期吃这种打虫药。我问村民们为什么，他们说，不用检验也知道肚子里会有钩虫。我下乡时随身带了一本《农村医生手册》，知道钩虫病只要不重复感染是可以自愈的。但光着脚泡在买来的人粪尿里或天天踩在浇了人粪尿的自留地里，重复感染钩虫病就无法避免了。

有一次，我光着脚修整自留地，回家后觉得脚面起了两个小包，就像被蚊子叮过一样，奇痒无比，我意识到那是因为混在粪便里的钩虫幼虫钻进我的皮肤里了。我也跟村民们学，大把大把地吃灭虫宁。

其实，灭虫宁的毒性和副作用都很大，村民们说，若吃多了就会感到头晕目眩。久病成良医——虽然村民们不知道如何防止感染钩虫病，但却能准确地知道如何根据大人、小孩的年龄及体重来计算服用灭虫宁的分量。

如果说施人粪尿的活儿比较恐怖的话，那撒农药的活儿则像是慢性自杀。有一次，因发现一块稻田有虫害，生产队长排工让我去撒农药。我问同去撒农药的村民要带什么工具，他们就嘱咐我带上一条手帕。我马上回家找到一条方形的小手帕，赶到田里与他们会合。

到了田边，那几个村民已从生产队的仓库里领来一大袋“六六六”农药和几只簸箕。我们把那袋农药打开，把黄色的“六六六”药粉倒进簸箕里，再把带来的小手帕对角折成一个三角形绑在嘴巴上当口罩，然后卷起裤腿，排成一横排走进田里撒农药。我们用一只手抓住簸箕的外沿，把它紧紧地顶在腰部，用另一只手从簸箕里抓，把农药粉往稻田里撒。村民们还聪明地知道我们要从风向的上游开始往下游走，一边撒药粉，一边前进。霎时间，稻田里一片黄尘滚滚，我们如同身坠云雾当中，谁也看不清谁了。这活儿倒蛮轻松，但人却被农药粉呛得眼泪鼻涕一起流。当我们撒完了农药，走上了那块稻田的田埂时，每个人的头发、眉毛、手和脸的皮肤以及那作为口罩的手帕上都沾上了一层黄黄的“六六六”农药粉。

“六六六”是一种毒性很大的农药，我不知道到底有多少药粉被我们吸进了肺里，有多少药粉从我们的皮肤渗进了体内。对于我来说，值得庆幸的是：那是我知青生涯中的第一次，也是唯一的一次撒农药的经历。可对于那些长年累月在田间劳作的农民而言，他们经常撒农药，不但自己吸了“毒”，而且还可能把毒性遗传给他们的下一代。

Chapter 10

Manure and Pesticides

It has been said that "Manure is gold to the farmer." Without manure, farmers would be like "Skillful housewives cooking without rice": It does not work. In our village, fertilizers could be obtained through three different means. One was to purchase the government rationed farm chemicals, such as carbamide (or urea), ammonium sulfate, and ammonium nitrate; the second was to find organic fertilizers locally, such as going to the rivers for the sludge at the bottom, collecting pig waste from the production team's pigsty, or harvesting deep mud from the production team's fish ponds; and the third was to go to nearby towns to purchase human waste.

One day, our production team purchased a boat-load of human feces and urine from a nearby town. The production team captain assigned me and several farmers to unload the boat and spread its content onto the jute fields. We connected the boat to the shore using a plank wide enough for walking, each of us carried two wooden buckets on shoulder poles and walked toward the hold of the boat. I had never unloaded feces before. I thought someone would be waiting for us by the hold of the boat to scoop the feces and urine into our buckets, which we could then carry to the jute fields.

How wrong I was! I could not believe my eyes when I got on board. My fellow manure carriers were all barefoot with their pant legs rolled up above their knees. Dangling two wooden buckets from their shoulder poles, they walked right into the hold of the boat, immersing their feet in the pool of feces and urine. Then they bent forward while tipping their buckets with their hands, and they pushed the buckets into the pool of human waste. When the buckets were filled, they straightened their backs and carried the buckets out of the boat and walked toward the jute fields.

Seeing that the boat was full of sluggish green matter, with clumps of light brown poop as well as pieces of white toilet paper and small sticks floating, I shuddered, and my feet refused to move. The smell was not too terrible because to make more money, the seller had diluted the human waste with water. How dark the human heart could be! I stood at the bow of the boat, my buckets and shoulder pole by my side. I simply did not have the guts to enter the hold of the boat. The other farmers noticed my hesitation. Without reprimanding me, they asked me to go to the jute fields to help spread the feces and urine that had been brought there. Ever since, I was never asked to do the same kind of work again.

Because the farmers worked with human waste year after year, hookworms were most prominent in our area. Every time we went home to the city, the farmers would ask us to buy a medicine called "Worm Extermination Tranquility" (bephenium hydroxynaphthoate). People in the village, neither the adults nor children, ever went to the doctors for hookworm treatments. They simply took the magic worm killing pills regularly. When I asked them why they never went to the doctor, they told me that they just knew they would have hookworms. I had brought a copy of the *Handbook for Rural Doctors* with me when I was first sent to the village. I knew from the book that the hookworm disease could be cured if one could avoid repeated hookworm infections. But for the farmers, who had to step in pools of human waste and who had to work in the human feces and urine soaked fields every day, they could not avoid being infected again and again.

Once I found two small bumps on the top of one of my feet after I had been working barefoot in my private plot. It was as if I had been bitten by mosquitoes. I realized that the bumps were caused by baby hookworms that had penetrated my skin while I was working with feces in the plot. I immediately swallowed plenty of Worm Extermination Tranquility, following the villagers' lead.

The reality was that Worm Extermination Tranquility was poisonous and had a lot of side effects. The villagers knew that if they had consumed too many of the pills, they would get dizzy and blurry eyed. It has been said that a long illness would make one a good doctor. Even though the farmers did not know how to prevent themselves from repeated hookworm infections, they knew how to calculate the dosage of the magic drug according to their own body weight and age. They became their own doctors.

If it was appalling working with human feces, it was simply committing slow suicide when working with farm chemicals. Once I was assigned by my production team's captain to spread pesticides when there were insect damages to the rice seedlings. When I asked the other farmers what I should bring as a tool, all they told me was to bring a handkerchief. I found a small handkerchief in my room and rushed to join the others in the field.

When I got there, several farmers had already brought back a huge sack of the 6-6-6 farm chemical (hexachlorobenzene) and several big winnowing baskets. We emptied the yellow 6-6-6 chemical into the baskets and covered our noses and mouths with the handkerchiefs we had folded into masks. We rolled up our pant legs and lined up horizontally at the edge of one field. Each of us held a basket tightly against our waists with one hand and with the other hand, we scooped the chemical and scattered it in front of us. Simultaneously, we walked while spreading the chemical. A yellow dust storm covered the rice field instantly. We felt as if we were in a thick cloud—no one was able to see anyone else clearly. Even though the work was not physically demanding, we were suffocating. The chemical made our eyes tear up and our noses run. By the time we got to the opposite end of the rice field, there was a thick layer of the 6-6-6 chemical on everyone's hair, eyebrows, hands and faces, and our skin as well as the handkerchief masks we were wearing.

The 6-6-6 chemical is extremely poisonous. I do not know how much chemical dust we breathed in that day or how much chemical penetrated our skin. For me, I was fortunate to encounter the chemical only once in my life—that was the first and last time I had to participate in the spreading of the 6-6-6. For the farmers, who worked in the fields year after year, generation after generation, they not only took in the "poison" themselves but it was also possible that they had been passing residuals of the poison to their children and their children's children.

十一

蔡大叔的眼泪

一天傍晚，生产队的副队长蔡大叔一个人孤零零地坐在我村附近的河边流泪，天黑了也不愿意回家。

第二天早上出工时，大家对此议论纷纷，不知道究竟发生了什么事情。原来，昨天是蔡大叔的妻子在公社卫生院分娩的日子。蔡大叔今年49岁，他和他的妻子已经生了5个女儿了，一直就盼着要生个儿子。妻子怀了第6胎，夫妇俩就觉得这回应该是个小子了。昨天一大清早，蔡大叔高高兴兴地摇着船把快要分娩的妻子送到了公社卫生院住

院部后，马上就赶回家给妻子熬鸡汤。下午时分，公社卫生院来电话，通知说孩子已经顺利地生下来了，大人、小孩都平安。蔡大叔知道消息后，连忙带上熬好的鸡汤，满怀喜悦地赶往公社卫生院看望妻子和孩子。当他来到住院部大门时，有个亲友告诉他，他的妻子生了个女儿时，蔡大叔大失所望，把鸡汤和罐子往地上一摔，妻子、孩子也不看了，转身就离开了公社卫生院。

回到村里，蔡大叔独自坐在河边痛哭，并自言自语地说：即使下一胎能生个儿子，也不是个能养老的儿子了。可不是吗？蔡大叔已经49岁了，等到儿子长大成人，他自己也起码70岁了。

Chapter 11

Uncle Cai's Tears

One evening, Uncle Cai (all of us zhiqing called him uncle even though we were not related to him), who was one of the vice-captains of our production team, sat crying by a river near our village. He did not want to go home even after dark. Everyone talked about the incident the next day, but no one really knew what had happened.

We found out later that Uncle Cai's wife had given birth earlier that day. Uncle Cai was 49 years old. He and his wife had brought five daughters into the world already, but they had hoped for a son. When Uncle Cai's wife was pregnant with their sixth child, both of them thought that it would be a son.

Early in the morning of the due day, Uncle Cai helped his wife to a boat and rowed her happily to our commune's clinic. After he settled his wife in the clinic, Uncle Cai went home immediately so that he could make some chicken soup for his wife. Then as soon as he received the call in the afternoon that his child had been born and both mother and baby were healthy, Uncle Cai was overjoyed. He went to the clinic full of happiness.

When he reached the clinic, he was told that his wife had just given birth to a girl. Uncle Cai lost it. He threw his ceramic pot onto the ground, spilling all the chicken soup in it. Without even seeing his wife and new baby, Uncle Cai left the clinic for the river. There he sat and cried. "Even if I get a son the next time," Uncle Cai told others later, "I cannot depend on him to take care of me in my old age." Uncle Cai knew he would be around 70 when his newborn—or his hoped-for son—would be old enough to take care of him. He did not think he could wait that long.

十二

狗　虱

我们插队的那条村，几乎家家都养狗。有狗就必然有狗虱——狗虱不但咬狗，更咬人。村里的环境卫生较差，乱草堆、烂泥巴、猪狗屎、鸡鸭粪便随处可见，狗虱可以说是无处不在，无时不在。只要你在村里走一小段路，就一定会有狗虱跳到你的身上开始肆虐，咬得你浑身是包，痒得难受。初进村那会儿，个个知青都得过“狗虱关”。

我们5个男知青住在一栋青砖小洋楼的二楼，瓷砖地板，条件不错。旧社会时这栋小楼是本村一个恶霸的房子，土地改革时就成了村里的公共财产。二楼有一房一厅，我们中有两人睡房，三人睡厅，床都是用知青安家费买来的两块床板放在两条长凳上搭成的。楼面虽然干爽，但因为每天人来人往，还是狗虱成灾。

每天晚上睡觉时，大家都被狗虱咬得翻来覆去，只顾着挠痒，根本无法入睡。身上被狗虱咬过的地方，都会长一个粉红色的大包，奇痒无比。包的最上端，还长着小水泡，一旦把水泡挠破了，就容易感染化脓。

我们听村民说有一种叫砂姜的中药能治狗虱，就到镇上的药材铺买回来一大包砂姜粉，撒在凉席底下，以为大功告成，可以安安稳稳地睡个好觉了。谁知道这招根本不灵，又是一个不眠之夜。有的村民教我们睡觉前把全部衣裤都脱下来使劲地抖几下，把粘在衣裤上的狗虱都抖掉再穿上衣裤睡觉。这个办法也无济于事，一会儿大家就被狗虱咬得人仰马翻。我们坐在床上，都能看到地板上布满了狗虱。为了不让狗虱跳到身上，我们在寝室内用长条木凳搭成桥，人在桥上行走。虽说跳蚤是跳高冠军，能跳到相当于自己身高几十倍的高度，但对高桥上的我们也只好望洋兴叹了。可好景不长，当我们从桥上下来洗脸刷牙，吃饭穿衣，扛着农具上工时，狗虱又跳了上来。

干活时，因为粗糙的衣裤不断地和身上的“狗虱”包摩擦，把“狗虱”包顶端晶亮的水泡磨破了，血水流成一片，磨破了的伤口被咸咸的汗水腌得发疼。就这样，旧的包还未痊愈，新的包又犹如雨后春笋般涌了出来，身上、腿上伤痕累累，惨不忍睹。

令我们感到惊讶的是，村民们并不像我们知青那样惧怕狗虱。有位村民说，他把裤腿卷到膝盖处，只要有狗虱跳到他的小腿上，腿上的汗毛就会有感觉，他就马上把拇指和食指放进嘴里沾点口水，然后把腿上的狗虱捏住。被唾沫粘住的狗虱再也不能蹦了，他就把被逮住了的狗虱用手指甲掐死。村民们被狗虱咬后，只会长很小的包，而且包上也不长小水泡，更有甚者——有的村民被狗虱咬后连包也不会长，只有一点痒而已。我想，村民们长期被狗虱咬，早就有免疫力了。

两年后，我们也开始对狗虱有些免疫力了——“狗虱”包明显变小了，包上也不长小水泡了。更令人欣喜的是，我们都成了空手套狗虱的高手，狗虱不再是我们的“灭顶之灾”了。

Chapter 12

Dog Fleas

In the village, almost every family had a dog or two. Dog fleas were everywhere and they bit not only dogs but humans as well. Sanitary conditions in the village were quite poor. Everywhere, one could see piles of organic matter, dirt buildup, and animal manure from pigs, dogs, chickens, or ducks. Dog fleas permeated the place. If you walked a short distance in the village, you would definitely get dog fleas that jumped to your body and bit you all over. The itch from such bites was excruciating. When we first arrived in the village, every zhiqing had to learn to deal with dog fleas—we had to pass the "dog flea test."

Five of us male zhiqing lived on the second floor of a brick, western style building. We had a tile floor—the living conditions were not bad. Before 1949, the building belonged to one feudal chief in the village, but during the Land Reform, the building became public property belonging to the village. One bedroom and one living room were on the second floor. Two of us male zhiqing shared the bedroom while the other three made the living room their bedroom. Each bed was put together by two wooden boards on two long benches—we bought the materials with the small sum of settlement money each of us got from the government when we were sent to the countryside. Even though our rooms were airy and clean, dog fleas were still a calamity due to the daily traffic we made between our rooms and the flea infested outdoors.

We could not fall asleep at night because of how itchy the flea bites were. We would toss and turn, scratching ourselves nonstop. Every dog flea bite would swell to a big pink bump, with the point of penetration forming a small blister. Infections would set in if or when the blisters broke. We heard from the villagers that sand ginger could be used as a dog flea dope so we went to town and bought a big bag of *shajiang* powder. We thought we could sleep at night after we spread the powder all over each straw mat on each bed, but it did not work at all. Other villagers told us that we should strip ourselves before we went to bed so that we could shake out our clothes before putting them on again. That did not work either. We suffered another crushing defeat. When we sat on our beds, we could see that our floor was covered with dog fleas. To prevent the dog fleas from jumping onto our bodies, we made convoluted bridges with long benches in our rooms. We walked on these benches to get around in the rooms so that the fleas on the floor, even though they were high jump champions and could jump to heights dozens of times their body length, could not get to us, who were too high for the fleas to reach. We imagined them sighing when looking at us who were full of the blood they were hungry for. However, we still had to get off our bridges every now and then to wash, brush our teeth, get dressed, eat, or go to work with our tools. The dog fleas knew when to jump onto us. When we worked, our coarse clothes often rubbed against the dog flea bumps on our bodies and the constant rubbing would break the blisters on the bumps. Pus and blood would ooze all over and when the open wounds met the sweat on our bodies, the prickle was penetrating. New bites were added to the old ones at the speed of bamboo shoots growing after the spring rain—instantaneously. The abrasions on our bodies and legs were a sorry sight to see.

What surprised us was that the villagers did not seem to be bothered by dog fleas. One villager told us that he usually rolled his pant legs to his knees so that whenever dog fleas jumped on his calves, he would feel them because of the hair on his legs. He would then put some saliva on his thumb and index finger so that he could catch the fleas because when touched by spit, fleas could not jump anymore. He would pinch the fleas to death with his finger nails. The villagers had only small bumps when they were bit by dog fleas. Their bumps did not have blisters. There were others who did not even have bumps after they were bit. They said that the bites would only itch a little. My guess was that they had built up their immune system against dog flea bites after having been bit year after year.

Two years after we had been in the village, our immunity against dog fleas began to take effect. Our bumps were considerably smaller and no blisters formed on the bumps. What made us really happy was that we had become expert dog flea catchers—we could capture dog fleas with our bare hands! Dog fleas were no longer our tormentors.

十三

厕　　所

为了给自留地积肥，我村家家户户都在自家的宅地范围内建厕所。因为是自家人用的，所以无男女厕所之分。有个别村民因为住在村会议室及碾米厂附近，就在自家的宅地建公厕以方便大家。当然，公厕里的人粪尿自然归其所有。

村民们修建的厕所很简陋。他们在泥地上挖个大坑，把一口直径约1米、高约1.5米的大水缸放进坑里，缸的顶部高于地面约5厘米，在缸顶横着放上两片比人的脚掌稍宽的木板，一个大小便两用的粪尿缸就建成了。有些占地面积大的厕所有两个大缸，有的还在地面上再放一口直径约0.5米、高约0.7米的小缸供男性小便用。厕所的周围，则用大块的泥砖砌墙围成一个矩形，在矩形的一条边上留个门，便是厕所的入口处了。所有的厕所都没有门扇，为了保护如厕者的隐私，厕所的门外加砌了一堵泥砖墙作为屏障。厕所的围墙约有1.6米高，一般人蹲在便缸上时，脑袋不会露出墙头。但若是个子稍高的男性站在厕所里的话，墙内墙外的风景便都可一目了然了。村里所有的公私厕所都是男女通用的，每个厕所的入口处都备有一根约1.5米长的小竹竿，如果看到有根小竹竿斜斜地拦着厕所的入口

处，则说明厕内已有人了。绝大部分的厕所都没有遮顶，下雨天人们就只好戴着斗笠如厕了。为了保持厕所的卫生，厕所的主人会定期挑来一对粪桶，把厕所粪缸、尿缸里的秽物掏干净。

村里的公厕可以男女通用只是名义上的。因为其结构简陋，为预防不测，妇女们是绝对不用任何公厕的。所以，实际上村里所有的公厕都是男厕。

我们这些知青没有自己的宅地，自然也就无法建自己的厕所。即使有自己的宅地，我们又哪有建造厕所的闲情逸致啊？幸好村民们都乐意让我们用他们的私家厕所，我们当然也是求之不得了。

相对来说，村民的私家厕所比村里的公厕干净，清理得也比较及时。但与城里的厕所相比，那可是天壤之别！这里的厕所实在是太简陋，卫生条件太差了。我们开始用这里的厕所时都很不习惯，每次如厕都觉得是一种受罪。特别是蹲在粪缸上大便时，两脚踩在那两条狭窄的木板上，脚下是满满的一缸黄澄澄的、散发着臭气的大粪，大粪的表面有一层厚厚的蛆在缓缓地翻滚着。那些雪白的蛆就像无数粒一头圆一头尖的大米，永远不知疲倦地蠕动着，令人十分恶心。

夏季骄阳似火，晒得厕所里热浪滚滚，热辣辣的氨味儿以及臭烘烘的大粪味儿呛得人都喘不过气儿来，还有一大堆在粪缸周围飞来飞去的绿头苍蝇。冬季天寒地冻，虽然臭味的浓度较夏天有所降低，但人蹲在粪缸上却被吹来的阵阵寒风冷得直打哆嗦。厕所的泥地面则是晴天硬得像一把刀，雨天烂得一团糟，加上有时地面上粪水横流，令人难以插足。我们知青们要上厕所，通常要寻访过好几个厕所，才能找到一个让人较能忍受的厕所。

刚进村不久的一天，我匆匆地走进村里的一间公厕，猛然间看见一条大黄狗正把脑袋伸到粪缸里吃大粪，嘴巴里发出“吧嗒吧嗒”的响声。听到我的脚步声，那条大黄狗马上抬起头来，转过身子看我。只见它两眼露出凶光，嘴巴微微张开露出尖尖的牙齿，威胁性地发出一阵低吼的声音，摆出一副要扑上来撕咬我的架势。更令人恐怖的是，它嘴巴的胡须上黏着的黄黄的粪汁正在往下滴，嘴巴的周围则沾满了黄黄的粪便和几条白白的蛆。我顿时感到毛骨悚然，非常恐怖，只觉得心跳加快，血直往脑门上冲。我想马上转身退出厕外也已经来不及了，说时迟那时快，只见那只大黄狗迅速地朝我冲

来，嘴巴里发出“嗷嗷”的叫声，从我的脚旁猛地一窜，夺路而逃。我被吓出了一身冷汗，便意全无了，转身就离开了那个厕所。

村民们上厕所大便后，基本上没有人用草纸擦屁股，大家都用一小撮稻草卷成团或一根小棍儿往肛门上一擦了事，所以厕所的粪缸里会有些稻草团和小棍儿。知青们便后都尽量用草纸，但有时没有草纸，也就用稻草团和小棍儿了。

为了逃避使用村里厕所时的那种令人难以忍受的折磨，男知青们都以本村的青年农民为榜样，喜欢在晴天的夜晚结伴到村外生产队的甘蔗地里大便，并向村民学会了用一截甘蔗叶的梗子做成小棍儿来代替草纸的技巧。仰望着满天的繁星，呼吸着甘蔗地里新鲜的空气，男知青们在这所大自然的厕所里心情舒畅，有时大便完事后还可冒着被生产队罚款的危险，顺手掰一根生产队的甘蔗嚼嚼。鲜甜的蔗汁流满了嘴，年轻人的心里乐开了花。

Chapter 13

Outhouses

In order to collect manure for their private plots, every family in my village built an outhouse next to their dwelling, and since it was for family use, there was no need to build one for the males and another for the females. Nevertheless, several families built public outhouses next to their homes because their land happened to be close to the village's meeting hall or rice mill. Of course, the human waste collected in those public outhouses would belong to the families that built the outhouses.

Thc outhouscs wcrc all simply constructcd. To build thc toilct, thc farmcrs first dug a huge hole in the ground. Next they put in the hole a barrel that was about one meter in diameter and one and a half meters in height, making sure that the top of the barrel stuck out about five centimeters higher than the ground surrounding it. Last they placed on the barrel two wooden boards, each of which was a bit wider than the width of a human foot. Some larger outhouses had two barrels; some even had an additional smaller barrel as a urinal, about point five meters in diameter and point seven meters in height. The outhouses were usually rectangular-looking and their walls were built with mud bricks. On one side of the outhouse, two walls with a space between them made the entrance—there was not a door. To protect the privacy of the person using the outhouse, a separate standalone wall would be erected in front of the entrance. The outhouse walls were all about one point six meters high. When squatting on the boards on a barrel, most people's heads would not show above the walls; however, for those males who were above average in height, they could have a good view of the inside and the outside when standing in an outhouse. All of the outhouses in the village, both the private and the public ones, were unisex. There was usually a bamboo stick about one and a half meters in length at each entrance. If the stick leaned across the entry way, blocking the entrance, it signaled that someone was using the outhouse. Most of the outhouses did not have a roof. When it rained, we had to wear our conical bamboo hats in the outhouses. To prevent the barrels from overflowing, the owners of the outhouses would use a pair of wooden buckets to scoop out the content of the barrels periodically.

Even though the public outhouses were unisex, no woman ever used them due to their crude construction and the possibility of the unexpected, so in reality, all of the public outhouses in the village were for males only.

We zhiqing did not own any land and therefore could not build our own outhouses. Even if we did own land, we probably would not have had the desire to build outhouses. Lucky for us, most of the farmers were more than happy to share their outhouses with us. We, of course, thought of the offering as something that could not have been gotten even if we had begged. Compared to the public outhouses, the private ones were much cleaner; but compared to what we were used to in the city, it was a world of difference. The outhouses in the village were just crude and dirty. At first it was always torturous for us when nature called. When purging on the two small planks on a barrel, one would be above a container full of stinky yellow poop. There would always be a thick layer of maggots churning in the barrel. The white maggots looked like grains of rice that had round heads and tapered tails—they were sickening and they squirmed continuously.

In the summer, when the sun scorched the earth as if everything was on fire, reeking heat waves and a fiery ammonia stench gagged those who were using the outhouses. And as if the smell was not enough, there would be swarms of green-headed flies hovering and jostling around the feces-filled barrels. In the winter, even though the stench was reduced, one would shiver when squatting on a barrel. The ground of the outhouses was another story. When the weather was good and dry, the ground would be as cold and hard as the sides of a cleaver, but when it rained, the ground would be a soupy mess. There would often times be urine and feces on the ground. It was difficult to know where one's feet should go. When we had to relieve ourselves, we would often have to inspect a few outhouses before choosing one that was tolerable.

One day not too long after I had arrived in the village, I entered one public outhouse in a rush. There I encountered a huge yellow dog who was slurping feces from a barrel. When it heard me, the dog turned to look at me. It bared its sharp teeth and glared at me, all the while making a deep glottal noise, as if it were going to attack me. But what frightened me more was not its demeanor; I was horrified by the yellow liquid that dripped from the dog's beard, which was covered with human excrement and white maggots. The hair on the back of my neck stood up instantly. I felt a rush of blood toward my head—my heart racing. I instinctively turned to run out, but I was not quick enough. Growling, the yellow dog leaped at me, landing next to my feet before dashing out of the outhouse. Needless to say, I did not feel like going to the bathroom anymore. I ended up drenched in a cold sweat.

It was customary for the farmers in those parts of the country not to wipe themselves with toilet paper; they simply rolled some straw together or used short sticks to scrape themselves. There were always straw rolls or short sticks floating in the outhouse barrels. We zhiqing usually used toilet paper but when there was none, we also learned to use shit sticks.

To avoid the nauseating smell and insufferable condition of the outhouses, we male zhiqing learned from the young farmers in the village. When it was nice out, we would go in groups to the production team's sugarcane fields to relieve ourselves. We also learned to use the ribs of sugarcane leaves to clean ourselves after bowel movements. In the natural outhouse, we could watch stars and breathe fresh air in the sugarcane fields while doing our business. We often enjoyed ourselves so much that we forgot to leave. Sometimes we would even chew on stalks of sugarcane, risking being punished if found out. At such times, we were happy.

十四

交 公 粮

我村的600多亩农业耕地全部为国家所有，其中大部分的农田每年都必须按照国家计划种植夏、秋两季水稻。当地农民根据水稻收获季节的先后，把春播夏收的夏季水稻称为“早造米”，而把夏播秋收的秋季水稻称为“晚造米”。

我村必须把全年收获的稻谷分成三部分：①公粮——每一亩水稻无偿给国家上缴75公斤稻谷。②口粮——按国家规定的数量留一部分稻谷作为全村人口一年的粮食。③余粮——除了公粮和口粮以外，剩余的全部稻谷必须以国家规定的价格由国家收购。

每年夏收一结束，我村就马上派工派船，把全年应交售的公粮、余粮全部运到镇粮食管理所的国家仓库去。开始，我不明白村民们为什么要这样做，觉得如果把全年的公粮、余粮分成夏、秋两季各交50%不是更好吗？后来向村民们一打听，才知道了其中的奥妙。原来，与早造米相比，晚造米的品种较好，生长期也较长，所以用晚造米煮成的饭比用早造米煮成的更香、更可口。农民们为了把较好吃的晚造稻谷留给自己作口粮，就尽量多交售早造稻谷给国家作为公粮、余粮。

1970年夏收结束后的一天，我村派我和农民青年阿友去镇粮食管理所交公粮。一大清早，我和阿友来到那条穿村而过的小河岸边，登上了生产队的一条中等大的木船，摇着橹把船驶向村里存放着公粮的仓库。我村的仓库都建在村大晒场的四周，离小河很近，村民们用船运输货物进出仓库十分方便。

到了大晒场，我们把船拴在码头上，在船舱底铺上一层干净的草席后，就向存放公粮的仓库走去。村的仓库保管员已经在仓库的大门前等候着我和阿友了，他用钥匙打开了仓库大门的锁，让我们跟随他进了仓库。

仓库里有几堆一人多高的稻谷，都是夏收刚刚收割下来、并已晒得干干的新谷子。一进仓库，我和阿友每人随手拿了一个竹簸箕和一个竹箩筐就干了起来。我们先把箩筐斜放在谷堆上，再用簸箕把谷子往箩筐里扒。装满了一箩筐的谷子后，我们就把箩筐扛在右肩上，同时用右手托住箩筐底部的一角，并用左手扶住箩筐的上沿，然后伸直腰杆向码头上的船走去。到了船边，我们用右手抓住箩筐的底部，接着左手一松，右肩膀一抖，就把整筐谷子倒进了船舱。一箩筐的谷子大约有25公斤重，而那条船的最大载重量是2500公斤。我和阿友每人扛了大约50箩筐的谷子，就把那条船装满了。

完成了装船的任务后，我和阿友就解开了拴船的绳索，顺手从仓库里拿了一个簸箕和两个箩筐放在船舱里为卸船用。我们把船轻轻地推离岸边后就跳上了船，阿友在船头撑篙，我在船尾摇橹，操纵着这条满载着公粮的船缓缓地沿着弯弯曲曲的小河前进。不一会儿，我们的船就驶出了小河，来到了水深流急的大江。这时，阿友的竹篙已无用武之地了，整条船只能靠我的橹来驾驶。我一边娴熟地摇着大橹，一边放眼远眺，只见蓝天上飘着朵朵白云，阳光灿烂，晴空万里；宽阔的江面上波光粼粼，白帆点点；大江两岸若隐若现的村庄和郁郁葱葱的田野，好一片令人陶醉的田园风光！我们的船快速地顺流而下，凉爽的江风迎面吹来，令人精神抖擞、心旷神怡。很快，我们远远地看到了在右前方的镇粮食管理所码头，就及时调整好船头的方向，斜斜地向着那个码头驶去。

到了镇粮食管理所码头，我们刚拴好船，粮食管理所的一位工作人员就带着一个质检器到我们船上检查这批公粮的质量。

粮食管理所工作人员所用的质检器看起来像一支用铁制成的“打气筒”，大约有一米多长。它的外壳形状是一个像笛子那样的薄圆筒，沿着长度方向有5个圆形小洞；这个外壳里面包着一根可以转动的实心圆柱体，沿着实心圆柱体的长度方向也有5个小洞，它们的大小、位置都与外壳上的小洞一样。若把实心圆柱体旋转到某个特定的位置，它上面的5个洞就会和外壳上的5个洞分别重合在一起。

粮食管理所的工作人员首先来到船舱前部抽查稻谷的质量。只见他熟练地旋转着质检器的实心圆柱体，使它上面的洞和外壳上的洞重合，然后把质检器几乎是垂直地从船舱谷堆的表面插到船舱底，停顿几秒钟，让处在谷堆不同深度的稻谷分别流进实心圆柱体的5个小洞里。接着，他把实心圆柱体旋转90度，它上面的洞就与外壳上的洞完全错开了，而那些原来流进了实心圆柱体小洞的稻谷就被外壳牢牢地“关在”了洞里。最后，那位工作人员把质检器从谷堆中抽出来，再旋转那个实心圆柱体，使它上面的洞和外壳上的洞再度重合，然后依次从每一个洞里取出几粒稻谷作为检查的样品，观察它们的色泽是否合格，并用牙齿把它们咬断来判断稻谷的干湿度是否达到规定的标准。如果稻谷的色泽或干湿度不合格，粮食管理所完全有权拒绝接受这船公粮。那位工作人员用同样的办法分别抽查了船舱中、后部等几个不同地方的稻谷后，对稻谷的质量表示满意，并同意我们把这船公粮运进国家的粮仓。

卸船开始了，我和阿友在船舱里用簸箕把稻谷扒进箩筐里，再把装满

稻谷的箩筐扛在肩上，走到国家粮仓的大门口处停下来，把箩筐放在一个与我们齐肩高的磅秤上，等坐在磅秤旁边的粮仓管理员称好并记录下每筐稻谷的重量后，我们再把箩筐扛在肩上走进仓库里，把稻谷卸在指定的谷堆上。

这个国家仓库比我村的仓库大几十倍，库内干净整洁，到处飘着一股刺鼻的陈年稻谷的味道。已入库的公粮都用一层层的谷围围成一座座圆柱形的稻谷山，有的稻谷山有几层楼那么高。我和阿友扛着装着25公斤稻谷的箩筐，脚踩着一层层搭成“之”字形的跳板，一步一步地往上走，最后把稻谷卸在稻谷山的顶部。

卸完了2500公斤公粮，我已累得汗流浃背，气喘吁吁了。我的身上、头发上都沾满了稻谷的芒刺和碎片，右肩膀还感到一阵火辣辣的疼。扒开衣服一看，我的右肩已经变得又红又肿了。

完成了交公粮的任务，我和阿友如释重负，兴高采烈地驾着空船循原路回村。我们俩一起在船尾摇着橹，一路上欢声笑语，迎着落日的余晖向我村驶去。

Chapter 14

Tax Grain

The over 600 mu of cultivatable farm land in our village were all government owned, and two crops of rice each year were assigned to the land. Depending on the time of the harvest, local farmers called the crop that was planted in the spring and harvested in the summer "early rice" while the crop that was planted in the summer and harvested in the fall "late rice."

All harvested rice grain each year had to be divided into three categories: ①tax grain—75 kilograms of rice grain from each mu of land must be paid to the government as tax grain; ②food grain—a portion of the rice grain—an amount determined by the government—could be kept as food provisions for everyone in the village; and ③surplus grain—what was left after tax grain and food grain had to be sold to the government according to the price set by the government.

Every year after the summer harvest, our village would send men and boats to bring our tax grain and surplus grain to the government granaries in town. In the beginning, I did not understand why the villagers did not pay what they owed the government with both the early and late rice, perhaps fifty percent of each. Later I found out there was a trick to what the farmers were doing. Compared to the early rice, the late rice was a better variety and had a longer growing season, resulting in better tasting rice when cooked. In order to keep as much of the late rice for their own food grain as possible, the farmers paid their tax grain and surplus grain with as much early rice as possible.

One day at the end of the summer harvest in 1970, I was assigned with a young farmer, Ah You, to bring our tax grain to the government granary. Early that morning, Ah You and I went to the river that ran through our village. We boarded and rowed a mid-sized wooden boat to our village's grain storehouses, which were built next to the village's grain sunning ground close to the river, making it convenient for the transportation of grain.

At the dock by the sunning ground, we secured the boat and laid a clean straw matt on the floor of the hold of the boat. The storehouse keeper was already waiting for Ah You and me at the gate. We followed him into one storehouse after he unlocked the door.

There were several mounds of rice grain in the storehouse, each was about the height of a person. It was all newly harvested and dried rice grain from the summer harvest. As soon as we entered the storehouse, Ah You and I each grabbed a bamboo basket and bamboo dustpan, and we started to load. We positioned the baskets against a mound of rice grain and used the dustpans to scoop the grain into the baskets. When my basket was full, I hoisted the basket onto my right shoulder, my left hand grabbing onto the upper brim of the basket while my right arm forming an L under the basket, supporting it on my right shoulder. Ah You did the same to his basket. We then straightened our backs and walked to the boat. When we got to the boat, we moved our right hands to the bottom of the baskets, let go of our left hands, gave our right shoulders a quick shrug, and we thus poured the baskets of rice grain into the hold of the boat. Each basket of rice grain weighed over 25 kilograms and the boat's weight limit was 2500 kilograms. Ah You and I filled the boat after each of us had carried over 50 baskets of grain to the boat.

After we loaded the boat, we took a dustpan and two baskets from the storehouse to the boat so that we could use them for unloading. Ah You and I then loosened the rope that tied the boat to the dock and jumped onto the boat after we detached it from the dock. Ah You punted from the bow while I rowed from the stern. Together, we guided the boat of our tax grain from a small winding river to a big river that was deep with its water flowing rapidly. In the big river, Ah You's pole lost its power. All depended on me and my oars. I rowed skillfully. Looking ahead, I saw a beautiful blue sky with white clouds extending to where the sky and water became one. The river sparkled under the sun. I felt dreamy on the river, seeing white sails dotting the river and villages and green fields lining both sides of the river. Our boat sailed rapidly downstream with the current. The cool wind rejuvenated me and lifted my spirits. Soon we saw the dock of the town's Grain Regulation Department so we guided our boat toward it.

As soon as we moored our boat, a representative from the Grain Regulation Department came over with his instrument to inspect our grain.

The instrument looked like a bicycle pump, about one meter in length. Its outer cylinder looked like a flute, with five round holes along one side. Its inner rod also had five holes, which matched the holes on the cylinder. The holes could be lined up by turning the rod inside the cylinder.

The representative first inspected the grain from the bow of the boat. He first turned the instrument so that its holes would line up, then holding the instrument vertically, he stabbed the instrument into the mound of grain in the hold. He paused for a few seconds to wait for the grain from the mound to fall into the holes of his instrument. Then he turned the rod ninety degrees so that its holes would not match the holes on the cylinder and the grains of rice that got into the holes would stay trapped. Last, the representative lifted the instrument from the grain mound, turned the rod so that its holes once again lined up with the holes on the cylinder. This way he could pick out each grain that was locked in each hole and inspect it. He looked at each one for color and he used his teeth to break each grain of rice in half to test its dryness. If our grain's color or dryness did not meet the standard set by the government, the representative could refuse to accept our boatload of grain. The inspector repeated his inspection from the middle, the stern, and several other locations of our boat. When he was satisfied with the quality of our grain, he told us to unload the grain into the government's granary.

Using the bamboo dustpan and baskets we had brought along, Ah You and I shoveled grain into the baskets with the dustpan and then carried the baskets to the door of the warehouse. There we put our baskets on a big scale, waited for the clerk next to the scale to record the weight of each basket, and then we carried the baskets into the warehouse and unloaded the grain onto the appointed grain mound in the granary.

The government granary was a few times larger than our village's grain storehouse. It was very clean and organized inside but in the air there was a pungent smell of aged grain. The tax grain in the warehouse was sectioned off into grain-mountains, some of which were as tall as buildings of several stories. Ah You and I had to carry each basket that weighed over 25 kilograms all the way to the top of a grain mountain by stepping on the zigzagging spring boards leading to the top.

I was exhausted after we unloaded over 2500 kilograms of tax grain. I could hardly catch my breath and I was drenched in sweat. I had grain bristles and husk all over me, from head to toe. My right shoulder burned. Lifting my clothes, I saw that my right shoulder was red and swollen.

Both Ah You and I felt a heavy weight had been lifted off our shoulders after we finished the task of delivering the tax grain. Happily, we rowed the empty boat together, bantering and laughing, sailing toward our village in the sunset.

十五

收获甘蔗

我村所在的地区属亚热带，全年气候温暖，雨水充沛，非常适合甘蔗的生长。甘蔗的生长期比水稻长，一般是春天播种，秋天收获。

在计划经济的政策下，国家对每个村庄种植甘蔗的面积、产量和销售价格都有严格的规定，并由国营制糖厂统一收购所有的甘蔗。蔗农只有超额完成规定的甘蔗产量，才能从国营制糖厂买到价格便宜的糖；否则，他们只能到自由市场去买比国营制糖厂的价格高几倍的高价糖了。

“上有政策，下有对策。”为了保证超额完成规定的甘蔗产量，让村民们能买到价格便宜的糖，我村的干部冒险擅自从国家规定种水稻的土地中，划出几亩地来改种甘蔗。这样的做法一旦被上级管理部门知道，不但全村人吃不上价格便宜的糖，而且那些村干部还会因为破坏国家计划经济而遭到撤职查办。因为事关全体村民的切身利益和村干部的前途命运，我村的男女老少都“深明大义”、守口如瓶，没有一个人向外界透露我村私自改种甘蔗的消息。全村人“同心协力”，筑成了一道密不透风的封锁墙。

下乡第二年的深秋，我村的秋季稻子已收割完毕，主要的劳动力都转入了收甘蔗的大忙季节。

12月初的一天清晨，当我带着蔗刀，沿着弯弯曲曲的河堤，来到离村不远的一块甘蔗地参加收甘蔗的劳动时，许多村民已经在那块甘蔗地的田头等候了。他们有的人在聊天，有的人在抽烟，人声嘈杂，好不热闹。

这块地的甘蔗长得又粗又壮，约有两米多高，像一片茂密的小树林一样。甘蔗主干的每一节上都长满了翠绿的甘蔗叶，宽宽的叶子表面有一层短短的毛，叶子的边缘布满了锯齿般锋利的小刺。村民们说，如果人的皮肤沾上了甘蔗叶上的那层毛会很容易过敏，弄得浑身又痒又疼；如果人的皮肤碰到了甘蔗叶边上的那些刺，就会被划破、划伤。我环视了周围参加收甘蔗的村民们，只见他们一个个都像全副武装起来的士兵一样：头上的草帽是他们的头盔；手上的手套、身上的长衣、长裤是他们防护甘蔗叶伤害的盔甲；肩上系着的一块黑布是他们盔甲上的披肩；手里握着的砍蔗刀是他们的战斗武器。村民们个个情绪高涨，跃跃欲试地等待着向那块甘蔗地发动进攻的号令。

早上7点多，生产队长挥手向大家发出了收甘蔗的命令。村民们迅速地散开来，在甘蔗地的田头排成一行，一边砍甘蔗，一边缓缓地向田尾推进。

我是砍甘蔗的新手，只能边学边干。我模仿着村民们的动作，一只手拿着蔗刀，另一只手握着甘蔗的主干，再用刀砍断甘蔗主干接近根部的部位，然后把砍下来的几根甘蔗放在一堆。

大家你追我赶，干得热火朝天，只用了一个多小时，就把整片甘蔗林放倒了。看到地面上到处躺着的一堆堆带着叶子的甘蔗，我心里一阵高兴，以为收甘蔗的任务已经大功告成了。这时，一位青年农民却幽默地对我说："砍甘蔗只是收甘蔗的三道工序中的第一道工序而已，'革命'尚未成功，我们仍需努力。"

收甘蔗的第二道工序是剥甘蔗叶和捆绑甘蔗。我们用手把甘蔗的全部叶子剥下来后，把五六根甘蔗放成一堆，再用几块甘蔗叶叠在一起扭成绳子，然后把那堆甘蔗的头部和尾部分别捆绑起来，以方便搬运和装船。我们在剥甘蔗叶时都格外小心，生怕皮肤会被甘蔗叶子弄得过敏或割破。不一会儿工夫，所有砍下来的甘蔗都被捆好了，每捆大约有25公斤重。在捆绑甘蔗的同时，我们还用甘蔗叶扭成的绳子把剥下来的甘蔗叶子捆成一捆捆的，留在地里晒几天太阳，等它们完全干透后再运回村里，分给村民作柴火。

中午时分，我们完成了第二道工序，生产队长便让大家回家吃饭，下午再回来完成收甘蔗的最后一道工序——把那些躺在地里的一捆捆甘蔗扛到船上。

午饭后，当我们回到那块甘蔗地时，我看到了一艘国营制糖厂雇来运送甘蔗的大船，停泊在离我们大约有200米远的江边，等候着我们把收的甘蔗装上船。因为戴着草帽扛甘蔗不方便，我和村民们二话不说，不约而同地把头上的草帽扔到了地上，把肩上绑着的那块黑色的“苦力”布解下来，披在头上和肩膀上作垫布，把一捆捆的甘蔗扛起来送到船上去。

我用双手把一捆横躺在地上的甘蔗竖立起来，然后弯下腰，用右肩顶住那捆甘蔗的中部，再用双手把那捆甘蔗的底部往上一抬，就把整捆甘蔗扛在了肩上。我扛着一捆沉重的甘蔗，踩着高低不平的田埂，踉踉跄跄地向着那条装载甘蔗的大船走去。到了船上，我把整捆甘蔗撂在船舱里，又马上快步回到那块甘蔗地里扛另一捆甘蔗。扛了几个来回，我的右肩就被又重又硬的甘蔗压得直生疼，我只好改用左肩来扛，以便让右肩得到喘息的机会。

经过两个多小时的紧张劳动， 我们终于把收的全部甘蔗都装上了船。看到那条吃水很深、满载着甘蔗的大船缓缓地离开岸边，张着满满的风帆向制糖厂的方向快速驶去时，我和几个村民都心照不宣地相视一笑，大家心里都明白：这回我村可以买到国营糖厂价格便宜的糖这件事，就像木板上钉钉子一样——跑不了啦。

在回村的路上，我突然感到两个肩膀一阵火辣辣的疼，扭头往左右一看，才发现肩膀都已经红肿起来了。

Chapter 15

Sugarcane

My village was located in an area where the climate was subtropical and the growing season was long. There was plenty of rain and warm weather, very suitable for growing sugarcane. We planted sugarcane in the spring and harvested it in the fall.

At the time, a planned economy was practiced in the entire country. That is, the state mandated how much land should be allotted for growing sugarcane, how much the total sugarcane output should be, and how much the sugarcane price should be set for. All sugarcane had to be sold to government-owned sugar processing mills. Farmers could buy sugar from the mills only after their sugarcane sales to the government had surpassed the required amount; otherwise, they had to buy sugar from the free market, where the price of sugar was usually a few times higher than that at the government-owned sugar mills.

There is a saying that goes like this, "When policies come from above, countermeasures spring up from below." To ensure a surplus of sugarcane production and to enable the villagers to buy inexpensive sugar, our production team leaders risked their positions and sectioned off a few mu of land that were required for rice production. They grew sugarcane instead. If found out, the consequences would have been dire. The villagers would not have had inexpensive sugar to buy and the leaders would have been demoted and punished as criminals who tried to sabotage the government's planned economy. Everyone understood the importance of keeping our "wrong doing" a secret. We kept our mouths shut about it and therefore built an impenetrable, invisible wall around our sugarcane.

It was the fall of the second year of my village life. We had finished our fall rice grain harvest. Most of the work then concentrated on the harvesting of sugarcane.

Early one morning in December, carrying the knife that I would use to harvest sugarcane, I walked along the meandering river embankments to my village's sugarcane field. By the time I got there, a lot of the villagers were there already. Some of them were talking to each other and some of them were smoking. There was excitement in the air.

The sugarcane in this field looked like small trees—they were big and healthy-looking, about two meters in height. The field looked like a dense forest. Looking at the sugarcane, one saw green leaves on each trunk of the sugarcane plant. The leaves were covered by fur-like short hair and the edges of each leaf had prickles that looked like the teeth of sharp saws. According to the villagers, most people would be allergic to the downy hair on the leaves. When touched, one's skin would itch and burn, and if one's skin encountered the prickles on the leaves, there would be slashes and gashes. I took another look at the villagers, and I realized that each of them looked like soldiers in full armor: their straw hats were their helmets; their gloves, long sleeved tops and long pants were their armor; the black cloths on their shoulders were their neck and shoulder guards; the knives for cutting sugarcane were their weapons. The villagers were all geared up and waited enthusiastically for the order to start the harvesting.

At about 7 a.m., the production team captain waved his hand to indicate the commencement of the sugarcane harvest. Quickly, we fanned out horizontally at the head of the sugarcane field. Together, we chopped down sugarcane as we advanced to the other end of the field.

I was new at harvesting sugarcane so I learned as I worked. Imitating the farmers, I grabbed the main trunk of each sugarcane plant and swung my knife at it. Afterwards, I put the chopped down sugarcane in a heap—a few stalks to a bundle.

We raced each other and worked cheerfully. In a little over an hour, we felled all the sugarcane in the field. Looking at the bundles of sugarcane on the ground, I was so happy that I thought the sugarcane harvest was over. "But the felling part is only the first part in the three-part sugarcane harvest," a young farmer said to me. "The 'revolution' has not been accomplished. We must continue the fight."

The second part of the sugarcane harvest consisted of stripping the leaves off the sugarcane and tying the sugarcane into bundles. After stripping all the leaves by hand, we arranged five to six stalks to a bundle. Then we twisted several leaves into a tie and secured both ends of the sugarcane bundles with these leaf-ties, making it easy for transporting and loading the sugarcane bundles onto boats. We had to be very careful when we stripped the leaves—we were afraid of touching the leaves or being slashed by them. Soon we finished tying up all the stalks. Each bundle weighed over 25 kilograms. While we bundled the sugarcane, we also used the leaf-ties to bundle up the sugarcane leaves. We left the leaf-bundles to be sun dried in the field so that we could collect and distribute the dried leaves as firewood to the villagers later.

We finished the second part of the harvesting around noon. The production team captain told us to go home for lunch. We were to return in the afternoon to finish the third part—transporting the sugarcane bundles onto a boat.

When we got back to the sugarcane field after lunch, I noticed there was a big rental boat from the government sugar mill. It was waiting for us on the river about 200 meters from us. Because our straw hats made it awkward to carry sugarcane on our shoulders, we threw our straw hats on the ground in unison. Each of us took the black cloth—known as coolie cloth—that was on our shoulders and put it over our heads, forming a cushion on our shoulders for carrying the sugarcane to the boat.

In the sugarcane field, I stood one bundle of sugarcane up, bent forward and put my right shoulder against the middle of the bundle while lifting up the bottom of the bundle. The bundle was thus hoisted onto my right shoulder. Carrying the heavy bundle of sugarcane, I took unsteady steps on the bumpy footpath to the boat. I took quick steps back to carry another bundle as soon as I placed the first bundle on the boat. After several rounds, my right shoulder was sore so I had to use my left shoulder to carry. I had to give my right shoulder a break.

After working intensely for a little over two hours, we finally finished loading all the sugarcane onto the boat. Watching the big boat full of our sugarcane leaving the shore, sailing toward the sugar mill rapidly under a full sail, we looked at each other and smiled. We knew that we would be able to buy the inexpensive sugar from the government sugar mill. We were as sure about it as we knew that when nails had been pounded into boards, the nails would not be lost.

On the way back to the village, I felt a burning sensation on my shoulders. Both of my left and right shoulders were red and swollen.

十六

那一年的冬至

南方水乡农村俗称农历的节气冬至为冬节。在我们插队的村子里，人们有“冬大于年”的说法——即指冬至是比春节还要隆重的节日。按农历算，每年的冬至大约在公历的12月21或22日。此时正值冬季农闲，秋收早在一个月前就结束了，口粮、稻草也分到了各家各户，剩下的就是积肥、平整田地等较轻的农活了——村民们真可谓是“刀枪入库，马放南山”，优哉游哉了。

过冬节，村里家家户户都毫无例外地做一种名叫“濑粉”的传统食物来吃，而每年也只有在冬节期间，人们才能吃上濑粉。可以说，吃濑粉是过冬节的标志，不吃濑粉就不算过冬节。

濑粉是用大米粉做成的一种雪白的圆“面条”。冬节前一两周，村里的妇女们就忙着舂米。搉子的结构就像一副跷跷板：用一根又粗又长的木头做成跷跷板的主干，主干的一端是一个重重的木锤子，另一端的顶部则做成一块脚踏的平板。在主干上有一个木头做的跷跷板支点，支点与脚踏平板端的距离大约是主干总长度的三分之一。木锤子下面有一个用花岗岩凿成的大石碗。舂米时，妇女们就把泡湿了的大米放在大石碗里，用脚把捧子的脚踏平板往下踩，捧子另一端的木锤子就高高地扬起，并在她们松开脚踏平板时重重地落下来，把那些放在大石碗里的米砸碎。就这样用脚一压一松，循环往复，把一粒粒的大米碾成了粉。每天傍晚时分，到处都可以看到穿着漂亮围裙的妇女们有说有笑，三五成群地在舂米。那有节奏的“咚咚咚”的舂米声此起彼落，和着妇女们那断断续续的打骂嬉笑声，谱成了一首令人心醉的舂米圆舞曲。

冬节全村休息一天。天刚亮，村里家家户户的烟囱都冒出了缕缕炊烟——大家都在忙碌着做濑粉。这天，我们知青不管路过哪家的大门，也不管平时与那家人是否相熟，该家的男女主人都会热情地邀请我们进门去吃濑粉——那份真挚和热情真是令人难以推辞。有些平时与我们知青交往较多的村民还特地让家人上门来请我们去吃濑粉。有时我在村里走一遭，就吃上了好几家的濑粉，真可谓是吃尽“百家濑粉”啊。

有趣的是，我们还能看到村民们是如何煮濑粉的。他们烧一锅开水，把舂好的米粉和水调成稠稠的糊状后用勺舀进一个圆柱形的金属容器里，容器的底部有一些直径约半厘米的小圆孔，然后再用另一直径稍小一点的圆柱形的金属容器去挤压那些糊状的米粉，就像用打气筒一样。一条条圆圆的米粉不断地落在锅里，在开水里被煮熟成粉条形，又马上被捞出来放进冷水里“过冷河”。据说这样才能保持濑粉的清爽可口。把过完冷河的濑粉捞起来放在盘子里备用，再烧好一锅高汤，要吃濑粉时则可把濑粉放进高汤里滚三滚，撒上点盐、油和葱花，然后把濑粉和汤盛到大海碗里，濑粉上面再放上几块烧鸭，真是香气诱人，令人垂涎三尺啊！

冬节这一天可谓是“世界大同”——不管平时谁贫谁富，过冬节家家都吃烧鸭濑粉。村里的小孩子们早早在秋收过后就盼望着过冬节，知青们也是如此。因为我们那天不用下地干活，不用自己做饭，还可以吃到那“百家濑粉”。

洁白如雪的濑粉，香味扑鼻的烧鸭和肉汤，还有那漂在肉汤上翠绿翠绿的葱花，真是人间仙境的美味佳肴，令人回味无穷。

Chapter 16

Winter Solstice

In the southern water villages, the winter solstice was considered a winter festival. In my village, people often said that the winter solstice was more important than the Chinese New Year. According to the lunar calendar, each year's winter solstice falls on December 21 or 22. The days around the winter solstice were usually a winter leisure time for the farmers in my village. The fall harvest would have been done over a month ago. Each family's grain ration and straw allowance would have been distributed. What was left of the farm work was manure collection and field maintenance, which was considered light work on the farm. It was a time "When the guns and knives are storcd and thc horscs arc lct loose on the southern mountain." It was a time when the farmers relaxed and did what they wanted, not what they had to.

During the winter solstice, every family would make a traditional dish called *laifen*. In those days, one only got to eat laifen during the winter solstice. It could be said that laifen symbolized the winter solstice. It would not be the winter solstice if there was no laifen.

Laifen is a fresh rice noodle that is round. During the years when I was in the village, usually about a week or two before the winter festival, the females in the village would be busy pounding rice. The contraption for such an activity looked like a teeter-totter: a big and heavy wooden hammer head was attached to one end of a long, hefty log while a flat board about the size of one human foot was attached to the other end of the log. The wooden support was located at about one third of the distance between the stepping board and the hammer head. A big stone bowl was stationed under the hammer head. To pound rice, women would put uncooked, soaked rice in the stone bowl. Then using one foot, they would push down the flat board to raise the hammer head. When they let go, the heavy hammer head would drop on the rice in the bowl. The repetition of lifting and dropping the heavy wooden hammer head on the teeter-totter would crush the rice into rice flour. Every evening, one could see groups of three or five laughing and chattering women pounding rice, all wearing pretty aprons. The cadenced sound of rice pounding and the women's intermittent bantering would form an intoxicating waltz of the rice dance.

Everyone in the village got a day off on the day of the winter festival. At day break, every chimney in the village would have smoke rising —every family would be making laifen. That day, no matter whose house we zhiqing passed—even if we did not know the people—we would still be invited to have laifen with the family. The farmers' hospitality and sincerity made it impossible for us to beg off. Those farmers who were our friends would send family members to our residence to invite us to their homes for laifen. Sometimes if I walked around the village on the day of the winter solstice, I would end up eating laifen several times with different families. I could say that I knew our village's laifen qualities. What was most interesting was watching how laifen was cooked. Usually a pot of water would be boiled first. The rice flour made earlier would be mixed with some water to make a thick batter. Then this batter would be spooned into a round metal tube that had several small holes (which had a diameter of about half a centimeter) at the bottom end. A metal bar of sorts would then be inserted into the tube to push the batter out from the small holes into the pot of boiling water.

What got pushed out by the bicycle-pump-looking contraption looked like round noodles. When the noodles were cooked, they would take a cold bath—or be put in a "cold river"—to keep the fresh taste and special texture of the laifen. The cooked laifen were usually kept on a plate so that whenever someone was ready to eat, there would be some laifen ready. To eat laifen, one only had to boil some soup stock with meat, and put the laifen in the broth to boil for a few minutes till the laifen was warm. One would then put the soup and laifen in a big bowl, sprinkle some salt, sesame oil, and chopped green onions, and put a few slices of roast duck on top. The fragrance was so appetizing that the bowl of laifen would make everyone's mouth water.

One could say that the winter solstice was World Equality Day because every family got to eat laifen with roast duck that day, no matter how poor or rich anyone was. All the children in the village looked forward to the winter festival as soon as the fall harvest was over. Zhiqing did the same. We knew that on that day, we would not have to work in the fields or cook for ourselves. We could eat laifen with a hundred families if we wanted to. The combination of the white-as-snow laifen, the aromatic soup stock with roast duck, and the fresh green onions—all contributed to this delicacy, which exists only in a fairyland.

I'm most nostalgic for laifen during the winter solstice.

十七

评　工　分

我们下乡插队的那个年代，全国正在掀起轰轰烈烈的“工业学大庆，农业学大寨”运动。山西昔阳县大寨生产大队被树为全国农业的样板，全国从上到下全面推广大寨精神和大寨的管理方法，大寨的陈永贵后来还当上了国务院的副总理。

在人民公社的体制下，全国农村实行人民公社、生产大队和生产队三级管理机制。生产队一般是由自然村组成，大的自然村也可分成几个生产队——我们村600多人就分成了5个生产队，基本是以同姓家族来划分的。生产大队一般由几个自然村组成，与“乡”的概念同级。人民公社一般由数个或十几个生产大队组成——我们所在的公社有18个生产大队，公社的上面就是县了。

在生产队一级的管理机制下，经济分配实行“按劳取酬”的原则——由生产队长安排每个劳动力每天的具体农活，年底生产队分红时，则按每个劳动力的贡献大小计算其应得的报酬。实行“按劳取酬”可以有各种各样的方式，但当时统一推行的是山西昔阳县大寨生产大队的“评工分”法。在我们村，一个劳动力出勤一天可挣的最高分是10个工分，大约值

人民币9毛钱，一般只有那些最强的老把式的男劳动力一天才能挣到10个工分。每年秋收过后，生产队就召开全体社员大会，采用“自报公议”的办法，给每个劳动力评出其出勤一天的工分值。工分值乘以出勤总天数就是该劳动力一年应分到的报酬。

下乡插队的第一年，我们是11月中才来到村里的，干了一两周活，秋收就结束了。12月初，我第一次参加生产队召开的全体社员评工分大会。早上8点左右，大家都来到村里的大礼堂开会。据说这个大礼堂是在1958年人民公社化时代建的，当时也是全村男女老少吃“大锅饭”的饭堂。大礼堂的正门有几扇涂了蓝漆的大门，墙是白色的，房顶很高，里面的地面是用橙红色的方砖铺成的。礼堂里没有椅子，大家都三五成群地席地而坐，有的妈妈们还把小孩带在身边。在队长宣布评工分开始后，大家就开始自由发言。每个发言的人首先自报自评工分，其他人则可自由发表意见，同意或不同意及理由，最后由大部分人的意见来决定，看来还挺民主的。

评工分的顺序一般是先评男劳动力，最高分是10分，他们是干活的中坚，重活和技术活一般都由他们承担。那些有家室的男性主要劳动力，一般都能评上9.7～10分。未婚的男性劳动力，强的也能评上10分，而一些刚出来参加劳动的十四五岁的男孩子，则只能评上6分、7分。

接着，是评“百花”的工分。“百花”是当地对未婚年轻妇女们的称呼。“百花”们是干农活的主力军，插秧、收割样样行。虽然她们与男性劳动力并肩战斗在农活的第一线，但根据村里的评分规定，她们的最高分是8.5分。在我们村， 除了驶牛翻土、耙田、用电动抽水机给田里灌水等农活外，百花们与男劳动力干的活是一样的。依我看，最高分8.5分是低了一点儿，但从未听到百花们对此不满。在“男尊女卑”的封建意识占主导地位的中国农村，男女之间的不平等处处可见，人们觉得这是天经地义的。与那些刚出来参加劳动的十四五岁的男孩子一样，那些小百花们也只能评上5分、6分和7分不等。

最后是评“后勤班”的工分。“后勤班”是当地人对已婚并生了孩子的妇女们的称呼，其出处也许是借用于军队的术语吧。“后勤班”的妇女们因为要照顾家庭和小孩，基本不参加插秧、收割等劳动强度较大以及一些离村较远的农活。拔秧、晒谷、除草等较轻的农活则主要由她们承担。“后勤班”的最高分是7.5分。

“自报公议”的评分过程总的来说都是比较平缓顺利的，特别是男劳动力和百花的评分争议不多，人们都是心平气和的，很快就评完了。争议比较多的是“后勤班”的妈妈们，有时也会大声地争吵起来，正如当地的土话说的 “三个妇娘一面锣” 。不管出现什么纠纷，最后总是由队长及其家族里有威望的人来帮忙解决。

我的感觉是，村民们基本能实事求是地、合理地评出每一个人应得的工分，有些本人是地主或地主家庭出身的劳动高手，也能评上10分，阶级成分对评分的影响不大。但其中不可否认的是，家族较大的人说话的底气会足一些，因为会有同族的人撑腰，所以会稍占优势。本人或家庭成分不好的人则一般不敢捍卫自己的权益，会稍稍吃亏一点。

当评我的工分时，我还未自报，同队的蔡锦明就站起来大声地对大家说，他觉得我应该评9.5分。他提到我离开城市，离开父母下乡，秋收割稻时把小拇指割伤了，流了很多血，但包扎后继续干活。记得当时是蔡锦明用烟丝洒在我的伤口上，并从他的衣服上撕下一块布条帮我扎住伤口。蔡锦明当年有30多岁，是队里的强劳动力之一，更重要的是他是家里的老大，在队里有三兄弟，还有几个叔伯堂兄弟，算得上是一族之长，所以讲话比较有权威，别的人一般不想得罪他。没有人反对他的提议，我就被评为9.5分。我想，有很多社员心里不服，只是敢怒而不敢言罢了。平心而论，我刚进村才一个月，啥也不懂，哪值9.5分啊！看看一起插队的几个男知青，最高的评为7.5分，有的还只有7分而已。幸好我那年只劳动了不到两个月，给我评9.5分不会占社员们太多的便宜。

往后的几年，我被评的工分分别是8.5分和9分。一直到我离开村庄那年，我也没有再被评过9.5的高分。

Chapter 17

Income Allocation

At the time when we were zhiqing in the countryside, there was a political movement called "Learn from Daqing in Industry and Learn from Dazhai in Agriculture." The production brigade named Dazhai in Xiyang county of Shanxi Province was made to be the model: Everyone in the country was supposed to be influenced by the Dazhai spirit and learn the management approaches used in Dazhai. The production brigade captain of Dazhai, Chen Yonggui, was also appointed to be a vice-premier of China.

In those days, a three-tier organizational structure was practiced in the countryside throughout China: production commune, production brigade, and production team. Villages were grouped into production teams, with larger villages being divided into several teams. Our village had over 600 people so it was divided into five production teams, with each team having members sharing the same family names. Production teams then formed production brigades, several of which could make a township. A commune was usually formed by over ten production brigades—the commune we belonged to had 18 production brigades. What came next in size to a production commune would be a county.

Within each production team, individual member's income was calculated according to the work each person performed. The production team captain was responsible for assigning work each day. At the end of each year, each person's compensation would be figured out according to his/her contributions. There were all sorts of ways to calculate the amount of "compensation according to labor contribution," but at the time, one popular method was what was practiced in Dazhai. It was called the *gongfen* or work-point method. In our village, the highest gongfen anyone could earn from a day's work was ten points, worth about nine jiao. After the fall harvest, there was always a production team meeting and the worth of each person's daily labor would be figured out according to a system called "self-reporting and public discussion," resulting in a value that could be used to multiply by the total number of days worked by each person. The result of such reporting, discussing, and calculating would be the amount of monetary income for each person.

We first arrived in the village in mid-November so after working for only one or two weeks, that year's fall harvest was over. In the beginning of that December, I participated for the first time in my production team's income allocation meeting. Everyone arrived in the village's meeting hall around 8 a.m. The meeting hall was built in 1958 when the production communal system was first introduced and the hall also served as the village's cafeteria where everyone ate their meals during the time of "eating from the big pot" —food was produced and cooked collectively and those who were in the commune were served food free of charge. The front doors to the hall were painted blue, the walls were white, and the ceiling was high. The floor was made of reddish orange square bricks. There were no seats in the hall. People sat on the floor in groups of three or five. Mothers brought their children along. When the production team captain announced the start of the meeting, people started to talk. Each person first suggested a gongfen amount for him/herself. The others then made comments and suggestions. The final gongfen for each person was the result of the majority vote. On the surface, the gongfen determination process appeared to be democratic.

Males usually got to get their gongfen figured out first. The highest was ten points. Those who received ten points were the males who did the hardest or most technical types of work. Those males who had families could usually get 9.7 to 10 points. Single males who were good workers could also get ten points, but those younger males, who were about fourteen or fifteen years of age, usually got six or seven points.

The next group was the "Hundred Flowers," which was a nickname given to the young, unmarried females in the village. The Hundred Flowers were valued laborers, who were capable of doing rice planting and harvesting, etc. However, even though they worked with the males on the front line, according to the village's income allocation policy, the highest gongfen they could receive was 8.5 points. In our village, we used water buffalos to plow and till the fields and we used electric water pumps to pump water into the rice paddies. The Hundred Flowers did every other kind of farm work just as the males did.

I thought giving them 8.5 points was low, but I never heard any complaints from the Hundred Flowers. In the countryside where the feudalistic thought of males being more important or valuable than females was a guiding principle, no one thought it unfair that females earned less than males when they did the same work. Inequality between the sexes was everywhere. The younger females—the young Hundred Flowers who were fourteen or fifteen years of age—received the same number of points as their male counterparts, about five, six, or seven points.

The last group was the "Logistics" group, whose membership consisted of mainly those married women with children. "Logistics" was a local name for the women and perhaps it was a title borrowed from the military for whatever reason. Because the women in the logistics group had to take care of their households and young children, they did not participate in the planting, harvesting or any other farm work that required them to work far away from where they lived or any work that was too demanding. They were mainly responsible for the comparatively light work, such as seedling preparation, grain sunning, and weeding. The highest anyone could earn in that group was 7.5 points.

The self-reporting procedures at such income allocation meetings were usually trouble-free without problems. There were usually no arguments from the males and the Hundred Flowers. People were even-tempered and points were assigned quickly. Nevertheless, the mothers in the logistics group usually had the most trouble, sometimes resulting in loud squabbles. The locals had a saying that described the situation: "If you want the sound of a gong, put three women together." However, no matter how involved the arguments were, in the end, the captain of the production team or the head of each family clan had the final say.

My impression was that most farmers were fair and honest when assigning labor points to each other. Even those who were land owners before the Land Reform or those who came from land-owning families could get ten points if they were good laborers. Social class divisions did not have any bearing on the gongfen method. Nevertheless, one fact that could not be ignored was that if one were from a large family clan, one would feel more confident and could speak louder because one would have the support of the other members of the family clan. People from large family clans certainly had an advantage. Those who were from what were considered bad families or those who had been classified into the not-so-desirable political classes were usually at a disadvantage, not daring to speak up to protect their interests.

I remember that when it was my turn to get points assigned to me that first year, even before I did the self-reporting, Farmer Cai Jingming from my production team stood up and proclaimed that I should be given 9.5 points. He mentioned that I had to leave my parents in the city to go to the village; he told everyone that I cut my small finger at the fall harvest but I continued working after I wrapped the wound and I had lost a lot of blood. I remember it was Cai Jingming who put tobacco on my cut and helped me dress my wound with a piece of cloth he tore from his own shirt. Cai Jingming was thirty-something at the time. He was one of the main hands on the production team, but what was more important was that he was the oldest in his family. He had two brothers and several cousins on the same team so he was like an elder in his family clan. He possessed the authority to speak and no one would want to upset him. No one countered his suggestion so I received 9.5 points. I knew that a lot of the villagers were not convinced that I deserved so many points, but they were afraid to speak up—they were dismayed but they dared not argue. Honestly, I had only been in the village for a month and I did not know much about farming. I really did not deserve to receive 9.5 points for my work. Other male zhiqing in my production team only got 7.5 points or even just seven points. Luckily, I only worked for a little short of two months that year. When my income was calculated by multiplying my 9.5 points to the number of days I had worked that year, my 9.5 points did not allow me to take advantage of the other farmers too much. I did not earn much that year anyway.

In subsequent years, I was only given 8.5 or 9 points. I never again got 9.5 points even during the last year I was in the village.

十八

打 篮 球

从中学时代起，我就爱好打篮球。学校停课期间，我和我的伙伴们搬回学校住，每天到学校的篮球场练球。下乡插队时，我随身带了一个藏青色的胶皮篮球，期盼着能在村里找到打篮球的地方。

进村的那天早晨，在生产队长的带领下，我们几个知青拎着行李，沿着弯弯曲曲的田间小路向村里走去。透过薄薄的晨雾，我们朦朦胧胧地看到了一片掩映在绿树丛中的房屋，生产队长告诉我们说，那就是我们的村子。当我们走近村子时，我不禁高兴地欢呼起来——“篮球场！ 篮球场！” 在一片房子中间，我看见了一块很大很大的水泥地，上面有一对高高耸起的篮球架。真棒，我又可以打球了！

进村以后，我有空就拿着球到村里的篮球场打球。仔细一看，原来这个篮球场是利用生产队的晒谷场建成的。在几百平方米大的水泥地上，画上篮球场的底线、边线、中线、禁区、罚球区等，再竖两个篮球架。球架、篮板、篮圈等也还算正规。6名男知青中，除了我之外还有两个人也打篮球，但他们的“球瘾”都没有我的大。村民们看到新来的几个知青会打篮球，觉得挺新鲜，大人小孩都围着看。有几个青年农民对我们说，邻近

的几个村子都有农民篮球队，打得很不错，咱村无法与他们较量。现在你们知青来了，咱村可以组织个篮球队跟他们比试比试。听了村民们的鼓动，我很兴奋，表示我们要尽快组队去邻村挑战。

我根据村民们提供的消息，知道本村民办小学的刘老师和本村一位在县城中学读书、名叫蔡锦森的青年也爱好打篮球后，就马上邀请他们参加我村的篮球队，准备挑战附近的几个村庄。我们3个知青加上刘老师和蔡锦森，正好凑够一队。我们根据各人的球技和特长，分了一下位置：由刘老师和知青小朱打后卫；蔡锦森打中锋；知青小刘打右锋；我打左锋。我们在村里的球场上练了几次，就向邻近的两个村中篮球水平较低的那个村送去了战书。

很快，对方就邀请我们去他们村比赛。由于我村的篮球队从未赢过他们，他们也不把我们放在眼里。结果，我们轻而易举地把他们打败了。村民们得知我村赢球的消息后感到很高兴，觉得我们为村里争了光。但这次的对手毕竟不是全大队最强的，村民们期盼着我们去打败全大队的篮球冠军村——彭辣村。

彭辣村与我村相距约半里路，鸡犬之声朝晚相闻，村民之间常来常往。该村有200多人口，只是我村人口的三分之一，是全大队的6个自然村中第5大的村子。站在村里远远望去，整个彭辣村被一大片茂密、翠绿的竹林遮盖着，村里的房舍若隐若现。村民们告诉我们说，彭辣村虽小，但篮球队却很厉害！该村生产队的一位副队长特爱打篮球，在村里组织了一支农民篮球队，打遍全大队无敌手。只要有人来挑战，那位副队长不惜让他的篮球队员们随时放下手中的农活去参加比赛。长期以来，篮球称雄于全大队是他们村的一大骄傲。

在我们插队的地区，每年农历5月举办村与村、乡与乡之间的划龙舟比赛有数百年的历史了。争得赛龙舟的胜利是关系到村子面子的大事，历史上曾有过不少村庄因为赛龙舟时的摩擦而发生大规模的械斗，导致伤人、死人的惨剧。不管是穷人还是富人，都把本村的面子看得很重很重。“文革”期间，赛龙舟被批判为“四旧”“封建迷信”，各村间一年一度的龙舟竞赛从此销声匿迹，农民们有条件组织的大型体育活动就只有篮球了。所以，对当地的农民来说，在一定程度上，村子之间的篮球赛就具有了昔日龙舟赛的意义。趁着第一场篮球赛的胜利，我村的村民鼓动我们马上向彭辣村挑战，夺取篮球冠军村的宝座，为我村争光。于是，我们就派人到彭辣村下战书，约好日期到该村比赛。

比赛那天，两村都有很多人前来为自己村的球队喝彩助威。彭辣村的球队果然名不虚传，队员个个人高马大，那位嗜球如命的副队长更是身材魁梧，浑身都是结实的肌肉。相比之下，我们虽然瘦小，但相信凭借娴熟的球技，定能以小打大，以柔克刚。我队的后卫

刘老师一次次的切入分球，为我们的上篮、跳投创造了很多机会，我从左边进攻得了很多分。最后，我们赢了。扳倒了全大队的篮球老大，村民们激动万分，人人都认为我们这帮知青为村里争得了大面子，很多村民都高兴地拍着我们的肩膀说：“你们知青真行！”为咱村夺得了篮球冠军村的宝座以后，村民们对我们几个知青比以前热情多了。

礼尚往来，彭辣村的篮球队不久也来我村挑战，但还是以失败告终。后来，在公社组织举办的村际及乡际的篮球赛中，我们打败了本大队的各路人马，牢牢地执着篮球冠军村的牛耳，我和刘老师还被选进了代表公社的农民篮球队中。

在那些艰苦的日子里，篮球给了我很多的乐趣。

Chapter 18

Basketball Games

I have been interested in playing basketball ever since my middle school days. During the Cultural Revolution, when we did not have classes, my friends and I lived at school and played basketball every day. When I went to the village, I brought along a dark blue basketball, hoping that I would find a place to play.

On the morning when we arrived in the village, we carried our luggage and followed our production team captain. As we walked on the serpentine footpath among rice paddies, we saw houses canopied by green trees and shrouded in the morning fog. The captain told us that our village lay where the houses were. "A basketball court!" I yelled for joy as soon as we entered the village. "A basketball court!" In the middle of a few houses, I saw a huge cement court with a pair of basketball stands jutting out into the air. Wonderful! I can play basketball again!

I played basketball whenever I had time while I lived in the village. The court was actually part of the production team's grain sunning ground, which was a few hundred square meters. On it, baselines, sidelines, the half-court line, the restricted area, and the penalty area were all marked. Two basketball stands safeguarded the court. The basket, the backboard, and the rim were all up to standard. Of the six male zhiqing in our village, two others liked playing basketball just like me, but they were not "addicted" to playing basketball as much as I was. When the villagers found out that we played basketball, they thought it was refreshing and they enjoyed watching us. A few younger farmers told us that the neighboring villages all had good basketball teams and our village could not compete with those teams. They told us that now that we were in the village, we should form a basketball team to compete with the others. I was overjoyed when I heard the encouragement from the villagers. I told them that we would form our own team and go challenge the others.

From the information given to us by the villagers, we found out that a teacher at the village's elementary school, Mr. Liu, and a student from our village, Cai Jingshen, who was attending the county's high school, both liked playing basketball. I invited them to join our village's basketball team and we prepared to play with the teams from nearby villages. We had just enough players to make a five-person team, three zhiqing plus Mr. Liu and Cai Jingshen. We chose our positions based on our individual skills and strengths: Mr. Liu and Xiao Zhu (a zhiqing) were the shooting guard and point guard, Cai Jingshen was the center, Xiao Liu (another zhiqing) was the power forward, and I was the small forward. We practiced a few times on our court and immediately sent a game invitation to the weaker team of the two teams from the two neighboring villages.

Soon after, we were invited to go to that village to play a match. Because our village's team had never beat their team in a game, they did not pay us too much mind. As a result, we beat them easily that time. When the villagers from our village heard that we had won, they were elated. They felt that we had brought honor to them. However, we all knew that the team we had just beat was not the strongest team in our production brigade. The villagers hoped that we could beat the basketball champion in our brigade—the team from Pengla Village.

Separated by merely half a huali (250 meters), Pengla Village and our village were so close that we could hear the barking and crowing of each other's dogs and roosters. The farmers of the two villages visited each other often. Pengla Village had about 200 residents, about one third the population of our village. It was the fifth largest village of the six villages that made up our production brigade. When we looked at Pengla Village from our side, the village looked as if it were cloaked by lush green bamboo, their houses not clearly visible. The farmers from our village told us that even though Pengla Village was small, their basketball team was superior. One of the vice-captains of their production team loved playing basketball so much that he built a team that had no rivals in the entire production brigade. Whenever any team wanted a match, the vice-captain would agree and he would even let his players skip out on their assigned farm work in order to play. Their team's victories had been a source of pride for their village for a long time.

In the area where we were zhiqing, there used to be a long standing—over hundreds of years—and fierce dragon boat race among villages every year around the fifth month of the lunar calendar. To win the dragon boat race champion was a matter of life and death for the villagers—it had to do with a village's honor. In the past, there had been huge fights among villages due to arguments over some misperceived unfairness of some race, resulting in injuries and even death. A village's face—honor—was of tremendous importance to every villager, rich or poor. During the Cultural Revolution, the dragon boat race was deemed "superstitious," one of the "Four Olds" that had to be eradicated. The dragon boat race—a once-a-year athletic event—saw its demise. The only large-scale sporting events that the farmers could afford to put together now were basketball games. To a certain degree, basketball games among villages carried the same significance with the farmers as the dragon boat races of the past. The farmers in our village urged us to play Pengla Village right away so that we would not lose our winning momentum. They wanted to be called the basketball champion village and they wanted us to win glory for our village. Immediately we sent a messenger to Pengla Village with our written challenge and when they accepted, we negotiated a date to play a match in their village.

On the day of the match, a lot of people from both villages came out to cheer for each team. True to their reputation, Pengla Village's players were all tall and strong. The vice-captain, whose life was basketball, was the biggest of them all. He was all muscles. Compared to him, we were small and scrawny, but we were confident that our skills would help us win and that our nimbleness would defeat their heftiness. Our shooting guard Mr. Liu made plays that provided us opportunities to make lay-ups and jump shots. My fast breaks from the left got us quite a few points. Needless to say, that day, we won the match and defeated the number one basketball team in the production brigade. People from our village were ecstatic. They thought that we had brought our village a tremendous honor—we had gained face for our village. "You zhiqing are really terrific!" many of them said to us, usually with a pat on our shoulders at the same time. The villagers were friendlier and more enthusiastic toward us after we had made our village the basketball champion.

Pengla Village's team soon came to our village for a rematch, but they lost again. We continued to defeat all the other teams from our production brigade at games organized by our commune. Our village was finally recognized as a basketball champion village. In the local language, we finally had a firm grip on "the cow's ears"—we took over the reins. Mr. Liu and I were chosen to be members of the basketball team that represented our commune.

In those harsh days, basketball brought me unimaginable joy.

十九

田鼠、水蛇和狗

俗话说“民以食为天”。在我们村，凡是天上飞的、水里游的、地上跑的动物，我们几乎都能吃进肚子里。

吃田鼠

有一年，秋收已接近尾声，一望无际的田野变得空荡荡的，我们生产队的社员们扑向了一块孤零零的稻田，打最后的歼灭战。随着“喳喳”的割稻声，那片稻田变得越来越小了。当我正在暗中庆幸秋收快要结束时，突然有几个村民兴奋地大喊了起来：“田鼠，田鼠！”我赶紧弯下身子往稻子下面看，只见好几只田鼠在里面惊慌失措地乱窜。

原来，大片稻子的消失，使这些吃粮食的“小偷”们失去了“黄纱帐”的掩护，最后都撤到这块还未被收割的稻田里来了。我村一位叫蔡狗的小伙子要大家放慢收割的速度，以免田鼠们受到过度惊吓夺路而逃。

我们本来只向一个方向往前收割，现在为了堵住田鼠们的逃路，我们把那小片稻子团团围住，从四面八方慢慢地向中央收割。随着那片稻子的逐渐缩小，只见那些被围的田鼠就像热锅上的蚂蚁一样，东西南北地来回乱跑，以寻找逃生之路。忽然，一只田鼠冲出稻田夺路而逃，蔡狗马上用手把它按住，只听见蔡狗“哎哟”地大叫一声，原来是那只被他按住的田鼠反过头来，在他手指上咬了一口，尖尖的牙齿在蔡狗的手指上戳了一个洞，鲜血直流。村民们马上大声提醒大家说：“不要用手捉，要用镰刀先把田鼠打死。”

最后，那片稻子收割完了，田里也躺着十几只被村民们打死的田鼠。吃稻谷的田鼠与家鼠不同，田鼠的个子较小，皮毛是浅灰黄色的，样子比黑咕隆咚的家鼠好看多了，而且因为田鼠吃的是稻谷，住的是泥洞，比爬房梁、钻沟渠的家鼠干净多了。也许正因为如此，当地的农民都有吃田鼠的习俗。村民们把田鼠带回家，用热水烫过之后去毛，再开膛除去内脏，用清水洗干净后，用两根小竹棍做成一个“十”字形架子，把田鼠的肢体撑开，用细绳把田鼠挂在通风处晾干，就像做腊鸭一样。有位村民给了我两只腊田鼠干，做饭时我把田鼠干放在饭面上蒸熟。蒸熟了的田鼠干呈浅黄色，透明发亮，散发出一阵阵腊鸭般的诱人香味儿。美中不足的是吃的时候，田鼠肉有一股浓浓的、像鸭尾巴的骚味儿，令我难以忍受。

吃水蛇

蛇是南方人的一大佳肴，不管是有毒的还是无毒的，不论是水里游的还是岸上爬的，一律通吃。南方城市里的一些蛇餐馆生意兴隆，顾客盈门。不言而喻，南方乡村的人们更爱吃蛇。从来没有吃过蛇的我，却在下乡后尝试了蛇的美味。

夏天的一个傍晚，村民大维来到知青楼告诉我们说，他们打死了一条一米多长的大水蛇，正准备煮来吃，问我们要不要尝一尝。我们几个知青都异口同声地说：“要。”大维说，等蛇煮好后他就拿些来知青楼给我们吃。大维离开后，我们就各干各的事儿，但一直等到晚上10点多了还是没有见到大维的影儿，我们也就关灯睡觉了。

半夜12点多，大维来到知青楼，手里拿着一个很大的搪瓷漱口缸子，里面装着蛇肉和蛇汤。他把我们一一唤醒，让我们逐个吃那缸子里的佳肴。我睡眼惺忪地用嘴往缸沿上一呷，一口甜丝丝的蛇汤让我顿时精神抖擞，睡意全无。蛇汤里还混夹着几条蛇肉柳，细细地嚼起来，那味道比炖鸡肉还要香一百倍。我还想再呷一口蛇羹，可大维已经把缸子递给了下一位知青了。我只好用舌头舔舔那残留在嘴边的几滴蛇汤，想重温那蛇羹的香味儿。我发誓，这是我有生以来吃到的最香、最甜的东西，那简直就是只有在蓬莱仙境才能找到的美食! 之后，我曾到城里的蛇餐馆吃过好几次蛇，可再也无法找回第一次吃蛇的那种感觉了。

吃狗肉

吃狗肉是中国南方一些城乡的饮食文化之一。俗话说："狗肉滚三滚，和尚站不稳。"按照当地的说法，天冷时吃狗肉能使人感到浑身热乎乎的，能补身子。村里的农民对我说："狗肉是穷人的人参。"在他们看来，狗肉能起到人参的功效。人们还普遍地认为，因为狗肉很补，很"热"，最适宜在冬天吃。若在夏天吃狗肉，则容易流鼻血。

南方的冬天，最冷的时候气温在几摄氏度，寒冷的北风加上蒙蒙细雨，那种"湿冷"能一直渗透到人的骨头里去。此时秋收早已结束，农闲时节活儿也不多，人们就三五成群地结帮成伙，带上钱，拿着棍子、绳索和麻包袋，到附近的村子去买狗。虽然本村家家都养狗，但村民们都不吃自家养的狗，只卖给别人。买到狗后，村民们就把狗绑起来放进麻包袋里，用棍子把狗抬回村里。每年冬天，村民们都要吃掉好几条从外村买回来的狗。下乡几年，我从没亲眼见过村民们杀狗和煮狗肉，也没吃过他们做的"穷人人参"。

Chapter 19

Field Mice, Water Snakes, and Dogs

A common Chinese saying says that of all activities in life, eating is the most important. In our village, people considered any animal that flew, swam, or walked to be suitable for human consumption.

Eating Field Mice

At the end of one fall harvest when we were battling in the last rice paddy among what seemed to be bare fields that went on endlessly, I was just happy that the fall harvest was about to be over. I could see that following the unison noise of sickles slashing rice plants, the rice paddy became smaller and smaller. All of a sudden, I heard loud yelps coming from a few villagers: "Field mice, field mice!" I took a look underneath the rice plants. Several field mice were scurrying in all directions.

What happened was after we had cut down the rice plants in all the other paddies, the "grain thieves" lost the "golden screen" that protected them so they all converged in the last rice paddy in which we worked that day. A young man named Cai Gou told us to slow our pace at cutting down the rice plants so that we would not disturb the field mice too much. We did not want the mice to leave.

Originally we were moving in one direction chopping down the rice plants, but now to prevent the field mice from escaping, we encircled the rice paddy and moved toward the middle of the field. The field mice were "ants on a hot pot," scurrying and scampering every which way, trying to escape. All of a sudden, one field mouse dashed past Cai Gou, but Cai Gou was quick. He pressed one hand on the mouse. "Ahh!" Cai Gou screamed. The field mouse bit him. The mouse's sharp teeth punctured one of Cai Gou's fingers. Blood dripped. "Don't use your hands," other villagers warned everyone. "Hit the mice with your sickles!"

By the time we finished harvesting in the last rice paddy, a few dead field mice also laid in the bare field. Compared to the house mice, the field mice seemed smaller and they had light yellow fur, which was more pleasing-looking than the usual black-furred house mice. Because they ate grain and lived in the fields, the field mice appeared to be cleaner than the house mice that lived in drains and on rafters. Perhaps it was due to their cleanliness, local farmers had a habit of eating field mice. They would bring the killed field mice home, use hot water to scald and remove the fur, cut open the mice to clean out the guts, and wash the mice clean before stretching them on small stick-crosses to dry. The mice on stick-crosses would be hung where there was a breeze, the same way the locals made dry-cured ducks. I received two such dry-cured field mice from a farmer once. I put the mice on my rice to steam-cook them. The mice looked slightly yellow when they were cooked and the meat became translucent, very fragrant, just like the dry-cured duck meat. What was unfortunate was that the mice had a distinct taste that I was not used to. I thought it tasted like a duck's rear.

Eating Water Snakes

Snake meat is a delicacy in the South. It does not matter whether the snake is poisonous, swims, or slithers—all snakes are good for eating. There are snake restaurants in southern China that never have to worry about getting enough customers. Needless to say, southern people like to eat snakes. I had my first taste of snake meat in the village.

One summer evening, Farmer Da Wei came to our residence to tell us that he and several of his friends had just killed a water snake that was over one meter long. They would cook it, and he asked whether we would like to have a taste. "Yes," we all said in unison. Da Wei told us that he would bring us some later before we all went about our own business. We waited but Da Wei did not come back. At around 10 p.m., we turned off the lights and went to bed.

At about 12 midnight, Da Wei came to our building with a ceramic pot of snake soup. He woke us up one at a time and told us to have a little bit of the soup from the pot. I could hardly open my eyes before I took a sip of the snake soup, but the fragrant and delicious soup was so delightful to my palate that I woke up instantly. There were slivers of snake meat in the soup and the snake meat was 100 times tastier than chicken meat. Savoring the snake meat in my mouth, I wanted to have another sip of the soup, but Da Wei had passed the pot to another zhiqing. All I could do was to lick my lips for the few drops of soup remaining there and treasure the flavor. I swear that was the most scrumptious and titillating dish I have ever had. It was something that one could only dream of finding in Penglai, the island of immortals! Since that evening, I have been to several restaurants that serve snake dishes in the city, but I could never get back the same taste that I had when I first had snake soup in the village.

Eating Dog Meat

Eating dog meat is a part of the cuisine culture in southern China. A common Chinese saying goes like this: "Monks can't be steady amid the fragrance of dog meat." According to local customs, eating dog meat in the winter could keep one warm and build up one's strength. "Dog meat is the poor man's ginseng," the farmers told me. They believed that dog meat was as good as ginseng, which is known to be good for the body's immune system. They also believed that the dog meat's nutritious value rendered it a "warm" food, which meant that dog meat should be eaten in the winter. If eaten in the summer, one might get a nose bleed.

In the winter in the South, it could get down to just a few degrees Celsius. When it rains and the north wind blows, the cold and humid air penetrates one's bones. Every year when I was in the village, the time to eat dog meat was when the fall harvest was over and there was not much farm work left to be done. In groups of three or five, people would then go to neighboring villages to buy dogs. They would bring money, sticks, ropes, and hemp sacks. Even though every family in the village had dogs, no one would eat their own dogs, which were often sold to buyers from other villages. After the dogs were bought, the dogs would be put into the hemp sacks and carried back to the village. Several dogs would be eaten each winter, but I had never seen how dogs were slaughtered or cooked in my village in the years I was there. I never got to eat the so-called "poor man's ginseng," either.

二十

乞丐阿鉴

阿鉴是一位在我们公社远近闻名的人物。下乡不久，就常常听见村里的成年人教训小孩和年轻人道："不要学阿鉴那样好吃懒做。"向村民们一打听，才知道阿鉴是河对岸镇里的一位居民，男性，单身，有一只手掌上长了6个手指，外号叫"孖指鉴"。阿鉴好逸恶劳，一直靠香港的亲戚寄钱来养活，整日游手好闲，抽好烟，吃香喝辣，日子过得挺滋润的。

可惜的是，好景不长，有一天，香港的亲戚终于对阿鉴烦了，不再给他寄钱，断了他的"米路"。失去了经济来源，阿鉴既无一技之长，长期以来养成好吃懒做的恶习又积重难返，于是就沦为乞丐了。

阿鉴多在镇里行乞，我们有时看见他满脸污秽，衣不蔽体地坐在街道边上，默默地等待路人的施舍。一旦讨得几毛钱，他就到镇里的茶楼买一碗米粉，狼吞虎咽地吃个精光。有时看见他倒在路边或茶楼正门的石台阶上蒙头睡觉，偶尔有几个调皮捣蛋的小孩笑着对他大喊几声"孖指鉴"后，便一溜烟地逃去，只看见阿鉴面有怒色，嘴巴微动，像是在喃喃自语地骂着一些什么话，却从不起身去追赶那些顽童。有时看见阿鉴正在茶楼的垃圾桶里寻找吃的，也许是太饿了。

阿鉴食不果腹，夜无宿处。夏天，他可以在镇里店铺橱窗旁的水泥地上和衣而睡。冬天，寒风呼啸，阴雨蒙蒙，天知道他是如何裹着他那床千疮百孔的破棉絮，度过那一个个寒冷的夜晚。

有一次，我意外地看见阿鉴坐在我村附近的一条小河岸上，手里拿着一只从河面上捞来的死小鸡，正在聚精会神地拔着鸡身上的毛，并不时地撕下一片肉放进嘴里细嚼起来。我顿时觉得浑身都是鸡皮疙瘩，马上快步离去。我实在无法想象阿鉴是怎样把那些鸡肉吞进肚里，又是如何不得病的。

阿鉴虽然长期以行乞为生，被当地的人们视为“懒”的典型，但村民们无不佩服地对我说：“别看阿鉴好吃懒做，但他从不偷东西。”在方圆几十里地的乡村里，阿鉴不偷东西的美德是大家有目共睹、一致承认的。所以，不管他到哪儿行乞，人们都对他宽容、放心，施舍的人也挺多的。

在我当知青的最后一年里，我再没有看见过阿鉴，也没有听到过有关他的消息，不知道他是否平安？

Chapter 20

Beggar Ah Jian

Ah Jian was a well-known person in our commune. As soon as I arrived in the village, I heard adults telling their children and other young people this: “Don’t be like Ah Jian. He likes to eat but does not like to work.” Later I learned that Ah Jian was a resident from the town across the river. He was single and he had six fingers on one of his hands. He was nicknamed “Twin-Finger Jian.” Ah Jian preferred leisure to work. He lived on the money sent by his relatives from Hong Kong. He wandered around all day, smoked good cigarettes, and ate good food—he lived well.

Unfortunately his good days did not last long. Ah Jian’s Hong Kong relatives got tired of supporting him and stopped sending him money abruptly one day, blocking Ah Jian’s “rice passage.” Without an income or any skill in any particular area, combined with his desire not to have to work for his food, Ah Jian became a beggar.

Ah Jian usually did his begging in town. We sometimes saw him sitting by the roadside, with a dirty face and tattered clothes, waiting for charity. As soon as he got some money, he would go to a restaurant, buy a bowl of rice noodles, and wolf down the food. We also saw him sleeping on roadsides or the steps in front of restaurants. Sometimes naughty children would taunt him. “Twin-Finger Jian,” they would yell and then run off. Ah Jian never chased those children—he would only appear to be angry or move his mouth as if cursing under his breath. We also saw him looking for food in store and restaurant garbage bins. Perhaps he did that only when he was most hungry.

Ah Jian never had enough to eat, nor did he have a place to sleep at night. In the summer, he slept on the cement pavement in front of store windows. In the winter, when the chilly wind howled and the rain trickled nonstop, no one knew how Ah Jian managed each cold night wearing his quilted jacket with gaping holes.

Once I ran into Ah Jian when he was sitting by a river near our village, plucking the feathers from a dead chick he probably fished out of the river. Every now and then, he would tear a piece of meat from the chick and put it in his mouth to chew. I got goose bumps right away and walked off as fast as I could. I could not understand how Ah Jian could eat the dead chick without getting sick.

Even though Ah Jian lived on panhandling and was considered a typical example of “laziness” by the local people, most villagers talked about Ah Jian with some admiration. “Ah Jian never steals,” they would say, “even though he is too lazy to work and only wants to eat for free.” Ah Jian’s good habit of not stealing was known in villages far and near; consequently, no matter where he was begging, people tolerated him and were at ease around him. People gave him what they could.

During the last year I was a zhiqing, I did not see Ah Jian again, nor did I hear anything more about him. Is he all right? I do not know.

二十一

卖草记

每年夏季的抢收、抢插，因为要赶农时，收割时田里还灌满了水，以便收割后马上犁地、耙田，抢插秋稻的秧。抢收时，我们把当天割下来的稻子连谷带秆的全都用船运回村里的晒场，晚上再用电动脱谷机把稻谷打下来。好好的稻秆从电动脱谷机里飞出来时，已被打成一缕缕软软的、短短的草丝，失去了正常稻草应有的许多用途，只能塞进炉灶里作燃料了。

与夏季不同，秋季收割后一般都会让农田闲着，次年开春才犁地、耙田、插秧。所以稻田里的水早早就放干了，太阳也把稻田晒得干干的，人们都可以穿着鞋在田里干活。我们在田里用电动滚筒把稻谷打下来，顺手将脱谷后的稻草捆成一捆捆，竖着扔在田里，远远望去，田里就像站满了稻草人一样。秋收的稻草基本是完整无损的，晒干后除了可以作柴火外，还有其他各种各样的用途，例如用来盖稻草房顶等。不言而喻，秋收的稻草比夏收的更值钱，所以村民们都把夏收的稻草留作自用，把多余的秋收稻草拿到市场上去卖。

村民们一般到两个地方去卖草，一是河对岸的镇上，二是离村10公里远的县城里。当然，到县城里去会卖个好价钱。我们知青去县城里卖草的那一年，是我们下乡插队的第三年，我村原来的6名男知青中，有一名已被招工到了县城，有一名去了香港，只剩下了4名。当年，生产队给每个男知青都盖了一间一室一厅一厨的房子。房子的墙是用泥砖砌的，只有正门的部分墙用红砖打点一下门面。按当地风俗，女孩子是要嫁人的，不需要有自己的房子，故生产队一律不给女知青盖房，而国家发给每个女知青的400元安置费，则被挪用来给男知青盖房子。每人400元的安置费哪够盖房啊？生产队为了尽量减少开支，把知青的4间房子建成连起来的一排，户与户之间只砌一堵泥砖墙。

以前没有自己的房子，知青们分到秋收的稻草后，就学着村民们那样，把一捆捆的稻草垒成一个遮风挡雨的草垛，以保证下雨天也有干草烧水做饭。有了自己的房子后，我就住在比较宽敞的厅里，把从队里分得的稻草堆放在房间里，以免稻草受风吹雨打后颜色不好看而卖不到好价钱。

12月初的一个星期六，我们几个知青商量了一下，决定星期天到县城去卖草。村里的几个农民青年知道我们的计划后，按照农历的方法计算了一下当地河水在海潮影响下的涨落时间，嘱咐我们要赶在星期六傍晚河水落潮前，把生产队停泊在村外大河上的一艘较大的木船弄进村里的小河里，停靠在我们房子前面的河岸边，晚饭后再把草扛到船上。否则，等到河水落潮时，我们的房子前面的小河就会变得很浅，生产队的那艘大木船就不能驶进这条小河里来，我们也就不能装船，无法按原计划在星期天拂晓出发了。

星期六晚饭后，我们4个男知青就开始把各家要卖的稻草装到船上去，村里几个与我们相熟的男青年也跑来帮忙，大家把一捆捆的稻草分层地垒在船舱里。不一会儿，船上就出现了一个巨大的长方形草垛子，在此重压下，那艘大木船的船沿离水面的距离就只有几寸了。我们为每家的草作好记号，就回家睡觉了。

第二天天刚蒙蒙亮，我就被调好的闹钟铃声惊醒了，飞身下床，匆匆地洗洗刷刷后马上生火做饭。霎时间，我们几家知青屋的烟囱都不约而同地冒出了一缕缕炊烟，响起了一阵阵锅碗瓢钵的碰撞声。饭后，大约是早晨5时左右，我们就起锚开船了。我们三个人在船后摇大橹，另一个人用竹篙在船头撑，那艘满载着稻草的大木船就摇摇晃晃地沿着弯弯曲曲的小河朝村外的大江驶去。穿过村里的水闸，水面豁然开朗——我们的船驶进了直通县城的大江。江面上风平浪静，江的两岸灰蒙蒙的一片，村庄、田野都还在酣睡着呢。船来到大江后，水变得很深，原来在船头撑篙的那位同伴也就“失业”了，只好跑到船尾来。我们4个人有节奏地摇着橹，有说有笑，一路向前。

我们花了一个多小时走完了10多公里的水路，在早上6时多驶进了县城里的一条小河。这条小河是县城里买卖稻草的市场，其河床呈一倒立的梯形状，上宽下窄，河床的两岸用大石块铺成30度左右的斜坡，装卸船都比较方便。河的两岸便是街道和民房。我们一边摇着船沿河缓缓前行，一边用当地的方言大声吆喝着“卖草啊，卖草”。

星期天早晨6时多，县城的大多数人还在梦乡中，河两岸街道上的行人寥寥无几，要买稻草的人倒是早早就来到了河边。有几个买主到船上来看看我们的稻草是否是新草且是否晒得够干，然后与我们讲价。根据村民的信息，我们的开价是50公斤草卖3.6元。围绕这个价钱，我们和买主们讨价还价。有的买主从我们的衣着和言谈中知道我们是知青，就说他们也有孩

子下乡当知青，也不杀价了。虽说是“鸟为食死，人为财亡”，但人还是有同情怜悯之心的。有的买主则斤斤计较，不但狠命杀价，还要我们称草时把称尾翘得高高地让称。

我们不是生意场上的老手，价钱差不多就可以成交。我们用一根扁担穿在秤上较粗一端的铁环里，在该端的铁钩子上挂上稻草，再用手拨秤砣，秤平衡后从秤杆上读出斤两，然后算出价钱来。这杆大秤是我们从生产队里借来的。

大概只用了一个多小时，整船草就卖完了，我们每人兜里都装了十几块钱，个个俨然成了大富翁的样子。我们把船在码头上拴好，就进城找了一家饭店吃了一顿丰盛的午餐。下午时分，我们4个人高高兴兴地摇着那条空船回村了。

Chapter 21

Rice Straw Sales

To do everything in a timely manner, water was not drained from the rice fields during the summer harvest, because harvesting, soil preparation, and summer planting all had to happen promptly one after another. When harvesting, we would cut the rice plants without separating the rice grain from the stems and transport everything to the village's grain sunning ground by boat. Then in the evening, we would use electric threshers to separate the grain from its stalks, which would become straw-like when they came out of the threshers. The straw would be short and soft, good for nothing but firewood.

Unlike the summer harvest, the fall harvest was followed by leisure. The rice paddies would be left alone until the coming spring when plowing, soil preparation, and planting would take place. Therefore, before the fall harvest, the water in the rice paddies would be drained so that the fields could be dried and the farmers could work in the fields with their shoes on. We would cut the rice plants, put them in an electric grain beater to separate the grain from the stems, then right away, we would bundle the stalks and stand them up in the rice fields. These stooks looked like straw men standing in the rice fields when one looked upon them from afar. The rice stalks from the fall harvest would not be damaged by the grain separator. After it had been dried, the rice straw could be used as firewood as well as other things, such as roof coverings. Needless to say, the rice straw from the fall harvest was more valuable than that from the summer harvest. Farmers liked to keep the summer harvest rice straw for their own use but sell the extra fall harvest rice straw on the market.

There were two places where the villagers liked to sell their rice straw. One was at the town across the river from our village, and the other was at the county market about ten kilometers from our village. Of course, the price at the county market was better than that in the town. The first year we sold rice straw was the third year we had been in the village. At the time, only four zhiqing were left in the village from the original six because one zhiqing managed to find employment back in the city and another one went to Hong Kong. Our production team had built a house for each of the remaining male zhiqing. Each house had a living room, a bedroom, and a kitchen. All the walls were made of mud bricks except for the walls where the front doors were set—those walls had a few fired red clay bricks, which made the house front showier. According to the local customs, females would all be married someday so they did not need to have their own houses. None of the production teams built houses for their female zhiqing. The money—400 yuan—the government gave each zhiqing as a settlement fee was not enough to cover the expenses for house building, even when the female zhiqing's allowance could be added to the male zhiqing's. To help reduce the cost, instead of building a free-standing house for each of the four male zhiqing, my production team built a quadruplex for us, separating each unit with just a mud wall.

Before we had our own living quarters, we did what the farmers did after we received our share of the fall harvest rice straw. We arranged the sheaves into stooks to create straw buttresses so that we would have dry straw for firewood during the rainy season. Now that we had our own space, I slept in the living room and stored my rice straw in the bedroom to protect the straw from changing color when exposed to the wind and rain—I wanted to guarantee a good price for my rice straw.

One Saturday in early December of the first year we sold straw, several of us talked it over and decided that we would go to the county market to sell our straw that Sunday. After they learned of our plan, a few young farmers in the village helped us calculate the low and high tide times of our local rivers according to the lunar calendar. They told us that, before low tide on Saturday evening, we should bring one of the production team's larger boats from where it was moored on the big river outside of our village to the small river in front of our house in the village. They said we could move our straw to the boat after supper. They said that we would not be able to bring the boat to the river in front of our house if we waited till low tide. The water in the river would be too low to float the boat and we would not be able to load the straw and go to the county market early on Sunday morning as planned.

So after supper on Saturday, we began loading straw onto the boat that we had borrowed from the production team. A few of our farmer friends came to help. We stacked bundles of straw in the hold of the boat and in a short while, we managed to create a rectangular straw mound, the heavy weight of which lowered the boat just to about ten centimeters above the river water. Before we went to sleep that night, we marked the straw so that we would know which layer of straw belonged to which one of us.

Early the next morning, when it was just turning light out, I was awoken by my alarm. I jumped off the bed and rushed to wash and light a fire to cook my breakfast. Seemingly all at once, light smoke rose from our chimneys and we could hear the clanking of pots and pans from each other's kitchen. After breakfast, at about five in the morning, we set sail. Three of us rowed the sculling oar at the stern while one of us poled with a long bamboo pole at the bow.

Meandering along the small river toward the big river outside of our village, our boat jolted forward. As soon as we passed our village's floodgate, the river became wider—we were in the big river that would lead us to the county market. The water was very calm that morning. The villages and fields along the river were still in a slumber in the early morning darkness. The water was deep in the big river. Our friend who was punting became jobless instantly. He came to the stern to row with us. We moved forward rhythmically, talking and laughing.

It took us a little over an hour to travel the more than ten kilometers of waterway. We reached the small river that was the county's straw market at about 6 a.m. As we entered, we noticed that the river was the shape of an upside down trapezoid. It got wider as we moved forward. Each side of the river had a 30-degree slope of big stone slabs, making it convenient for loading and unloading boats. Streets and houses lined the river. "Straw for sale," we yelled in the local dialect while rowing our boat slowly. "Straw for sale."

Most of the townspeople would have been dreaming in bed still at 6 a.m. on Sunday mornings. There were not too many people in the streets; however, those who were interested in buying straw were already by the river. Several of the buyers came on board our boat to inspect our straw—to see whether the straw was new and dry. From there, the straw price negotiation would begin. According to the information we collected from the farmers in our village, we opened our negotiation with the asking price of 50 kilograms of straw for 3.6 yuan. Some of the buyers recognized us as zhiqing by the way we talked and the way we dressed. They paid us what we asked for as they said that they had children who were zhiqing also. We experienced human compassion even though we had been told in folktales that "Birds would die for food while men would die for money." However, other buyers were quite manipulative—they did not only cut our price but also demanded that we give them more straw than they had paid for. We were not experienced businessmen so when the price was close to what we had asked for, we would stop haggling. We would then use the steelyard (scale) that we had borrowed from our production team to weigh the amount of straw sale. Each bundle would be hooked to the steelyard. Two of us would then lift each bundle of straw off the boat with a shoulder pole that had been threaded through the steel ring above the steelyard's hook. The steelyard's weight would then be moved left or right till the steelyard and our boat paralleled each other. One of us would then read out loud the marking on the steelyard where the weight rested and calculate the total price of the straw sale.

It did not take us more than one hour to sell the boat-load of straw. Each of us had a little over ten yuan in our pockets afterwards. We felt rich. After mooring our boat at the dock, we went and had a good lunch in one of the restaurants in town. Then happily, we rowed our empty boat back to the village in the afternoon.

二十二

一上水濂山日记摘抄

我们有几个孩提时的伙伴儿在邻近的一个公社插队，他们的公社地处大岭山山区。大岭山是一条绵延上百里的山脉，水濂山是其中一座有500多米高的山峰，而他们落户的生产队就在水濂山山脚下。

我们插队的地区是水乡，顾名思义，只有水，没有山。每当我们遥望着云雾缭绕的水濂山时，总觉得那座山充满了神秘感。我们一直盼望着有机会去水濂山探访我们的老朋友，登上水濂山，撩起她那终日遮盖着云雾的面纱，看看其真面目。

下乡不久，我们终于如愿以偿。这里，还是让我的知青日记来叙说我们的故事吧。

1969年6月2日　星期一　晴

清晨，唤醒家福，我们匆忙地洗把脸，收拾了一下东西就出发。我们从镇里乘电船到县城后，因为我前段时间一直感到胃部不舒服，就先到县医院挂号看中医，由于是上午8时的号，时间还早，我们就到商店为村篮球

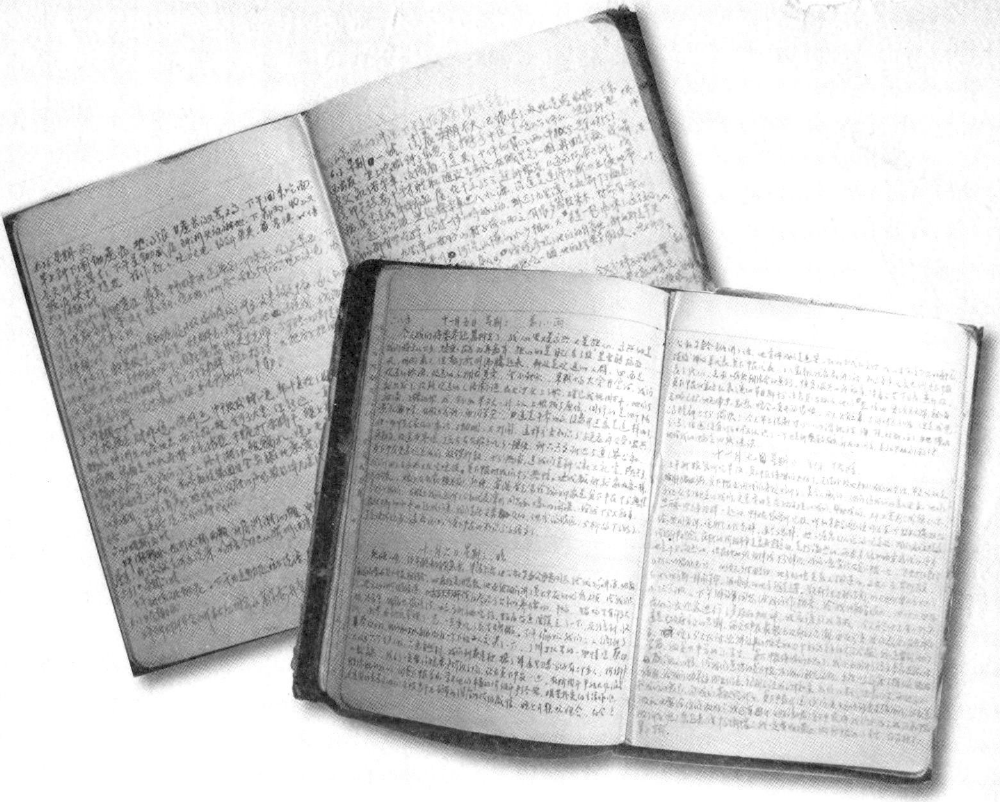

队买了10件白背心。我们把背心送到印号码的铺子，但要十号才能取，于是，我们去邮局寄信，又在城里转了一圈，8时再到医院看病。医生说我的身体很弱、较虚。在上午10：35，我们如约赶到县城的船站时，我们的两位在水濂山九里潭村插队的伙伴儿已经到了。我们一起去饭店吃了饭，然后骑上自行车向水濂山进发。

见到沿途都是连绵不断的丘陵山岗，来自水乡的我和家福都感到惊讶。经过一个多小时的行程，我们到达九里潭时都十分疲倦了，大家在床上躺了一会儿。

九里潭四面环山，村子倚山而立，有很多荔枝果木，村前有一条山溪流过，同万里平川、河流纵横的水乡相比，又另是一种风味。这里很僻静，宛如世外桃源。

傍晚，我们参观了知青们的自留地，种的都是芋头、豆角、丝瓜等。我们从自留地里摘回来豆角和丝瓜，美美地饱吃了一顿。他们这里取柴草很方便。

晚上到村边的小溪洗完澡后，我们就早早睡了。

1969年6月3日 星期二 雨

早上起床，天上阴雨蒙蒙，我们的心都凉了，今天看样子不能去攀登水濂山了。早餐，我们吃了煮红薯、煎饼，后来又吃了午饭，饭后睡了一会儿。我征求大家的意见是否要上水濂山。因为天上下着小雨，当地的两位伙伴都不太愿意。但我和家福坚决要去，大家也就拖拖拉拉地带上雨具出发了。山上的灌木丛又多又密，有时要用刀从中砍出一条路来，尽管没能从村民那里借到砍路用的刀，我们还是决定上山。

一路上大家的情绪都不高。远望水濂山，顶峰笼罩着云雾，我们穿过了两个村子才到了山脚下。开始上山时我们走错了路，后来才找到了上山的路。我看见大家的情绪都不高，就说点笑话想让大家振奋振奋，但大家还是乐不起来，我只好领先在前面开路。

密密的灌草中有一条被人踩出来的小路隐隐约约，山涧的溪水哗哗作响，山谷中回荡着一种不知是什么动物的叫声。我是第一次上山，心里有些不安，突然，大家又发现了一头像山羊的黄色动物……草上的水把我们卷到膝盖高的裤子全打湿了，我们上身打着赤膊往前走。穿过一片松林，到处弥漫着松脂的芳香，我看见了一棵笔直的小松树，就砍下来作为拐棍，另一个伙伴则要了小松树上面的一截，因为到顶峰还有一段很陡的山路。

我们一走出蔽日的松林，往身后一看，眼前出现一幅壮丽的图画。东莞县珠江三角洲的水网已历历在目，绿绿的田野上一条条纵横交错的白带子织成了网，连远在百里外的莲花山也看得清清楚楚。再往近看，一个个小山岗，山间有几个大水库。往北看，数百里外的罗浮山高耸入云，东江像一条白带子。东莞城的楼房若隐若现，只看见工厂冒出的白烟，大家都赞叹不已。我们不敢久留，继续上山。

到了山顶，其半径不过10多米，只有几丛蒿草。天下着细雨，我们都穿上雨衣，向远处眺望——山的背后是更宏伟的大岭山。我找到一棵最靠近顶峰的松树，用刀子刻上了“知青万岁”。这时狂风大作，只见北面的乌云滚滚而来，一下子把整个山顶罩住了，四周灰蒙蒙的一片，什么也看不清了，一缕缕的云烟从我们的周围掠过。没经历过这种情景的我，心里免不了有些吃惊，但看见大家非常镇定，我也就不怕了。风大得很，令人有几分寒意，大家都裹紧了雨衣。一会儿，风把云雾吹到南面去了，云消雾散。大家再看了一会儿，有人提议下山，于是大家都同意了。可下了不到50米，大家又都不约而同地停下来，留恋地向山顶望去，心里有点埋怨建议下山的人。大家望了一会儿，才继续下山。

下山时，一位伙伴拾到了一支箭猪的毛刺，送给了家福。下山一会儿就到了地面，回头望水濂山的顶峰，又是云雾弥漫的了。回去的路上，大家都有说有笑，兴高采烈的。

我们回去后马上动手做饭，饭后天已黑了。这里没有电灯，点的是煤油灯。村里的都是客家人，他们对外来人似乎有点好奇，但他们也会讲本地话，与我们交谈时讲得十分流利。他们的房子都很宽敞，三房一厅，但全是泥砖砌的。

这里的水田很少，全村200多人，有100多个劳动力，但只有200亩水田，水稻亩产200公斤左右，比水乡低。我们去看了他们的稻田，稻子长得不及水乡的壮，但他们的旱地很多，可种花生、木薯、绿豆、红豆等。这里还有很多荒地可开垦，又有砖窑烧制红砖，发展副业也是大有可为的。

晚上开社员大会时，我们与一个农民谈话，了解了这里的情形。他们每天上午6:30开工，10:30收工；下午2:30开工，6:30 收工，开工、收工都以击鼓为号。

这里的消息比较闭塞，文化也比较落后。

客家人十分爱清洁，每天晚上都习惯用热水洗澡。

Chapter 22

First Time to Mount Shuilian

A few of our childhood friends were zhiqing in a neighboring commune, which was in a mountainous area called Da Ling. The Da Ling mountain range covers over 50 kilometers, and Mount Shuilian is one of the peaks that is about 500 meters high. Our friends' production team happened to be at the foot of Mount Shuilian.

The area where we were had no mountains but plenty of water—it was a water village. Every time when scoping out Mount Shuilian, which was usually in the clouds, we were filled with wonderment and yearned to have an opportunity to visit our friends. We wanted to climb to the top of Mount Shuilian so that we could lift its cloud-fog veil to see it for real.

Not long after we settled in our village, our wishes were granted. Here I will let the diary I kept at the time tell my stories.

June 2nd, 1969, Monday (Sunny)

Woke up Jiafu early in the morning. Washed and packed a few things. Then we were on our way. From town we took the electric boat to the county.

Because I had been having a discomfort in my stomach, first I went to the county hospital to make an appointment with a traditional Chinese medicine doctor. The appointment was at 8 a.m. We had plenty of time so we went to a store and bought ten jerseys for our basketball team. We took the jerseys to a shop that did screen printing and we were told to wait till the tenth of the month to pick up our jerseys. We then went to mail letters at the post office, walked around, and went to the hospital for my appointment. The doctor said I was exhausted but not sick. At 10:35 we went to the county ferry as planned and met up with our two friends from Mount Shuilian's Jiulitan Village. We had a meal in a restaurant first before we biked to Mount Shuilian.

All along the way, we saw hills and mountains one after another. Jiafu and I were quite surprised since we came from a water village. After about an hour of paddling, we reached Jiulitan Village. We were tired so we lay down to rest.

Jiulitan Village was surrounded by mountains. The village stood right next to a mountain. There were a lot of lychee trees, but only one stream passed in front of the village. Compared to the water villages that had rivers crisscrossing everywhere, the landscape in the mountains was different. It was very quiet in the mountains. I felt as if I was in a retreat from the world.

In the evening, we visited several zhiqing's private plots. They planted taro, string beans, and squash. We picked some string beans and squash from their plots and had a good meal. It was easy to collect firewood.

We washed ourselves in the stream in the evening and went to bed early.

June 3rd, 1969, Tuesday (Rainy)

It was rainy and cloudy when we got up in the morning. We were disappointed to realize that we might not be able to climb Mount Shuilian that day. We ate sweet potato pancakes for breakfast and we took a nap after lunch. I asked everyone if they thought we should climb Mount Shuilian. Because it was raining, the two friends didn't want to go, but Jiafu and I were still eager so we brought some rain gear and dragged everyone along. The bushes on the mountain were lush and dense. At times we had to make a path by cutting bushes with our knives. Even though we could not borrow machetes from the farmers for path making, we managed.

We were in low spirits most of the time. Looking at Mount Shuilian from the distance, we saw that its peak was covered by clouds and fog. We had to pass two villages to get to the foot of the mountain. At first we went a wrong way. It took us a while to find the right path that would lead to the mountain top. When I noticed the somber mood among us, I thought I would tell a few jokes to cheer everyone up, but that did not work. I decided to lead the way instead. There was a hidden footpath among the shrubs. Streams made loud noises and there were echoes of animal calls that were unknown to us. That was the first time I climbed a mountain so I was a little nervous. Suddenly, we came across a yellow animal that looked like a goat. . . . Our pant legs were all wet from the dew even though we rolled them to our knees. We walked on with our shirts off. After we passed a small pine forest, bathing in the fragrance of the pine, I saw a small but very straight pine tree. I cut it down to make a walking stick. One of my friends took the top half of the tree because he knew we would have to walk on a steep mountain road before we could reach the top.

As soon as we passed the pine tree forest that was blocking our view of the sky, looking back, we saw a beautiful scenery. The water networks of Dongguan County in the Pearl River Delta appeared before our eyes. White ribbon-like footpaths traversed the green fields as if a massive net had been cast over the land. We could even see Mount Lianhua clearly. It was over 50 kilometers away! Close by, we saw small mountain peaks, among which were several huge reservoirs. To the north, Mount Luofu, which was several hundred kilometers away, penetrated the clouds, and the East River looked like a white ribbon. Buildings and houses in the city of Dongguan were faintly discernable. We could only see white smoke rising from factory chimneys. We were all in awe but we did not dare to stay long. We continued our climb.

When we got to the mountain top, we found that the radius of the top was only a little over ten meters, and there grew several clumps of tall grass. It was still raining and we all had our rain coats on. Looking afar, there were taller mountains behind us. I found a pine tree that was closest to the peak of our mountain and I carved these words on the tree trunk: "Long Live Zhiqing!" All of a sudden, a wild wind started to blow and dark clouds rolled in from the north, covering the mountain top in an instant. Everything was dark and we could not see anything except threads of white fog around us. I was scared since I had never been in a situation like that, but seeing that my companions were all calm, I stopped worrying. The wind blew hard and we felt cold so we wrapped our raincoats around us tighter. In another instant, the wind blew the fog to the south and all became clear suddenly. We stayed a little longer before someone suggested that we should go down. We all agreed, but after we descended about 50 meters, we all simultaneously stopped to look back up the mountain, and we silently blamed the person who suggested that we go down. We looked around for a while before we continued descending.

When we were climbing the mountain, one of our friends found a bristle of a wild boar and gave it to Jiafu. It did not take us a very long time to get to the bottom of the mountain. Turning around to look at the top of Mount Shuilian, we noticed that the top was masked by clouds and fog again. We were in high spirits on the way back, laughing and talking all the way.

We started making supper as soon as we got back to our friends' village. It was already dark after supper. There was no power in the village. Everyone used kerosene lamps. The villagers were all Hakka people. They seemed to be quite curious about outsiders and they knew how to speak Cantonese so when they talked to us, they were quite fluent. Their houses were pretty big, usually with three bedrooms and a living room, and the houses were made of mud bricks. The villagers did not have a lot of paddy fields, only about 200 mu. Of the over 200 residents in the village, their labor force had only about 100 people. Their per mu rice grain production yield was about 200 kilograms, lower than that of the water villages. We went to see their rice paddies and we found that their rice plants did not grow as well as ours in the water villages, but they had a lot of dry land, which could be used to grow peanuts, yucca, mung beans, and azuki beans, etc. They also had a lot of uncultivated land and a brick kiln, which could all be used to develop their secondary livelihood.

At the evening meeting of the commune members, we struck up a conversation with a farmer and got some information about how people lived. They would go to work at 6:30 in the morning every day and they would be done at 10:30 a.m.; in the afternoon, they would begin work at 2:30 p.m. and be done at 6:30 p.m. They would beat a drum to signify the beginning and ending of their daily work periods. The place was isolated so it seemed quite backward.

Hakka people valued cleanliness so it was their custom to bathe with hot water every evening.

二十三

二上水濂山日记摘抄

我们6月曾到水濂山一游。11月，因为我弟弟从城里来我村玩，我们再次到水濂山探访我们的老朋友。

1969年11月12日 星期一 晴

凌晨我们乘阿瑞的船去县城。1时多出发，2时多就到县城了。等到天亮，家福去医院挂号。然后我们去吃早饭，再去买到水濂山的汽车票。中午在华侨大厦吃午饭，饭后乘车到水濂。到了九里潭，我们的老朋友去开工，我们由于昨晚没睡好，都躺下睡了。

1969年11月13日 星期二 雨

本来想早上登水濂山，但天气很坏，牛毛细雨下个不停。我们一直睡到10时多。我们躺在床上聊天儿，不时看见有些老鼠在房顶的木梁上蹿来蹿去。我们的朋友就躺在床上用打鸟的气枪瞄准老鼠射击，基本是一枪一只老

鼠，弹无虚发，只见鲜血四溅，一只只被击中的老鼠从房梁上掉下来。幸好知青房子是泥土地面，地上的血迹用泥土一盖就可打扫得干干净净了。

饭后雨停了，我们步行去附近的水库玩。我们沿着一条小溪向前，到了水库，我们看见岸边拴了一条船，便上去摇船。在水库里游玩真快活，但山乡船的橹真难摇，我们几个人才把它勉强驾驭住了。

水面上有很多水鸟会潜水，再加上“船夫”们摇起船来都很不熟练，我们的船无论如何也追不上它们。船前进了1000多米，水库也望到尽头了，我们正要把船往回摇，看见两个农民推着单车从岸上追赶我们，态度很凶地问我们要船，还威胁说要把我们作为偷渡犯处理。我们便靠岸把船还给他们。

山区的景色别有风味，到处是连绵起伏的丘陵，山坳间郁绿的荔枝树环绕着村庄。庄上大部分是泥砖房子。泥砖是用田里的泥打制的，比较粗糙，比水乡的泥砖大。

群山环抱着的一潭清水，便是他们的水库。客家村的大人们对孩子比较溺爱、迁就，所以山村里的小孩子都有一些任性、调皮，他们不惧怕任

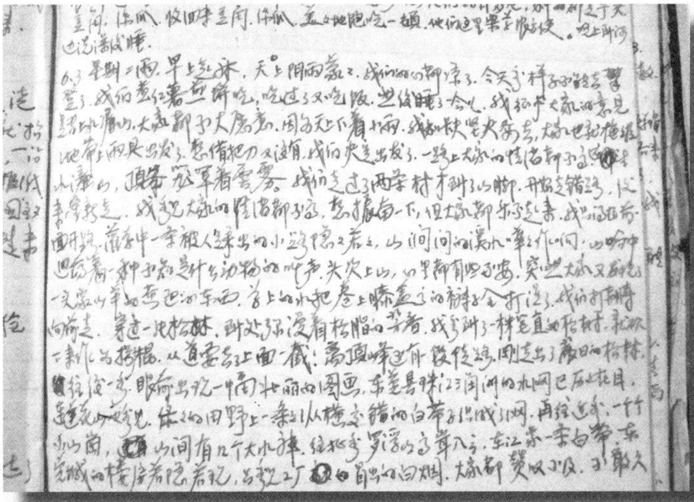

何人。

水濂一带曾是革命根据地，这里的地形、人情都很适宜，物产也不少。除了水稻外，旱地有红薯、木薯、花生、红豆、绿豆，果木有荔枝。这里有稀疏少见的山塘，还有烧窑制作的砖瓦，自给自足毫无问题。但是交通不大方便，通到山里来的公路也很难走，司机的技术得较高超才行。

客家人跟本地人的矛盾很大，他们常遭本地人欺负而只得忍耐。客家人长得矮小，但善于用肩膀挑东西，大多会说本地话。

我们的伙伴杀了一只鸡来招待我们。

1969年11月14日 星期三 雨

昨晚商量好，我们今日早上起床后攀登水濂山，中午离开九里潭。但伙伴们却再三挽留，无奈只好再小住几天。

午饭后，天气不大景气，阴云层层。远望水濂山，顶峰被云雾遮住了，但我们还是兴致勃勃地带上气枪和伙伴们养的那条黑狗出发了。

上山很累，几经休息才上到顶峰。四周远眺，云海茫茫，什么也看不见。我又在上次刻过字的那棵松树上刻下了“知青劲”，而上次刻的“知青万岁”已被松脂填平了，只得再加加工。我们在山顶上打了一会儿气枪，坐了一会儿，四周也没什么可看的，只好下山。

雨后的山路较滑，我们都不时地打滑，下山很快。人们说“上山容易下山难”，我们却相反，“上山辛苦下山易”，一会儿就下到了山脚。天色越来越阴暗，我们不由地加快了脚步，刚走到村的供销社，雨就下起来了。我们在供销社看看报纸，一会儿雨小了，继续往回走。到村小学借扑克，借不到，只得冒雨回去。

回到村里，外衣、裤已湿了，肚子又饿，吃了煎饼，和衣睡觉。

Chapter 23

Second Time to Mount Shuilian

We went to Mount Shuilian once in June. Then in November, because my younger brother came to visit me, we went to Mount Shuilian together to visit our friends.

November 12th, 1969, Monday (Sunny)

We boarded Ah Rui's boat to town early in the morning. We left at 1 a.m. and got to town a little after 2 a.m. We waited for day break and then Jiafu went to get an appointment at the hospital. Afterwards we went to have breakfast before buying our bus tickets to Mount Shuilian. We had lunch at Huaqiao Hotel and got on the bus to Mount Shuilian from there. When we arrived in Jiulitan Village, our friend went to work while we took a nap because we did not get enough sleep the night before.

November 13th, 1969, Tuesday (Rainy)

We had planned to climb Mount Shuilian in the morning but because the weather was bad, raining nonstop, we slept to sometime after 10 a.m. We talked as we lay in bed watching mice scurrying here and there on the rafters. With his air rifle and while lying in bed, our friend fired at the mice, one shot per mouse—no misfires. Blood splattered everywhere while mice dropped down to the floor from the rafters. Thankfully it was a dirt floor. The blood stains on the floor could be easily covered by sweeping some dirt on them.

The rain stopped after lunch. We walked to a nearby reservoir to have fun. We followed a stream along the way. When we got to the reservoir, we saw a boat so we decided to give it a try. We had lots of fun at the reservoir, but the boat was difficult to row compared to the ones we were used to in our village. It took several of us to handle the boat properly.

A lot of water birds were at the reservoir and they knew how to dive. We tried chasing them but we could not catch up with them, especially when we, the "boatmen," were not too skilled at handling the boat. After advancing for about 1000 meters, we got to the other side of the reservoir. As we were turning the boat around to go back, we noticed that on shore, two farmers were pushing their bicycles, running. They were chasing us. They wanted their boat back and they were not friendly. They threatened us by saying that they would report us as criminals who wanted to escape China. We rowed the boat to the shore and returned it to them.

The scenery in this mountain district was special: Rolling hills dominated the landscape and lychee trees surrounded the villages in the mountain valleys. Most of the houses were made of mud bricks, which came from the dirt in the fields. The mud bricks were not as big or polished as those in the water villages.

Their reservoir was a pond in the hollow of the mountains. The Hakka adults pampered their children so the mountain village children seemed stubborn and mischievous. They were not afraid of anyone.

The district of Shuilian used to be a base for the Chinese revolutionary army. It was a good location as the lay of the land and the people's temperaments were all suitable for the need of the army. There was also an abundance of produce that grew in the area. Besides rice, there were sweet potatoes, cassava, peanuts, azuki and mung beans. Lychee also grew there. We saw ponds in the hollows of mountains and the villagers could fire bricks and tiles in their kilns. The farmers had to be self-sufficient because transportation was inconvenient in the mountains—the roads were difficult and demanded good skills from the drivers.

There were conflicts between the Hakka people and the local people. The Hakka people had to endure abuses from the local people. The Hakka people were short, but they were good at using their shoulder poles to carry things. Most of them could speak the local dialect.

Our friend butchered and cooked a chicken to treat us.

November 14th, 1969, Wednesday (Rainy)

We decided last night that we would climb Mount Shuilian this morning after we got up and we would leave Jiulitan Village at noon, but our friends kept asking us to spend more time with them so we decided to stay for a few more days.

After lunch, the weather turned bad and dark clouds rolled in. Looking at Mount Shuilian in the distance, we saw that its peak was completely covered by clouds, but we were not deterred. We set out with our air rifles and our friends' black dog. The climb was exhausting. We had to take a few breaks before we got to the top. Looking around, we saw nothing but clouds. I added the words "Zhiqing Power" to the pine tree on which I had carved the words "Long Live Zhiqing." The original words had faded because of sap collecting on them so I retraced the words. We fired our air rifles on the mountain top for a while, rested, and then we came down as we could not see much on the top in the heavy fog.

The mountain passages were very slippery after the rain. We came down the mountain very fast, slipping and sliding. We've heard people say that it's easier to go up a mountain than to come down one, but we proved them wrong that day. For us, it was difficult to go up Mount Shuilian but easy to come down. It did not take us very long to get to the foot of the mountain. The sky got darker and darker so we walked faster and faster. It started to rain as soon as we got to the village's co-op. We read newspapers there for a while. We continued on our way when the rain died down a bit. We went to the elementary school to borrow playing cards, but we could not get any. We had to go back to the village in the rain.

By the time we got back, our outer clothes and pants were all wet. We were starving, too. We ate some pan fried flatbread and went to bed.

二十四

麻风病

我们插队的地区是水乡，到处河汊纵横，出门便与水打交道。在我村方圆几十里的水网地带，小的河涌上都建有木桥或石拱桥，把各村之间的大路小路连接起来；大的江河两岸则有渡口和渡船，由船夫日夜摆渡来驳接两岸的交通。当然，乘渡船的人必须付过渡费给船夫，钱的多少则视江河的宽窄而定，由一分钱到一毛多不等。

水面稍宽的江河，两岸的渡口一般都建有一座小屋，以方便等候过渡的人们躲避风雨和寒冷。这种小屋一般只有三面墙，面向渡口的那面是一个完全敞开的入口。入口的左右两侧墙上一般都有两个矩形的窗口。这种小屋一般都没有门扇和窗扇，有点像个简陋的候船室。虽然各处盖候船室的材料不尽相同，有砖瓦的，也有泥砖茅草的，但它们都毫无例外地在屋内外最显眼的地方写有“提防卖疯”的警告字句，有的是用红色或黑色的字写在墙上，更多的则是刻在一块嵌在墙内或竖在渡口的石碑上。

向村民们一打听，才知道此地区在旧社会的时候，长期麻风病流行，人们缺医少药，一旦染上此病，家散人亡，故人们视麻风病为瘟疫。此地民间流传一种说法：麻风病人若能与100个不同的人性交就会不治而愈。男人们还说，得了麻风病的女子比以前更漂亮，脸色红润，犹如出水芙蓉，娇艳欲滴，让男人们不能自拔。而这些麻风病的女子经常出没的地方就是渡口小屋了。特别是夜深人静、风雨交加之时，渡口小屋里只剩下一孤男面对一含情脉脉、以身相许的漂亮女子，真是天时、地利、人和——要不上钩也很难啊。此外，这里民间还相信此说法：麻风病人与不同的人性交的次数越多，病情就减轻得越多。所以，这地区麻风病长期流行，经久不衰。为了让人们不上卖疯的当，防止麻风病的传播，各乡各村都在渡口处警告人们候船时不要失去理智，要“提防卖疯”。

新中国成立后，这个地区的麻风病人都被政府送到附近江心的一个小岛上的麻风病院治疗，基本与外界隔绝。当地民众对麻风病的知识和预防措施也得到了很大的提高，麻风病及“卖疯”行为基本绝迹，唯有那在每一个渡口依然耸立的“提防卖疯”的石碑依然随处可见，成了当地一道历史的记忆。

Chapter 24

Leprosy

A water village was where I lived among farmers for a few years. Rivers crisscrossed everywhere. People had to deal with water as soon as they stepped out of their houses. Villages were connected by rivers and bridges. To go from one village to the next, one very often had to travel by both water and land. For about a ten-mile radius in the vicinity of our village, there were wooden or arched stone bridges crossing all narrow rivers, but on wider rivers, there were ferries that brought people across day and night. Of course one must pay a fee to the boatman. Depending on the width of the river, fees ranged between one to ten fen.

On the banks of the wider rivers, at the ferry docks, there were small huts that sheltered travelers from bad weather. The huts typically had only three walls—the side to the ferry crossing was an open entrance. The walls to the left and right of the entrance had two rectangular openings. Such huts did not usually have doors or window sashes. The huts served as simple waiting rooms for ferry passengers. Some huts had brick walls and tile roofs while the others were mud huts with thatched roofs. Even though these ferry waiting rooms were constructed with different materials, they all had, without exception, these words written inside and outside in easy-to-see places: "Beware of Leprosy Whoring." These words were written on walls in red or black ink, but most places had these words carved on walls or on a stone slab by the dock.

From the villagers, I learned that leprosy was a problem in the area before 1949. Due to the lack of doctors and medicine, once anyone contracted the disease, death and a broken family would be inevitable, so the locals viewed leprosy as a plague. A regional belief said that a leprosy patient could be cured of the disease if he or she had sexual encounters with 100 people. Local males also said that females who had contracted leprosy would become prettier than before. These females' faces would be rosy red, comparable to lily flowers—fresh, tender, and seductive—making men lose control of themselves. They said that

female lepers liked to hang around ferry huts, especially on stormy nights. If a man was in one of the huts on such a night, he could not resist the temptation of a passionate pretty girl who would promise herself to him. All conditions would be right for him to be fooled. Additionally, the locals also believed that the more people a leper had sex with, the sooner the leper would get better. Because of the hearsay, leprosy had been an epidemic in the local area for a long time. In order to stop fornication and prevent the spread of leprosy, a notice had been put at every ferry crossing, warning people not to lose their heads and to beware of "leprosy whoring."

After 1949, local lepers were all quarantined and treated on a small island in the middle of a nearby river. People were also educated on the causes and prevention measures of leprosy. The disease was eventually eradicated and "leprosy whoring" was stopped. The only things left from the past era were the stone slabs with the words "Beware of Leprosy Whoring." These stone tablets stood at every ferry crossing, serving as unique, local historical memory.

二十五

村选举

1969年秋收后的一天，村里召开全生产队社员大会，投票选举生产队长、副队长、会计、仓库保管员等干部。生产队长、副队长主管生产安排及每天的派工；会计管账目、记工分及计算各家的年终收入；仓库保管员则管生产队仓库里物资的进出。这些干部人选的好坏都关系到各家各户的生计，所以大家都想让自己信得过的人来担任这几个角色。据说这是村里第一次举行的民主选举——每个社员都有一票。

全体社员集中在村里的礼堂开会，大家席地而坐。男人们有说有笑地抽着烟，妇女们大声小声地哄着怀里和身边的小孩子，会场里好不热闹。会议正式开始了，现任队长做了个简短的开场白，就把选票发给大家，并由大家自由提名各个位置的候选人。

我村的村民由几个不同的姓氏家族组成，其中陈姓及蔡姓是最大的两个家族，其他还有温姓等几个小家族。传统上，每逢村里有大小事要全体社员讨论决定时，每个家族都会有个固定的发言人发表意见，该家族的其他人则附和。所以，小家族的权益很难占主导地位。不过，同村的小家族与大家族总是有联姻关系的，故小家族也可以通过与大家族结成联盟来体

现自己的利益。我所在生产队的副队长就是来自温姓小家族的。

这次“民主选举”，大家还是“外甥打灯笼”——照旧（舅）。各家族的代表出面提名候选人，接着是填选票。此时，我只见各家族的代表堂而皇之地吆喝着收集自己家族成员的选票，填好后交给唱票人。不言而喻，这次的选举结果就是村里各家族之间角力的结局而已。

Chapter 25

A Village Election

One day after the fall harvest in 1969, our village held an election meeting. We were to choose our production team captain, vice-captain, team accountant, warehouse custodian and so on. The production team captain and vice-captain would be in charge of the daily work assignments; the accountant would be responsible for the team's finances, recording gongfen and calculating every family's annual income; the warehouse custodian would keep track of the goods and supplies entering and leaving the production team's storehouses. People in these positions could make decisions affecting the livelihood of each family in the village. Everyone wanted to elect the people that they could trust. I heard that this election was the first democratic election in the village. Each villager had a vote.

On the day of the election, all members of the production team gathered in the village's meeting hall, taking a seat on the floor. Males talked to each other and smoked; females cooed and scolded their babies and children in their arms and around them. The meeting place was full of commotion and chaos. When the meeting began, the then-captain gave a brief introduction and passed out ballots. Everyone was free to nominate candidates.

My village consisted of several family clans. Two of the larger clans were the Chen clan and the Cai clan. The Wen clan was one of the smaller ones. Traditionally, whenever decisions had to be made in the village, each clan would have a representative as its spokesman while the other clan members would support the representative's opinion. Consequently, it was difficult for smaller clans to have a say in anything. However, there had always been marriages between people from larger and smaller clans, so a smaller clan could protect its interest by siding with a particular larger clan. At the time, the vice-captain of our production team was from a smaller clan in the village, the Wen clan.

At this particular "democratic election," everything was done the same way it had always been done—"nephews holding lanterns for their uncles" —family members helping each other. A representative from each clan would make a nomination before ballots were filled out. I saw each clan's representative actually collecting blank ballots from the members of his clan and filling out the ballots himself before casting the ballots to be counted. Needless to say, the result of this election was the outcome of the power struggle among clans.

二十六

水 轮 泵

我村地处东莞水乡地带，城镇、村庄和田地被纵横交错的大江小河分割开来，形成一片片四面环水的绿洲。因靠近江河的出海口，海水涨潮时，江河的水位比这些绿洲的地面还要高出一大截，故人们兴修堤坝，像筑城墙一样，把这些绿洲围起来。当地人把这些大大小小被堤坝围起来的陆地叫作“围”。

每个围内都有四通八达的小河与围外的江河相通，以解决围内的饮水、灌溉及运输需要。在小河与围外的江河接口处，一般都有一座水泥结构的水闸。水闸有两扇大门，可在涨潮时关上，以保护围内的房屋、田地不受水淹； 在退潮时打开，以利水路交通。

千百年来，围内的农民世世代代用人力水车从小河里抽水灌溉农田。从60年代初开始，电动水泵就取而代之成为主要的农田水利工具了。

大约在1969年与1970年之间，有人提出了在水乡地区建造水轮泵的主意，即利用河水涨潮时围内外的水位差来推动一个泵从小河里抽水灌溉农田。村干部们听了这个主意后十分兴奋，觉得这是个一本万利的投资——以用之不竭的潮水来抽水灌溉农田，既省电力又省人工，何乐而不为！说干就干，村干部们找了村里最有经验的一位泥瓦匠，任命他为建造水轮泵的主要技术负责人，并从公社水利会得到技术咨询和帮助，选了一座离村不远的水闸作为建水轮泵的试点。村里大量的主要劳动力分成白天和晚上两个班次，夜以继日地挖土方，浇水泥。当时作为知青的我们也参加了挑灯夜战的抢建工程。那位村里最有经验的泥瓦匠的年龄大概是40出头，最多是小学文化水平。他的经验也只是建简单的农村砖房，并无机械、物理等方面的知识。我只听他提过曾到公社水利会找技术员商量及审查施工图纸，但这已足以镇住所有的村民，让大家对他佩服不已。

经过几昼夜的奋战，水轮泵终于建成了。据我的观察，我们当时是在水闸旁建了一口水泥井，井中装有一个水泥水轮泵。水轮泵有一条轴，轴

上有螺旋式的叶片。这个井有一条水泥渠道通到水闸外，其入水口有木闸板控制流进井里的水流量。涨潮时，把水闸的大门关起来，等到门外的水位比门内河面的水位要高出一米多到两米时，再用人力抽出入水口的木闸板，水就冲进水泥井里，驱动水轮泵转动，把水抽到田里。但是，据说这个水轮泵只转了几圈儿就再也不动了，从来就没抽上来一滴水。原来，放水进井的次数多了，水里沉淀的泥沙把那个水泥水轮泵的转轴和叶片都塞得死死的，纹丝不动了。据说村里花了6万多元修这个水轮泵，最后是鸡飞蛋打了。

后来我每次下地经过那个静静地竖在那里的水轮泵时，心里都有一种难言的怅惘。村民们辛辛苦苦用血汗赚来的6万多元，就这样葬送在那位不知深浅的泥瓦匠和那些不学无术的公社水利会技术员手里！我不禁地在心里呐喊道：农村需要知识！农村需要文化！农村需要技术啊！

Chapter 26

A Water-Powered Pump

My village was located in the coastal water village districts of Dongguan, where towns, villages, and farmland are separated by crisscrossing rivers big and small. One sees everywhere clusters of green oases surrounded by water. Due to the close proximity to the sea, the water level in the rivers rise above the land mass whenever the tide comes in. Locals built dykes to protect the green oases, and the rimmed land parcels, big and small, are called "surrounds" by the locals.

To provide water for consumption, irrigation, and transportation, there are extensive tributaries and watercourses inside each surround and these watercourses lead to rivers outside in every direction. There are usually cement floodgates where the tributaries meet the rivers. There are two gates at each connecting point. When the tide comes in, the gates are closed to protect the houses and farmland inside the surround from being flooded; when the tide goes out, the gates are lifted open for transportation between land and water.

For thousands of years, the farmers inside the surround had used manpower to draw water from the tributaries to irrigate their farmland, but starting in the early 60s, electric water pumps have been in place and they have been a major farm tool ever since.

However, around 1969 or 1970, someone suggested that water-powered pumps be built in water villages to take advantage of the power generated when the tide came in. Village cadres were all excited about the idea. They thought building such pumps would definitely be a profit generating investment—the water-powered pumps would save electricity and manpower as there would be an endless supply of high tide to irrigate the farmland. Why not? They started the project right away. The village cadres found the most experienced mason in the village and appointed him to be in charge of the pump building. They got some technical information and assistance from the commune's Irrigation Board and found a floodgate not too far from the village as a test site for the new water-powered pump. We were all assigned to work on the project, taking day and night shifts. We dug holes and poured cement, joining in the rush to build our first water-powered pump. The village mason was about 40 years old at the time. He had no more than an elementary school education. He was a skilled mason who could build simple brick farm houses, but he did not know anything about mechanics or physics. I heard that he had been to the commune's Irrigation Board to consult the technicians there and to get his construction drawings checked. Nevertheless he was admired by the villagers and regarded as an expert.

The pump was built after a few days of round-the-clock shifts. From what I could see, we actually just built a cement well with a water-powered pump next to a floodgate. The pump had a shaft with a few spiral blades attached. It sat in a cement tunnel that led to the outside of the floodgate. The outside opening of the cement tunnel had a wooden gate that could be used to control the amount of water coming into the well. When the tide came in and the water level outside the surround was between one to two meters higher than the water level inside the surround, someone would have to lift the gate so that the high tide water would rush into the well to turn the pump, which would then pump water into the farmland inside the surround. Unfortunately, after several turns, the mud and sand that came into the well with water packed the shaft and spiral blades, making it impossible for them to turn. I heard that the village spent nearly 60 000 yuan building the so-called water-powered pump, but in the end, the result was like "having one's hen fly away and her eggs all cracked"—we worked for nothing.

Every time I walked past the nonworking pump, I could not help but be disheartened. The farmers' 60 000 yuan of sweat and blood money were wasted due to the ignorance of the mason and the incompetence of those so-called specialists at the commune's Irrigation Board. I could not help but scream silently: Rural areas need knowledge! Rural areas need information! Rural areas need technology!

二十七

老 知 青

1968年秋，我们下乡来到农村时，村里已经有4位1964年从城里下乡务农的街道知识青年了。据说她们是考不上初中或高中的学生，在城里又没有找到工作，成了街道居民委员会管辖下的“闲散人员”，由街道居委会直接动员并安排下乡插队的。

我们公社先后接收了100多名1964年知青，分布在全公社的几个比较富裕的生产大队。到了1968年，大规模的知识青年上山下乡运动在全国掀起，我们公社又接收了1000多名知青，遍布在全公社的18个生产大队。为了区分两个不同时期下乡的知青，人们把1964年下来的那批知青称为“老知青”。

我们所在的生产大队有6个自然村，分配到我们生产大队的老知青则分别在4个比较富裕的村子里插队落户。我村的4位老知青都是女孩子，其中阿英的文化最高，读过初中，其他的3位叫阿莲、阿妹和阿女，都只有小学文化水平。由于我村人多地少，所以开展了用水草织草篮的副业，即用染了五颜六色的水草织成各式各样的草篮出口到国外，供水果商装水果用。村里15岁以下的女孩，基本都织草篮而不下田干活。4位老知青因为是城里来的女孩子，受到了生产队的照顾，她们平时织草篮，农忙时才下田干活。同样，我村1968年来的女知青也受此待遇。

尽管受到村里的一些关照，但4位老知青还是吃了不少苦，她们一直都期盼着离开农村回到城市的那一天。好不容易苦熬了4年，1968年不但转机未见，又下来了1000多人，看来回城是无望了。在1968年以后的几年里，4位老知青不断挣扎，各寻出路，可命运和结局却令人感慨甚多。

阿英，人长得端庄秀丽，脸庞白里透红，身材稍胖，村里人都亲切地叫她“肥英”。在4位老知青中，阿英下地干活比较能吃苦，村民们对她评价最高。村里有一个初中文化的帅小伙子叫阿德，出自本村一大家族，有兄弟6人，势力较大，其本人又是生产队的会计，平时基本不用下地干活。他长得白白净净的，村里的姑娘们都希望得到阿德的垂青，可阿德数年来

却唯独苦追阿英不舍，多次碰壁也不放弃。后来，阿英看到回城无望就嫁给了阿德，次年就生了一大胖儿子。结婚后的阿英，装束打扮就完全转型了。她穿得跟当地的已婚妇女一样，一身黑衣黑裤，昔日常穿的小碎花衣服也不见踪影了。按照当地的民俗，因为阿德在兄弟中排行第五，村民们对阿英的称呼也变成“五嫂”了。

阿莲，人长得五官端正，肤色较白，个子比阿英稍高，有人说她比阿英漂亮。但她除了织织草篮，基本不下田干活，农忙时多数回城躲避，所以村民们觉得阿莲不能吃苦。阿莲一直在等回城的机会，可到了二十七八岁也没有希望，她就结婚了。据村民们说，她嫁给了一个四五十岁的“香港客”。阿莲结婚后，我们就再也没见过她了。按当时的政策，她要申请到香港定居是遥遥无期、希望十分渺茫的。但村民们说，阿莲可以待在城里靠“八分钱”过活了，即在信封上贴一个八分钱的邮票寄到香港去，香港的老公就会寄钱到内地来养她了。她再也不需下地干活了。

阿妹，人长得比较矮小结实，一双小眯眯眼加上塌鼻梁，模样不算好看。但阿妹为人诚恳憨厚，据说她下乡那年只有15岁。阿妹干农活也挺卖力的，后来她看上了村民阿德的弟弟阿光，经常到阿光独居的一间狭小的小泥屋里与阿光幽会，最后嫁给了阿光，被村民们称为“六嫂”，与阿英成为知青加妯娌，亲上加亲。

阿女，人长得瘦小，有点“哨牙”。有个已婚的男村民不怀好意地百般照顾阿女，让阿女在他家“搭食”，即一日三顿吃在他家。不用自己买菜、做饭，离乡背井的阿女十分感激那个男村民。那个男村民的老婆讲话时有点粘舌根、口齿不清，平时很怕她老公，他们育有几个子女。“天下没有免费的午餐”，村民们背后都议论纷纷，为阿女担心。果然不久，阿女就被那个男村民搞大了肚子，只好去做人流。村里人觉得阿女真傻，从此叫她“懵女”。与阿莲的命运相似，阿女后来嫁给了一个比她大二三十岁的男人，但她的老公不在香港，而是省城里的。婚后的阿女再也没有回过这条让她伤心痛苦的村庄了。

1971年全公社第一次有知青招工名额时，各生产大队召开知青大会宣布招工政策，其中有一条规定是与当地农民结婚的知青不能被招工。

在我们生产大队的知青会上，与我同组讨论的一位穿着一身黑衣黑裤、嫁了当地农民的老知青愤愤不平地说："我下乡这么多年了，即使是劳改也应该到期了！我要招工回城！" 当有人问她说："若你招工回城，那你的孩子怎么办呢？" 她狠狠地夹着粗言烂语说道："我就把那几个孩子扔回给他（她那个农民丈夫）！"

我们生产大队的几位男性的老知青则一直过着单身的知青生活，或是终日劳作，或是经常往返于城乡之间，日复一日，年复一年，无以穷尽……

老知青的命运归宿，让我们这些新知青仿佛看到了我们那可怕的明天，不寒而栗，不甘心，却又感到无可奈何、无能为力，不知等待着我们的命运是什么？

Chapter 27

Old Zhiqing

When we were sent to the village in the fall of 1968, there were already four zhiqing from the city who had been there since 1964. We heard that they were students who could not pass the entrance exams to junior high or senior high schools and consequently could not find employment in the city. They were nicknamed "free and idle folks," who became burdens to their respective neighborhoods. The four of them were eventually sent to our village by the committees in their neighborhoods that were responsible for finding employment for residents.

My commune received about 100 such early zhiqing in 1964. They were assigned to several relatively well-to-do production brigades within the commune. Then in 1968, when the large scale Sent-Down Movement took place, our commune received over 1000 zhiqing, who were then assigned to the eighteen production brigades within the commune. To distinguish the two groups of zhiqing, people usually referred to the earlier zhiqing as "Old Zhiqing."

Our production brigade encompassed six villages. The earlier zhiqing who were in our production brigade resided in the four relatively wealthier villages. The four Old Zhiqing in my village were all girls, one of whom, Ah Ying, was better educated than the others. She was a junior high student. The other three were Ah Lian, Ah Mei, and Ah Nv, all of whom had only an elementary school education. Because our village had more people than what the farmland could support, we engaged in a sideline business that made baskets of reed that had been dyed into different colors. These baskets were exported overseas to be used as fruit containers. Most of the girls under 15 years of age were basket weavers; they did not have to work in the rice fields. The four earlier zhiqing were also assigned to weave baskets. In consideration that they were female and from the city, they were only asked to work in the fields during busy farming seasons. Likewise, the female zhiqing that came to the village later in 1968 enjoyed the same treatment.

Even though they had been cared for in the village, the four Old Zhiqing still had to endure a lot. They longed for the day when they could return to the city, but after four years, when it was 1968, instead of being granted a change in their circumstances, they saw over 1000 zhiqing joining them in the commune instead. They did not see any hope of their returning to the city. They struggled and looked for an escape from their circumstances but the results were all discouraging.

Ah Ying was courtly and beautiful with rosy cheeks. Because she was plump, people in the village gave her an endearing name, Plump Ying. Of the four earlier zhiqing, Ah Ying was the best at bearing her sufferings. Villagers thought highly of her. There was a handsome young man in the village, who had a junior high education and was from one of the larger family clans in the village—the family had six boys. The young man was the village's accountant so he did not have to work in the fields. He had a good complexion and a lot of girls in the village hoped to catch his attention. Ah De, however, was only interested in Ah Ying. He did not give up even after several rejections. Eventually, when Ah Ying realized that there was no hope of her returning to the city, she consented to marrying Ah De, and they had a healthy son the following year. Ah Ying's appearance changed completely after she got married, however. She wore what local married women wore, a black top and black bottoms. No longer did she wear tops that had small flower prints. According to the local customs, because Ah De was the fifth son in the family, everyone addressed Ah Ying as "Fifth Sister-in-Law."

Ah Lian was nice-looking, had a good complexion, and was a little bit taller than Ah Ying. Some people said that she was prettier than Ah Ying. Most villagers did not think Ah Lian was a good worker because she often went back to the city during busy farming seasons. Besides basket weaving, she hardly ever worked in the rice paddies. Ah Lian had been waiting for an opportunity to move back to the city permanently, but when she got to be 27 or 28, she gave up hope. She got married. According to the villagers, she married a "Hong Kong Guest" who was between 40 and 50. We never saw Ah Lian again after she got married. According to the policy at that time, there was no way that Ah Lian could establish residency in Hong Kong. The villagers said that Ah Lian could stay in the city with the support of "Eight Fen" —at the time, an eight-fen stamp would send a letter to Hong Kong so that Ah Lian could ask her Hong Kong husband to send money to support her. She no longer had to do farm work.

Ah Mei was short and stout with small eyes and a flat nose. She was not good-looking but she was earnest. I heard that she was only 15 when she arrived in the village. She worked hard, and eventually, she fell in love with Ah De's younger brother, Ah Guang. She used to meet up with Ah Guang in his small hut, and then finally she got married to Ah Guang. The villagers called her "Sixth Sister-in-Law." She and Ah Ying were then doubly related as they were zhiqing together first and then sisters-in-law.

Ah Nv was small and slim with buckteeth. A male villager tried every scheme to "take care" of her. He invited her to board with his family, which meant eating three meals at his house. For a girl far away from her family in the city, not having to shop and cook was quite an attraction. Ah Nv was most grateful to this farmer, whose wife seemed to have a knot in her tongue that made her lisp. The wife was cowed by her husband even though they had several children together. “There is no free lunch under the sky”—the villagers knew what was going on and they were worried about Ah Nv. Not surprisingly, Ah Nv got pregnant and had to get an abortion. Ah Nv was thought to be a fool and got the nickname, “Muddleheaded Girl.” Like Ah Lian, Ah Nv later got married to a man 20 to 30 years her senior, but the difference was that Ah Nv’s husband was not from Hong Kong; he was from a nearby city. After getting married, Ah Nv never once came back to the village where her heart had been broken.

In 1971, when for the first time our commune had a quota for possible city employment for zhiqing, we heard that the policy stated that those zhiqing who were married to local farmers would not be eligible. At our production brigade’s meeting where the announcement was made, an Old Zhiqing, wearing all black, who was married to a local farmer, got up and said angrily, “I have been in the countryside for many years. Even if I was imprisoned, I should have been eligible for parole by now. I want to work in the city!” “But what about your children?” someone asked. “I’ll leave them with him!” she said curtly. She would not hesitate to leave her children with her farmer husband so that she could return to the city.

We had a few male Old Zhiqing on our production team. They all remained single, and some of them worked all day long while the others traveled often between the village and the city. Day after day, year after year, they did not know what their future held.

From the lives of the Old Zhiqing, we younger zhiqing could see our own hopeless future. We felt chills running down our spines. We did not want to settle for a harsh life in the country, but we felt helpless and hopeless. We did not know what was waiting for us—what tomorrow would bring.

二十八

养猪、养鸡、养鱼、养鸭

在我们下乡插队的那个年代，城里人买猪肉是凭票供应的，即由国家统一发放猪肉票，每人每月半斤定量，可到国营市场按规定的价格购买。若要多吃猪肉，则要到自由市场去买，那里的价格通常是国营市场价格的3～4倍。城里国营市场所卖的猪肉是从哪里来的呢？下乡前的我从来没有想过这个问题，也不知道这个问题的答案。

养猪，是农民生计中的一件大事。农民没有由国家统一发放的猪肉票，那占中国人口绝大多数的农民要吃猪肉怎么办呢？众所周知，长期以来，国家对农村的生猪采取统购统销政策。按此政策，农民要自己花钱买猪苗饲养，猪养大后要卖时必须送到公社经营的屠宰场，由那里的专职人员过秤、屠宰后，把猪肉按“去六留四”的办法分成——即国家用公价收购六成的猪肉，其余的四成则留给农民本人自由处理。农民可以以高于公价的所谓市价把猪肉卖给国家；也可以留作自己食用。留作自己食用的部分，可以换取等量的肉票和钱，需要吃猪肉时则到国营市场凭票购买。那时，私自屠宰或收购农村的生猪都是非法的，一经发现就会受到严厉的惩罚。由此可见，农民不养猪就没有猪肉吃，因为他们吃不起自由市场的高

价肉。尽管我听到我村的农民们都抱怨说，“去六留四”的政策使他们养猪亏本，但为了吃猪肉，基本上还是家家都养猪。

养鸡，则是农民比较自由的副业之一。因为国家对农民养鸡没有统购统销政策，故大多数农家都养鸡。鸡蛋、鸡肉既可以自己食用，也可以拿到自由市场去卖钱帮补家用。城里的居民平时买鸡肉只能到自由市场去，只有在春节期间每户才能从国营市场买到国家配给的一只公价鸡，且不是每年春节都有。

养鱼和养鸭，因为没有上缴国家的任务，是我村农民享有完全自主权的副业。我们村里、村外都有鱼塘，由生产队放上各种鱼苗，年底时干塘捞鱼，按每户人口的多寡分鱼到户，吃得皆大欢喜。作为知青，我每年年底都能一次分到几斤活蹦乱跳的鱼，大打牙祭，好不过瘾！我村也派专人养鸭。养鸭人每天划着小艇，赶着几百只鸭子在江河里畅游，在收割后的稻田里觅食，晚上则和鸭群一起，睡在远离村庄的鸭寮里。因为养鸭人不能经常回家，一般都由上了年纪的老人来干。养大的鸭子可拿到市场上卖或分给村民。鸭子下的蛋一般都用来换谷子等作为鸭饲料。我们知青为了补充营养，都喜欢用分作口粮的稻谷去鸭寮换鸭蛋，1公斤谷子可以换4个鸭蛋呢！

Chapter 28

Pigs, Chickens, Fish, and Ducks

At the time when we were in the countryside, people in the city had to use ration coupons when they wanted to purchase pork; that is, the government distributed pork ration coupons, allowing each person to buy half a catty of pork each month from government-run markets at set prices. If one wanted to eat more pork, one would have to buy it from the free-market, where the price was usually three to four times as high as that at the government-run markets. Where did the pork in the government-run markets come from? I never thought about it, nor did I know the answer until after I had been a farmhand for a while.

Raising pigs was crucial to the livelihood of the farmers, who were not entitled to any pork ration coupons from the government. Where could the farmers, who made up the majority of the Chinese population, get pork when they wanted to eat some? For a long time, the government had a policy of monopolizing the buying and selling of live pigs. According to this policy, farmers had to use their own money to buy piglets if they wanted to raise pigs. When the pigs were ready to be slaughtered, they had to be sent to the slaughter houses run by the government. There, government-appointed people would weigh and slaughter the pigs, and they would divide the meat according to a "Six-Four Formula" —that is, the government would purchase sixty percent of the meat according to a set price and leave forty percent of the meat for the farmers, who could then sell the meat back to the government at a price higher than the set price or keep the meat for self-consumption. The portion that the farmers kept for themselves could also be exchanged for pork ration coupons so that when the farmers wanted pork later, they could buy it from the government-run markets with their ration coupons. At that time, slaughtering or buying pigs privately was illegal and the punishment was steep. Farmers would not have pork to eat if they did not raise pigs—because they could not afford to buy the expensive pork from the free-market. Even though I had heard complaints from the farmers from my village that the "Six-Four Formula" forced them to lose money raising pigs, basically every family still raised pigs in order to have pork in their diet.

Raising chickens was one of the sideline businesses the farmers were allowed. Because the government did not have a policy monopolizing the buying and selling of chickens, most farming families raised chickens so that they could keep the eggs and meat for self-consumption or so that they could sell the eggs and meat at the free-market to supplement their family income. City residents could only buy their chicken from the free-market. However, once a year, but not every year, at Chinese New Year, each family could purchase one whole chicken from government-run markets at a set price.

Fish farming and duck raising were two sideline businesses that the farmers had total control over because they did not have any obligation to pay the government anything they raised. There were fish ponds in and outside of our village. Our production team would stock the ponds with various types of fry and fingerlings. At the end of each year, the ponds would be drained and the fish raised would be distributed proportionally to each family according to the number of people in each family. Everyone was happy. As a zhiqing, I received a few live fish at the end of each year to satisfy my craving. I could eat to my heart's content! My village also assigned specific people to raise ducks. Rowing their boats behind the ducks, usually numbering in the hundreds, the duck keepers would herd their ducks on the rivers every day; and after each harvesting season, they would bring the ducks to the then bare rice paddies to feed. In the evening, the duck keepers had to sleep with the ducks in the duck shacks far away from the village. Because the duck keepers could not go home often, most of the duck keepers were elderly farmers. When the ducks were full grown, they could be sold at the free-market or be distributed among villagers. Duck eggs were usually used to exchange for grain to be used as duck feed. To help supplement our diet, we used to go to the duck shacks to exchange duck eggs with our rationed grain. We could get four duck eggs with just one kilogram of rice grain.

二十九

听收音机

在那个文化生活极为贫乏的年代，全国只有《沙家浜》《智取威虎山》《红灯记》《红色娘子军》《海港》等几个样板戏流行，广大农民喜闻乐见的地方传统戏剧要么跟着潮流演样板戏，要么就干脆销声匿迹。听粤曲、看粤剧是广东农村的一项主要文化生活，但当时传统的粤曲、粤剧到处受禁，不仅在戏院里看不到粤剧，在收音机里也听不到粤曲，农民们对此极为不满。

有一次，我到村民阿根家玩，看到他的大哥跷着二郎腿，坐在院子里的一张椅子上抽烟，旁边摆了一张桌子，桌子上放着一壶热茶和一台晶体管收音机，收音机里正在播放着美妙动听的粤曲。阿根的大哥看见我，就热情地

跟我打了招呼。我问阿根的大哥听的是哪家的电台，他说是澳门的绿村电台。他很平静地说，国内的电台没有粤曲听，农民要听粤曲就只好收听香港、澳门的电台了。

那时，收听港、澳电台是被严禁的。港、澳电台被强大的电波干扰，一般来说，大城市里的收音机是收不到清晰信号的，只有一阵“沙沙沙”的干扰声。可农村是“山高皇帝远”，不但没有被电波干扰，也没有那些无处不在的告密者。 我村人人都收听港、澳电台的粤曲，大家对此都心照不宣地形成了“统一战线”，从来没有发生过有人告发他人的事件。农民们聪明地意识到：只有和平共处，互相保护，大家才能无忧无虑地继续享受他们所喜爱的粤曲这一文化生活。

Chapter 29

Radio Listening

No private entertainment industry existed during the Cultural Revolution. Watching or listening to the government's model plays and operas, such as *The Sha Village*, *Capturing Tiger Mountain, The Legend of the Red Lantern*, *The Red Detachment of Women*, and *The Harbor*, was the only entertainment. What was loved deeply by the farmers—the traditional local plays and musicals—either got changed into the eight model plays and operas or disappeared completely. Listening to Cantonese songs and watching Cantonese plays used to be important cultural activities in rural areas in Guangdong, but after the beginning of the Cultural Revolution, Cantonese songs and plays were banned. No longer could anyone watch Cantonese plays in theatres, nor could anyone listen to Cantonese songs on the radio. The farmers in my village were not happy at all about not being able to get their daily dose of Cantonese music.

Once when I visited Ah Gen, I saw his older brother sitting cross-legged in a chair in the yard, smoking. There was a table next to him, on which sat a pot of hot tea and a transistor radio, which was broadcasting some beautiful Cantonese music. When Ah Gen's brother saw me, he greeted me warmly. I asked him which radio station he was listening to. He said it was Radio Vilaverde from Macao. He also told me calmly that there was not any radio station in China that had Cantonese music. When farmers in the village wanted to listen to Cantonese music, they had to listen to the radio stations from Hong Kong or Macao.

At that time, listening to Hong Kong and Macao radio stations was forbidden. Programs from Hong kong and Macao radio stations were interrupted by strong radio waves, so under normal circumstances, radios in urban areas could not receive any signal from the "enemy stations." All one could hear would be noises from the interfering radio waves. However, in the countryside, where as the saying goes, "The emperor is far away"—things were different. There were no intrusive radio waves, nor was there any snitch. Everyone in my village listened to Hong Kong and Macao radio stations for Cantonese music programs. People formed a united front—no one would report anyone for listening to the "enemy stations." The farmers realized wisely: The only way they could enjoy, without worrying, their beloved Cantonese music—which was the only entertainment available—was to live peacefully with each other and help protect each other's interests.

三十

搭　食

我在种了一年的自留地后，就再也没有心思继续种下去了。与农民们不一样，我们绝大多数的知青种自留地只求有菜吃，而不是为了把菜拿到自由市场去卖钱。村民锦胜是我的好朋友，他提出若我把我们姐弟俩的自留地无偿地让给他经营，他可让我随时到他的自留地里任意地拿菜吃。于是，在村里划分自留地时，锦胜就代表我向生产队要求把我和姐姐的自留地分在他家自留地的旁边。

在姐姐因眼睛被稻谷打伤回城治疗期间，我每天收工回来得自己做饭了。看到我每天收工回来疲惫不堪的样子，锦胜的妈妈松姨就让我到她家“搭食”。名为“搭食”，实际上我不用交任何菜金，只需把大约相当于我饭量的谷子碾成米和谷糠给她家即可。若不是交情很深，哪有这样“搭食”的呀！我从心里由衷地感激松姨一家对我的关照！

松姨有三个儿子，除老大锦胜已婚并有一个两岁的儿子外，老二、老三都未婚，全家六口人一起吃、住。松姨家是下中农成分，住的房子是土地改革时分到的一房一厅的地主房子。该房子是连在一起的三间房子中的一间，据说这三间房子过去是我村蔡姓地主三兄弟的房子，土地改革时分给了三户贫下中农。房子前面的门面是青砖砌成的，其余的墙除墙基外都是用泥砖砌的。一进正门是一个小天井，天井的左侧是一座大炉灶；右侧则是水缸和放厨具、碗筷的地方。从天井再往里走是一个20平方米左右的厅；从厅里再进去是一间10平方米左右的卧房；厅和卧房的地面都是黑乎乎的泥地。厅里摆了一张方形的小饭桌，加上几把椅子，就是全家吃饭的地方了。

与村民们一样，为了节省柴火，松姨家基本上都采用“一锅熟”的做饭方式，即用一口大铁锅做饭，在饭基本熟时，把盛在几个瓦钵里的菜放在饭面上蒸熟。饭菜做好后，就把盛菜的瓦钵放在饭桌上，再用一把小铁铲子把大铁锅里的米饭铲进一个小圆木桶里，再把小圆木桶端到饭桌上，全家就可以开饭了。偶然要加菜，则用水洗刷煮过米饭的大铁锅后再下油炒菜。

那几个瓦钵里一年到头盛的几乎都是一钵咸鱼，一钵自家腌制的咸菜，一钵从商店买回来的腌制咸橄榄加油和糖。有时也有青菜，但村民们都宁愿把自留地的青菜拿到自由市场上去卖钱，以帮补日常的家庭开支。

开始到松姨家“搭食”的第一个星期，有一件事让我很不习惯。松姨家养了一条狗和一只猫。每次吃饭时，家里人都拿来一摞碗筷，随手从中拿两个碗盛上饭、菜，一个碗用来喂狗，另一个碗用来喂猫。饭后，他们把人和猫、狗用过的碗放在同一个洗碗盆里洗干净后又摞在一起。每天如此，循环往复。因为曾目睹村中的狗在厕所里吃大粪的恐怖情景，再加上松姨家的那条狗长得脏兮兮的，身上的毛有一块、没一块的，让人看了恶心，我是一万个不愿意用猫、狗用过的碗吃饭。但无奈之中，我只好自我安慰地说，松姨家的人与猫、狗共用碗筷，不也活得健健康康的吗？！所有的村民都是如此这般，不也是安然无恙吗？！为了不用自己做饭，也只好入乡随俗，睁一只眼，闭一只眼。况且，有道是“不干不净，吃了没病”。这样，我找到了心理的平衡点，就十分坦然地与猫、狗天天共碗了。

自从到松姨家“搭食”后，我每天上工前和收工后都能吃上香喷喷、热乎乎的饭菜了。

“搭食”期间，我深深地感受到“男尊女卑”的封建习俗在农村根深蒂固。按当地的风俗习惯，烧火做饭纯是女人们的事，男人是不会做的。吃饭时，不论辈分高低，所有的女人都是不能坐在饭桌旁吃饭的，她们只能坐在炉灶边等远离饭桌的地方吃饭，当媳妇的女人尤其如此。有一次，一位生产队长为其祖母八十大寿举办家宴，请我们几个知青到他家吃饭。吃饭时，他的寿星祖母也不能上饭桌吃饭，只能和队长的老婆和女儿们一起蹲在炉灶旁吃。因生产队长知道城里的习惯，破例安排了几个女知青和男人们一样上饭桌吃饭。当我姐姐看到当地的女人们都在炉灶边吃饭时，她也端着碗离开饭桌，加入了她们的行列。

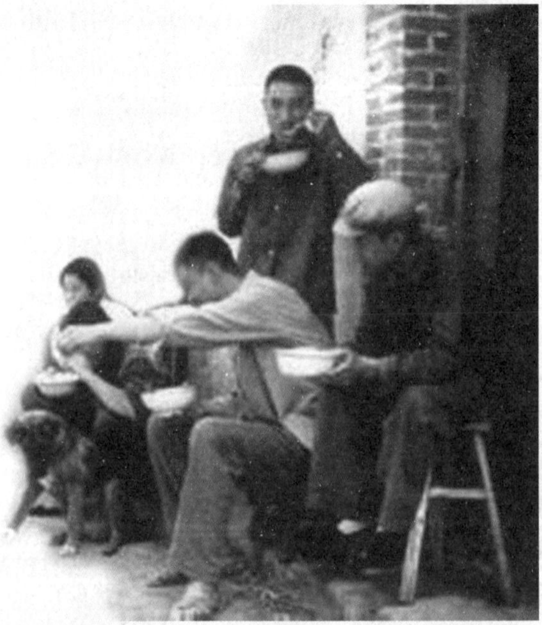

Chapter 30

Meals with Host Family

I did not want to have a private garden plot any more after I toiled in mine for a year. Unlike the farmers, who sold the produce from their private plots at the free-market, most of us zhiqing only wanted to grow enough vegetables for self-consumption. Farmer Jinsheng was my good friend so he suggested that if I let him farm the plot that was allotted to my sister and me, he would let us take vegetables from him anytime. When it was time for assigning private plots, Jinsheng asked for our plots to be next to each other.

During the time when my sister was back home in the city recovering from her eye injury, I had to cook for myself after work each day. Seeing how tired I was, Jinsheng's mother, whom we called Aunt Song, asked me to board with her family. She did not ask me for any boarding fees. The only thing I had to do was to mill the amount of grain that I would be eating and bring her the rice and husk. Where could one find such a good boarding deal if it weren't for the deep friendship we had? From the bottom of my heart, I'm grateful to Aunt Song and her family for taking care of me those days.

Aunt Song had three sons. Besides Jinsheng, the oldest, who was married and had a boy who was one or two years old, the other two sons were still single.

The family of six lived and ate together. Aunt Song's family was classified as a lower-middle peasant family so they were given a house with one bedroom and one living room that used to belong to a landlord in the village. Their house was one of the three houses that belonged to the three brothers of the landlord family named Cai. During the Land Reform Movement, the houses were given to three poor and lower-middle peasant families. The front walls of the houses were built with greenish blue bricks while the other walls were of mud bricks. There was a small court yard right inside the front door. To the left of the yard was a big stove; to the right of the yard was a place for a water container, pots and pans, and bowls and chopsticks. A room of about 20 square meters made up the living room while a room of about ten square meters was the bedroom. One must go through the yard to get to the living room and then through the living room to the bedroom. Both rooms had dark dirt floors. There was a small square table and several chairs in the living room. The table was used as the family's dining table.

Like the other villagers, to conserve firewood, Aunt Song's family used a "one pot" cooking approach: They used one big cast iron wok to cook their rice. When the rice was almost done, they would put several ceramic containers of dishes on the rice to steam. When everything was done, they would use a serving-spoon-sized iron shovel to scoop the rice into a small wooden pail before putting the pail on the table. Occasionally, when additional dishes were called for, they would wash the iron wok in which the rice was cooked and add cooking oil to the wok for stir frying. The ceramic containers had the same dishes in them all year round. One had cured fish, one had pickled vegetable, and the third had store-bought preserved olives in oil and sugar. Sometimes there would be fresh vegetables, but the farmers usually preferred to sell their fresh produce at the free-market so that they would have more cash for their family expenditures.

During the first week when I boarded with Aunt Song's family, there was one thing that bothered me. Aunt Song's family had one dog and one cat. At meal time, her family members would bring out a stack of bowls and some chopsticks. They would take any two bowls out of the stack, put some rice and other dishes in them, and give one bowl to the dog and one bowl to the cat. After each meal, they would wash all the bowls together and put them away. They did this daily. Because I had seen the horrid sight of dogs eating feces in the outhouses in the village, and because the Song family's dog was very dirty-looking with patches of hair missing, I certainly did not want to eat from the same bowls as the cat and dog; however, I did not have a choice. I had to convince myself by thinking this way: Isn't everyone in the Song family healthy even though they share bowls with their cat and dog? Aren't all the villagers all right even though they all do the same as the Song family? In order not to have to cook for myself, I must observe the custom of the family and turn a blind eye to the bowl situation. Besides, isn't there a saying that states "*Bugan bujing, chile meibing*" (a little dirt would not hurt anybody)? Thus, I found my mental equilibrium by rationalizing myself into sharing bowls comfortably with Aunt Song's dog and cat every day.

In boarding with Aunt Song's family, I was able to get a warm and delicious meal before and after work each day.

During my time boarding with Aunt Song's family, I also witnessed the deep-rooted traditional feudal view of men being superior to women. According to the local customs, women—not men—were responsible for cooking meals but at meal time, no women, especially those daughters-in-law, were allowed to eat at the table, no matter what family status a woman occupied. Once, when our production team captain hosted a birthday banquette for his eighty-year-old grandmother, he invited several of us zhiqing to dine at his house. When we started eating, his birthday grandmother could not eat at the table; she had to eat squatting next to the stove with the production team captain's wife and daughters. Because the captain knew something about how family members sat at dining tables in the city, he arranged for a few female zhiqing to eat at the table with the males, but when my sister noticed other female villagers eating by the stove, she picked up her bowl and left the table. She went to join the other women on the floor.

三十一

知青文艺宣传队

下乡后的第三年，公社管理知青的干部在全社召开了上山下乡先进知青代表大会后，决定组织一个知青宣传队到公社所属的各个大队或生产队去宣讲公社上山下乡先进知青代表大会的精神，以促进、落实知青的安置和接受贫下中农再教育工作。公社一共点了我们6位男知青和5位女知青的名字，临时集中住在公社机关招待所，以编排表演节目，为期一个月左右，而在生产队记工分的报酬，则由公社负责。

不知何故，从来没有参加过文艺宣传队或展示过文艺才华的我和姐姐都在名单之中。管他那么多，虽说是没干过宣传队，但冲着不用下田干农活就值了！

要搞宣传队，就得有节目。于是，大家就马上讨论如何编排表演节目。红屋窝大队的知青老何是本县老高三，文采不错，写得一手好字，篮球也打得不错，被选入公社农民篮球队。 因为家庭成分是地主，他高中毕业后的唯一出路就是上山下乡当知青，于是就投奔他那在红屋窝大队小学当教师的哥哥来了。在他的主笔下，一个反映农村知青接受贫下中农再教育的生活小话剧就成型并进行了排演。一个外号叫“肥仔强”的省城知青，虽然身材胖而矮小，但在当学生时曾经是文艺宣传队的骨干。他下乡后还被地区汉剧团招去演样板戏《沙家浜》中的胡传魁，可后来不幸被筛选回来重当知青。“肥仔强”毕竟是受过专业训练的人，其功底不错。在他的带领下，我们很快又排出了《大刀向鬼子们的头上砍去》，《游击队之歌》，乐器小合奏，男、女声合唱等节目，可以连续表演一个多小时。

为了取得更好的演出效果，我们还从公社领来经费买化妆品。从未化过妆的我也学会了在上妆时首先在脸部涂上一层凡士林打底，然后再画眉、涂红，等等。若没有凡士林打底，卸妆时就无法把颜色洗掉，而且那些颜色还会渗进皮肤里。演出用的服装，除了话剧外，一般都是当时风行的军装、军帽加军皮带。

排好了一台节目，经过公社的领导们观看、审查及批准，我们就下到各村去巡回演出了。在那文化生活极为贫乏的年代，电影、剧院、广播里看到的和听到的，除了样板戏还是样板戏。所以我们的知青宣传队每到一个地方，都受到了当地农民和知青们的热烈欢迎。有的村子有礼堂、舞台，我们就利用晚饭后的时间为大家表演；有的村子没有礼堂，也没有舞台，我们就在灯火通明的晒谷场上表演，外面围满了黑乎乎的一大群人。我村还特地邀请了我们知青宣传队回去演出呢。

我们知青宣传队的名声越来越大，传遍了全公社，也传到县里去了。县里要在某公社召开全县贫下中农代表大会，点名邀请我公社的知青宣传队去演出。

一个多月的时间一眨眼就过去了，我们真希望那不用“修理地球”的日子能再长一些。可惜好景不长，知青宣传队要解散了，无奈之中，我们只好互相惜惜道别，又回到了那个令人不寒而栗，浩瀚而冷漠的广阔天地之中。

Chapter 31

A Zhiqing Performing Arts Squad

Three years after I was sent to the countryside, the commune office in charge of all the zhiqing in the commune organized a meeting of the representatives of the exemplary zhiqing. It was decided at the meeting that a performing arts squad of the zhiqing should be formed and sent to all the production brigades or teams throughout the commune to help inform everybody of the meeting's resolutions, assist in the placement of zhiqing, and help share the zhiqing's experiences with the farmers in the commune. Six male and five female zhiqing were named to form such a performing arts squad. We were to live at the commune's guest house for about a month, during which time we were to create, rehearse, and perform a repertoire. The commune would be responsible for paying our production teams the gongfen we would have earned.

I do not know why but my sister and I were both chosen to be on the team even though we had never been a part of a performing troupe or demonstrated any performaning talents. But no problem! We would perform as long as it meant we did not have to do farm work for a while.

Propaganda teams ought to have programs. We got down to business right away. Zhiqing Lao He from Hongwuwo Production Brigade had a high school education.

He had some literary talents and his calligraphy was good. Additionally, he was a good basketball player and had been chosen to be on the commune's basketball team. However, because his family had been classified into the landlord category, he had to become a zhiqing after he graduated from high school. He chose to be with his older brother, who was an elementary school teacher in Hongwuwo Production Brigade. Under Lao He's editorial leadership, we soon put together and began rehearsing a play about how zhiqing were re-educated by farmers. There was another zhiqing, nicknamed "Fat Boy Qiang," who used to be a lead-performer on his school's performing arts propaganda team even though he was short and paunchy. He was chosen (by the district's Drama Regiment) to play the part of Hu Chuanqui of the model play, *The Sha Village*, but unfortunately, he was sent back to be a zhiqing. Because "Fat Boy Qiang" had had professional training in acting and he was familiar with the fundamentals of acting, under his guidance, we soon put together a repertoire that included short plays (*Hacking the Japanese Invaders and Song of the Guerrillas*), instrumental ensembles, and male-female duets, all of which yielded us over an hour's worth of performance.

In order to get better results, we applied for and received funding from the commune to purchase stage make-up. I learned to put Vaseline on my face before darkening my eyebrows and applying rouge to my face. I learned that without Vaseline, I would have a hard time removing the make-up and the color of the face paint could even get under my skin. Except for when we did plays, which had various characters, the costumes we normally used for singing and dancing were simply the popular military uniforms at the time—olive-drab tops and bottoms, hats, and belts.

After we got our repertoire ready and after we passed the inspection of the commune cadres, we traveled to different villages and performed our repertoire. We were welcomed everywhere by farmers and other zhiqing due to the fact that all they could watch in movies and theaters or listen to on the radio were the eight model plays—people were craving to be entertained differently. In those villages that had an assembly hall or stage, we gave our performances after supper; in those villages that did not have an assembly hall or stage, we performed on the well-lit grain sunning ground while the audience sat in the dark surrounding us. My village even made a special effort to invite my performing arts squad there for a performance.

Our squad's reputation grew quickly, and we became known throughout the commune—even in the county. When the county held its meeting of the representatives of the poor and lower-middle peasants from different communes, we were invited to perform.

Our month was up and it passed in the blink of an eye. How we wished we could prolong the days when we did not have to trim and prune the earth—toil in the fields. But our good fortune did not last long. Our performing arts squad had to disband. Helplessly, we said goodbye to each other and returned to the vast farmland that made us tremble. The farmland was boundless and showed us no mercy.

三十二

偷渡香港

我们插队的农村毗邻香港，很多村民都有亲戚朋友在香港定居，有的村民每月都收到香港亲友的汇款或邮寄包裹，日子过得比较滋润。

我村与香港相距八九十公里，虽然不算是边防地带，但出入该地区也要持有证明。知青回城探亲、购买往返的车船票都必须有生产大队革委会以上权力机构的证明。若要进入边防地区，则必须持有边防证，否则无法通过由民兵和边防军组成的层层关卡。

由于内地与香港生活水平的差距很大，在大批知青下乡插队前，当地农民偷渡去香港的事就偶有发生。在靠近香港的边防地区，农村的男性青壮年都在香港谋生，留在村里的是老弱病残的男人、妇女和孩子。我曾到一个离香港只有20多公里的农村访问，当地的农民告诉我，这一带地区的妇女是田间的主要劳动力，村里的男性年龄都是15岁以下或60岁以上。当地的农民家庭依靠香港亲戚的汇款作为主要经济来源，人们过着比较富裕的生活，而农作物收成的好坏对他们的生活影响甚微。我在前往该边防地区的沿途时看到：越靠近香港的村庄，房子就盖得越好；一条村子的富裕程度与该村子到香港的距离成反比。在我访问的那个农村的中学里，我看到的是一群清一色的女中学生，她们都穿着漂亮的蓝花白底的衣服，学校大门旁边停着一大排崭新的自行车，这在城里也很罕见。

大批的知青来到这一地区插队落户，艰苦的劳动生活和前途渺茫的将来使相当一部分知青对他们的明天失去了信心，有的更是铤而走险，置个人安危于不顾而偷渡香港。当时知青中极为流行的一句话是：我们知青的一条命只值两分钱。两分钱一条命！连农村中最赖的痞子也不敢跟知青拼命啊！

香港地区与内地接壤的地带很窄，外围有各村武装民兵的层层岗哨，内围有河流和带电铁丝网的屏障，还有边防军和狼狗的严密把守，要想从陆地非法进入香港地区简直比登天还难。

偷渡的知青都选择从海路游泳到香港地区——即先徒步到距离香港地区稍远的海边，然后在海里游5000～10000米到香港。一般而言，在离香港越远的海边下水偷渡，被武装民兵和边防军抓住的概率就越小，但在海里出危险的概率也就越大。因此，要练就一身高强的游泳本领。因为经过数天担惊受怕的长途跋涉，到达海边时体力已经消耗很大，还要马上下海游几千米，一不小心就会前功尽弃，甚至会葬身大海。偷渡的知青都不敢在农村当地苦练游泳，以免引起农民干部的怀疑。他们一般都在回城期间苦练。有一次我回城，当时正值盛夏，几个朋友相约到江边游泳。我们游累了就坐在岸上的树荫下休息，但有一个朋友还在江里奋力地搏击风浪，逆流而上。我在岸上看着他那认真执着的样子感到大惑不解，觉得出来玩玩不必太认真。后来知道他偷渡成功才恍然大悟，原来他那时是在练游泳啊。

夏天天气炎热，在山林、田野里风餐露宿尚可忍受，海水的温度也较高，是知青偷渡的旺季。我插队的那个公社有1000多名知青，偷渡去香港的有数十人。有的是一次偷渡成功，有的是数次才成功。我认识的一位知青，偷渡了10次都被抓住了，第11次才成功。知青偷渡被抓住，就会被送到县的收容所关十天半月，然后由县里通知公社派出所来领人。

我孩提时代的一个朋友小安，下乡插队后不久就去偷渡。他一路上东躲西藏，走了好几天才到海边。由于路上体力消耗太大，下水后游到离香港不远的海域就再也游不动了，肚子又饿，海水又冷，只好抱着随身携带的救生圈随波逐流地在海上漂浮了几个小时，人都几乎冻僵了，他对生存已完全绝望，只能听天由命了。后来，他被一香港渔船发现了，船员们把他捞上渔船时，他已浑身冰凉，不省人事。船员们把他搁在滚烫的柴油机外壳上烤，才把他救活了过来。最后，这艘渔船把小安送到了香港。小安离船前一再询问船员们的名字，以便日后报答他们的救命之恩，但船员们说，他们只是做了他们应该做的事情。

现在内地的生活水平已经大幅提高，粤港两地居民来去自由，“偷渡香港”的现象已经绝迹。

Chapter 32

Hong Kong Getaway

My village bordered Hong Kong. A lot of the villagers had relatives or friends in Hong Kong and some of the villagers received monthly money transfers or packages from their relatives in Hong Kong, making life comparatively easier for them in the village.

The distance between my village and Hong Kong is about 80 to 90 kilometers. Even though our village was not considered a border zone, we had to have special permits to leave or enter our area. When we went back to the city to visit families, we had to get permission from the production brigade's revolutionary committee or its higher-ups before we could buy our bus or ferry tickets. When people wanted to travel to the border zones, they would have to have border zone identification cards; otherwise, they would not be able to pass the layers of check points guarded by the people's militia and the border patrol.

Due to the difference in living standards between mainland China and Hong Kong, before the large number of zhiqing arrived in the border villages, there had been occasional incidents of local farmers swimming to Hong Kong. In those areas that were considered border zones, most of their young men made a living in Hong Kong. They left behind the older men or those who had health problems, in addition to the women and children. I once visited a village that was a little over 20 kilometers from Hong Kong. The local farmers told me that women were the main work force in the fields because all the males in the village were either under 15 or older than 60. Families depended on money sent from Hong Kong. People there lived well and whether they had a good harvest or not from the farmland did not affect how they lived. I noticed while traveling to the border villages that the closer a village was to Hong Kong, the better their houses; how wealthy a village was varied inversely with the distance the village was from Hong Kong. I noticed that the village high school had only female students. They wore pretty clothes with blue flowers on a white background, and there were brand new bicycles parked at the school entrance. Such a sight could seldom be seen even in the city.

A large number of zhiqing were sent to the border villages, but due to the harsh farming life and the hopelessness for their future, some of the zhiqing took the risk of swimming to Hong Kong. A common sentiment among us at the time was this: Each of our lives was only worth two fen. Two fen equal one life?! Even the village scum would not want to risk his life to fight us!

The land mass that connected Hong Kong and the mainland was very narrow. On the outskirts, there were guards from the people's militia and along the interior boundaries, there were rivers and electric fences, in addition to the border patrol and their dogs. At the time, it was simply harder than reaching the sky if one wanted to get to Hong Kong by land.

Those zhiqing who wanted to get to Hong Kong had to choose to swim there. They first had to walk to the part of the sea that separated the mainland from Hong Kong; then they had to swim for about 5000 to 10 000 meters to get to Hong Kong. Normally, the chance of being caught was smaller if one were willing to swim farther but one would have a higher risk of running into danger while at sea. So, excellent swimming skills had to be gained. After several days of long distance walking, people were usually exhausted by the time they reached the sea. Careful preparations had to be made if one did not want to end up dying at sea or wasting all prior efforts. Those zhiqing who wanted to swim to Hong Kong never dared to practice swimming in the villages because they did not want any village cadres to be suspicious. They usually practiced in the city while they were visiting their parents. One summer when I was home visiting, a few friends and I went for a swim in a river. We stopped and took a rest under some trees when we got tired, but one friend kept going, swimming upstream and battling the waves and currents. I could not understand why he was so serious about swimming while the rest of us were just having fun. It was not until I learned later that he had successfully swum to Hong Kong when I realized that he was training himself that time.

Summer time was a high season for swimming to Hong Kong because it was not too difficult to camp out in the woods and the water was quite warm. Out of the over 1000 zhiqing in my commune, a few dozen of them swam successfully to Hong Kong. Some of them swam successfully the first time while some of the others had to embark on the journey several times before succeeding. I knew one zhiqing who was captured ten times before he succeeded the eleventh time. When zhiqing were caught swimming to Hong Kong, they would be jailed at the county detention center for ten days to half a month. Then the commune's police station would be notified and the offenders would be transferred back to the commune.

Xiao An was one of my childhood friends. I was told later that Xiao An swam to Hong Kong not long after he was in the countryside. He walked for several days before he reached the sea, hiding here and there along the way. Because he was exhausted, Xiao An could not swim any longer when he was almost to Hong Kong. He was starving and the water was cold. The only thing he could do was to hang on to the life preserver he had brought along and float in the water. After several hours of drifting in the water, he was almost frozen, and he lost all hope for survival—he resigned himself to fate. However, he was discovered by a Hong Kong fishing boat. When he was brought onboard, he was ice-cold and unconscious. He eventually came to because the crew warmed him next to a hot diesel engine. In the end, the fishing boat brought Xiao An to Hong Kong. Before he left the boat, Xiao An asked the crew for their names so that he could repay them for their life-saving kindness later, but the deckhands only said that they did what they could and must do.

Living standard in Mainland China has increased a lot since my zhiqing days, and residents of Guangdong Province and Hong Kong can travel freely to either area. "Swimming to Hong Kong" is no longer a thing.

三十三

“忆苦思甜”

在那个年代，开“忆苦思甜”会、吃“忆苦饭”等活动盛行。“忆苦思甜”，即忆旧社会的苦，思新社会的甜。吃“忆苦饭”，即吃旧社会时吃过的饭。

记得下乡前，我们在大城市里的名牌中学也搞过“忆苦思甜”会、吃“忆苦饭”等活动：一边由学生中的贫下中农子弟诉说旧社会的悲惨家史，一边吃用米糠和树叶煮成的“忆苦饭”。“忆苦饭”难吃极了，粗糙的米糠和着带着碱味儿的树叶让人难以下咽。若说旧社会人们就得一辈子吃这样的食物，那真是打死也不能让旧社会复辟。最后，这样的“忆苦思甜”会在一曲凄惨的“天上布满星，月牙亮晶晶”的歌声中结束。学校当时还组织我们到学校附近的农村去访贫问苦，也和当地的农民一起吃“忆苦饭”——那是用少量米糠和番薯做成的，比我们在学校吃的“忆苦饭”好了不知多少倍了！

下乡后，我对吃“忆苦饭”还心有余悸，就向村民们打听他们的“忆苦饭”是什么样子的。下中农成分的松姨告诉我，这里的“忆苦饭”是用番薯和大米煮成的稀饭。这下我可高兴了，番薯大米稀饭绝对不会难吃！

同很多同龄的知青相比，我们有幸来到了一个被称为“鱼米之乡”的地区插队。因为是“鱼米之乡”，不管在什么时代，这里的生活水平总是比大多数的农村地区要高。可不，这里连“忆苦饭”也比别处的丰盛、易吃。我问松姨他们旧社会一般吃啥东西，她说一般都有米饭吃，困难时则吃一段时间的稀饭。我又问她村里有否开过“忆苦思甜”会，她说村里曾搞过一个“忆苦思甜”会，有一个苦大仇深的贫农上台发言，他先讲了旧社会挨饿受冻的苦，进而又声泪俱下地谈到了“大跃进”、“人民公社化”时没饭吃的苦，搞得台上台下一片哗然，最后发言未完就被主持人赶下了台。

虽然事隔十多年了，但当农民们谈论起当年搞“大跃进”“人民公社化”的荒唐事时都感到深恶痛绝。

有的村民说，当时搞“行动军事化”——把全村的劳动力分男、女集中住在生产队晒场旁的集体宿舍里。不管婚否，男的只能住在男宿舍，女的只能住在女宿舍。每天天亮集队出工，天晚集队收工。

有的村民说，为了使甘蔗“高产”，生产队要他们趁着黑夜，把几亩地里快要成熟的甘蔗用人工移到一亩地里，然后向上级报甘蔗亩产的“高产卫星”，并由上面组织各方面的人士来参观、拍照、取经。由于甘蔗密度太大，不通风，田中央的很多甘蔗都死了，只有靠近田周边的甘蔗还长得高大粗壮。为了掩盖“高产卫星”的谎言，生产队就每天派人往甘蔗田里浇上一层厚厚的河泥浆，使想走进蔗林里面参观的人望而却步。

有的村民说，当年的口号是“人民公社好，吃饭不要钱”。全村男女老少都在村生产队的饭堂吃饭，而且是不限量地任吃。很快，未到年底，全年的口粮所剩无几了，全村人只好吃稀饭，难怪有人“忆苦思甜”时忆出了公社化时的苦！

Chapter 33

The Past and the Present

In those days, having meetings to "Remember Bitterness and Appreciate Sweetness" and having meals to "Remember Bitterness" or having meals that were called "Remember-Bitterness Meals" were common activities. "Remembering Bitterness and Appreciating Sweetness" meant remembering how life was miserable for the masses before 1949 and appreciating how life had been a blessing ever since 1949. To have "Remember-Bitterness Meals" meant to eat what the masses used to eat before 1949.

I remember before I was sent to the countryside, my school, which was, academically, one of the top middle schools in the city, also hosted remembrance meetings and meals. Those students who were from the families of the poor and lower-middle peasant classes talked about how their families suffered before 1949 and we ate a mixture of rice bran and tree leaves. The remember-bitterness meal was difficult to eat because the coarse rice bran and the tree leaves, which tasted of alkaline, were extremely hard to swallow. If people ate that stuff all the time before 1949, we definitely would rather die than go back to living in that society! Our meetings would always end in the sad tune of "The Sky is Full of Stars and the Moon is Bright." Our school also brought us to nearby rural areas to visit the poor so that they could tell us about their sufferings. When we had "Remember-

Bitterness Meals" with the farmers, however, we found the meals much better than the stuff we ate at school. The farmers made their mixtures with sweet potatoes combined with a little bit of rice bran.

After I got sent to the countryside, I still had a lingering fear of the "Remember-Bitterness Meals," so I asked the villagers what their meals were like. Aunt Song, who was classified as a lower-middle peasant, told me that the "Remember-Bitterness Meals" in the village were a soupy mixture of sweet potatoes and rice. I was overjoyed, knowing that the sweet potato and rice combination would not be too bad. Compared to a lot of zhiqing of our age, we were fortunate to be sent to an area known as "the Land of Fish and Rice," which meant that no matter what was happening elsewhere in the country, the living standard in "the Land of Fish and Rice" was higher than that of every place else. Even their "Remember-Bitterness Meals" were better than those elsewhere. I asked Aunt Song what they used to eat before 1949. She said that they had rice to eat most of the time, but on occasion, they would have a diet of rice porridge only. I also asked her whether the village had held "Remembering Bitterness and Appreciating Sweetness" meetings. She said that once they held a meeting, at which a villager spoke. He suffered a lot and harbored a deep hatred toward the old society. He first talked about how he was cold and hungry before 1949; then he cried and talked about how he did not have enough to eat during the periods of the Organization of the People's Commune and the Great Leap Forward. His talk brought about an uproar and he was chased off the stage by the meeting organizers before he could finish talking.

Even though it had been over ten years, the farmers still hated the absurdity of the Great Leap Forward and the Organization of the People's Commune whenever they talked about those two events.

People in my village told me that at that time, "militarizing" was all the rage.

They had to live in male/female dormitories next to the village's grain sunning ground. Everyone had to live in the dormitories, even those who were married. People had to work together in the morning and finish work together in the evening.

They also told me that in order to claim a high yield for their sugarcane production, they were ordered to transplant, in the dark, sugarcane from several fields into one field when it was about time to harvest the sugarcane. They then could report that their sugarcane per mu production yield was sky high. Upper administration would then organize groups to visit our village, take photos, and ask the farmers to share their experience. Because the extreme density in the sugarcane field caused poor air circulation, most of the sugarcane in the middle of the field would die, leaving only the plants on the outer edge of the field surviving. To cover up the lie of a high yield, the production team had to send farmers to pour mud into the sugarcane field so that those visitors who might want to venture into the middle of the sugarcane field would stop going farther at the sight of the mud.

The villagers also said that the slogan at that time was this: "People's communes are good. We do not need to pay to eat." Everyone in the village ate without limits at the production team's dining hall, but soon, way before the end of the year, there would not be enough provisions left. Everyone had to eat rice porridge instead. No wonder that man, while "Remembering Bitterness and Appreciating Sweetness," remembered how he suffered during the period of the Organization of the People's Commune.

三十四

两次招工

1968年下乡插队时的口号是“接受贫下中农的再教育，扎根农村干一辈子革命”。下乡的头两年，知青们靠着一股热情，还能扛得住繁重的体力劳动和艰苦的物质生活。但久而久之，大家都对农村的生活厌倦了，觉得无法在农村熬一辈子，可又回城无望。于是，知青们看不到前途出路，意志消沉，以各种不同的形式潜移默化地滑向社会的反面。

1971年，我县宣布在全县范围内招收几百名知青到县供销系统工作，基本是分配在公社、大队及生产队一级的供销社当售货员，属集体所有制职工。

县供销系统的销售网遍布全县各地。

在农村地区，公社、大队及生产队各级大小不等的供销社星罗棋布。我村供销社的铺面只有20平方米左右，村民们可以在供销社里买到油盐酱醋糖等日常食品以及手电筒、电池、针线等简单小百货。供销社里只有一名售货员，每月有若干元固定工资。对于一些离城镇较远的乡村，这些简陋的小店确实给农民带来了很大的方便。

尽管此次招的是集体所有制的售货员，且绝大多数的工作岗位是在大队和生产队一级的供销社，但知青们还是翘首以待地希望自己能被招上工，从此可以不用干繁重体力劳动的活。我当时对这次招工不感兴趣，因为我觉得，回省城才是我所要的。一旦进了县供销系统，以后有回省城机会也轮不到我了。

这次知青招工主要是由生产队及大队推荐，最后由公社批准。我大队6个自然村有100多名知青，其中有3名知青被招了工：一名1968年的知青和两名1964年的知青。那名1968年的是我村一名老高二的知青，他大概是分配在县城里的供销社工作。

1972年底，省城的港务局来我县招工。我公社1000多名知青只分到了十几个名额，僧多粥少，我大队则只有一个名额。我当时想让我姐姐先回城，就去找公社管知青的干部，但他说，我姐姐的表现不如我突出，让她招工别人会有意见。无可奈何，我只好自己被招工回省城了。

就这样，我终于回到了省城，且当上了一名吃商品粮的国家职工——码头工人。

Chapter 34

Employment Opportunities

In 1968 when we were sent to the countryside, a prominent slogan at the time told us this: "Obtain a re-education from the poor and lower-middle peasants. Take root in the countryside for revolutionary work." During the first two years, our enthusiasm helped us endure the heavy physical labor and the poor living conditions, but very soon, we were all tired of what we were doing in the rural areas. We did not think we could live in the countryside for the rest of our lives, but we did not have any hope for ever returning to the city, either. Consequently, we saw no future and became despondent, turning to different means to cope. Some of us even became unlawful.

In 1971, there came an announcement in our county about an opportunity that would affect a few hundred zhiqing, who could be recruited to work in the county's supply and marketing cooperatives, probably becoming salaried sales clerks at different co-ops at the commune, production brigade, or production team levels.

The county's supply and marketing cooperatives were wide spread. There were co-ops big and small all over. The co-ops were located in communes, production brigades, and production teams. They were very convenient for the farmers in rural areas. The one in our village occupied a storefront of about 20 square meters. Villagers could buy cooking oil, salt, soy sauce, vinegar, sugar, and other basic daily necessities, as well as flashlights, batteries, needles and thread, and other small articles for daily use. There was one sales clerk at our village's store. The clerk drew a fixed salary of a few yuan a month.

Even though the recruitment was for sales clerks in the co-ops at the production brigade and production team levels, a lot of zhiqing were hopeful and yearned to be hired so that they could escape the heavy physical labor in the fields. I was not interested in the recruitment at the time as I wanted to be able to return to the city. I did not think opportunities of returning to the city would come my way if I had entered the county's merchandise system.

To qualify for the sales clerk employment opportunity, one had to be recommended by one's production team before one could get an approval from the commune. Out of the over 100 zhiqing in the six villages of our production brigade, three zhiqing got hired at that time. One was a zhiqing of 1968 while the other two were of 1964. The one from 1968 was from my village. He was a high school junior before coming to the village. He probably got assigned to work in a store in the county.

At the end of 1972, when the provincial port authority from our province's capital city came to recruit in our county, out of the over 1000 zhiqing in our commune, we only received between ten to twenty slots—too many monks for too little porridge—not enough positions to go around. My production brigade got only one slot. I wanted to let my sister go back to the city first so I went to talk to the commune cadre who was in charge of us zhiqing. He told me that my sister's performance in the village was not as outstanding as mine. Others would complain if she got hired. Reluctantly, I got myself hired and returned to the city.

Thus, I finally returned to the city and became a government employee, who would buy his food instead of growing it himself. I became a dock porter.

词汇索引

Vocabulary Index

chijiao 赤脚

0. barefoot

0. barefoot doctors were medical personalities during the Cultural Revolution. They did not have much medical training, and they mainly worked in the countryside alongside farmers

dawei 大围

0. a local name for the parcel of land in the middle of embankments surrounded by water

Dazhai 大寨

0. village in eastern Shanxi province that was made to be an example for all farming communities throughout China in 1963

0. Dazhai was glorified during the beginning of the Cultural Revolution. Their practice of self-sacrifice for the good of the community or country was emphasized and revered throughout China

fen 分

0. Chinese penny

0. also a land measurement equivalent to 1/10 of a mu

gongfen 工分

0. points indicating the value of one's work performance; income was calculated by multiplying one's gongfen to the total hours one worked during a particular period of time

gou 狗

0. dog

heqiao 禾撬

0. shoulder pole with tapered ends used for carrying bundles of rice straw in southern China

hebaojie 禾包结

0. straw knot or tie

huali 华里

o. chinese distance measnrement

o. l huali=500 meters

jiao 角

0. Chinese dime

laifen 濑粉

0. fresh rice noodle popular in southern China

li 厘

0. traditional Chinese land measurement

0. weight unit for grain

meinv 美女

0. good looking girl

0. an endearing term for any young woman

Mianyinchen 绵茵陈

0. Virgate Wormwood Herb, a Chinese herbal medicine, often used as a diuretic

mu 亩

0. Chinese unit of area

0. 1 mu = 0.0667 hectares

nv 女

0. girl, female

qi 气

0. body energy, the flow of which dictates one's well-being

shajiang 沙姜

0. sand ginger or aromatic ginger that has medicinal properties

Wuqi Ganxiao 五七干校

0. May 7th Cadre School

0. rural areas to which Chinese intellectuals were sent to be re-educated by farmers during the Cultural Revolution

yuan 元

0. Chinese dollar, same as kuai

zhiqing 知青

0. Educated Youth

0. junior or senior high school students who were sent to the countryside to be farmers during the Cultural Revolution